She stiffened, signaling he'd reached a point where she'd stop talking. He was okay with that. He had enough to go on for now. Another determination took over.

Pressing his body to hers, he slid his hand to the back of her neck so that he could satisfy an intensifying curiosity about how her mouth would feel against his. When her hands glided up his arms to his shoulders, he deepened the caress. Full. Warm. She fit him well. They kissed well together. He touched her tongue with his. Only their tongues were in contact for a brief moment, and then he kissed her fully again.

She made a sound that sent him into an eddy of fevered passion. The strength of it sent caution scattering.

Dear Reader,

The Ivy Avengers miniseries is a new concept for me, and an interesting change from the All McQueen's Men miniseries, which features heroes or heroines working secret military ops. Quite a difference!

Here in book two of Ivy Avengers, Lincoln Ivy becomes embroiled in his neighbor's trouble. He's a steady, fairly ordinary guy who's capable of protecting her in a subtly tough kind of way. Other than the plot, one of the best parts about writing this story was bringing these two characters together and making them confront the emotional trials of their pasts. Another great part about writing this story was Maddie, the dog. Maddie is likened after my yellow lab, who I lost to cancer in 2012.

Enjoy this suspenseful and romantic ride. May it be all you expect and more.

Only my best,

Jennifer Morey

ARMED AND FAMOUS

—

Jennifer Morey

HARLEQUIN® ROMANTIC SUSPENSE

Recycling programs
for this product may
not exist in your area.

ISBN-13: 978-0-373-27859-6

ARMED AND FAMOUS

Printed in U.S.A.

JENNIFER MOREY

Two-time 2009 RITA® Award nominee and a Golden Quill winner for Best First Book for *The Secret Soldier,* Jennifer Morey writes contemporary romance and romantic suspense. Project manager *par jour,* she works for the space systems segment of a satellite imagery and information company. She lives in sunny Denver, Colorado. She can be reached through her website, www.jennifermorey.com, and on Facebook.

For Maddie.

Chapter 1

Soft clawing on the back patio door made Lincoln Ivy put the steaming pan of cheesy chicken casserole down. Turning from the stove, he saw Madeline's paw lift for another series of attention-getting noises. *Tap, tap, tap.* Toy hamburger in mouth, tail wagging, nose smudging the glass and breath fogging the early-autumn air, her sweet brown eyes zeroed in on him with unabashed excitement. Chuckling, Lincoln walked to the door. She was a beautiful Labrador retriever. Show quality.

"Hey, there, girl," he said in greeting after he opened the door. The dog began squeaking her toy and bounding all around him. She squeaked a tune using her jaws, her eyes playful and looking up at him.

He got in a pat on her head before she trotted over to the pantry and sat, her white tail thumping the floor, whites of her eyes flashing in an upturned plea and cheeks wrinkled around the burger.

"Yeah, you're adorable." He went to her and got a biscuit from the pantry.

Madeline dropped the stuffed burger and chomped for the treat.

"Be nice," he admonished. "Don't be such a pig."

The tip of her tail wiggled faster.

"Nice." He slowly brought the treat closer.

Madeline's eyes blinked as though communicating her deep gratitude as she gently took the biscuit. Then she hungrily crunched away. It was devoured in seconds.

The gate next door was broken, and Madeline could open the latch on his. Over the past couple months, her visits had been sporadic. But this past week they had become an everyday occurrence. She wasn't his dog. She belonged to the mean lady next door.

Well, he used to think she was mean. A few things had changed recently.

He crouched in front of the still-sitting dog. "You know, for having such a troublemaker for an owner, you sure are a good girl."

Madeline gave him one of her white paws and stretched her head to lick him. He moved just in time to avoid a wet kiss on his mouth.

"Thanks, but you're taken. I don't cheat."

He scratched her ears as his doorbell rang. Right on schedule. Remy Lang was here to get her dog. Sighing, he stood and went to the door, Madeline trotting beside him.

He opened the door. A siren of a redhead stood there with a humble face framed by long, wavy hair. Beautiful face. He wasn't sure if it was just him or if everyone couldn't stop staring at her whenever she came into view. She was in light blue jeans and a Stanford University sweatshirt. No makeup, but her striking green eyes didn't need any.

"Uh…is Maddie here?"

She shifted from one foot to the other, stuffing her hands in her pockets. Awkward. She'd been a bitch when he'd first met her. He'd gone over to her house after he heard her fighting with a man. The man had hit her. Lincoln had beaten him for it, and she'd been angry…*at Lincoln*. Ever since then, she'd been uncomfortable in her own skin around him. She never could get away fast enough. But he always sensed her desire to blurt out an excuse for her behavior. And every time something stopped her. Fear.

What was she so afraid of? He found himself wondering more and more.

"Uh," she stammered again, this time leaning to see around him.

Madeline had gone into the kitchen and sat by the pantry again.

He swung the door open wider. "Sorry. Why don't you come in for a while?" Maybe this time he'd get some information out of her.

"Maddie," Remy called, stepping inside.

The dog stayed there, tail thumping, panting happily.

"Her name tag says Madeline." This was the first time he'd heard her call the dog by name. Until now, she'd only referred to Maddie as "my dog," and all she ever said were things like "sorry to have bothered you" to him, or "come on" to her dog. Whenever he tried to talk to her, she always said she "had to get going. Bye." Awkward and embarrassed. Why had she been angry with him for beating up the guy who'd hit her? She was afraid of that man, of course, but Lincoln wanted to know the reason.

"I call her Maddie most of the time." She bent and patted her thigh, a long, lean thigh. "Come on, Maddie."

"Do you want me to fix your gate?" he asked.

"No. Maddie!" she snapped, in a hurry to get away.

The dog's ears slumped, and her eyes drooped. Getting Maddie out of his house worked better when Remy waited on the front porch and he brought the dog to her.

"Come here, girl," Lincoln coaxed.

Maddie's ears perked, and the smile returned to her face as she trotted over to him.

Remy gaped at him with the hint of a smile. "What have you done to my dog?"

Seeing her begin to relax, he patted Maddie. "She's a great dog."

Remy crouched, and Maddie went to her, sitting before her with that tiny wiggle of her tail and going in for a few licks. Remy sank her fingers into the fur of her chest.

"Yeah, she is." The soft smile that shaped her lips captivated Lincoln.

When she looked up from Maddie's love-drunk eyes, she caught him staring at her. As her gaze took in his chest and arms and then returned to his eyes, he burned.

"Ah…" She stood. "I should probably get going."

Lincoln was a little disconcerted over his reaction, as well. A familiar, old pain overtook him for a few seconds before he could control it, hide it away where he always did, safely out of mind.

Remy didn't move for the door. She seemed on the verge of saying something that was hard for her to say. "I've…I've been meaning to…apologize for the way we met."

Finally. He waited for her to go on.

"Wade… That whole…thing…"

"Is he your boyfriend?" he asked.

"No!" she answered instantly and adamantly. "He's... sort of a friend."

"Sort of?"

She waved her hands and then let them hang at her sides. "I thought he was a friend when I first met him. He turned out to be something else."

Lincoln nodded. "Why did he hit you?"

"It's complicated," she said. "I don't expect you to understand."

How could he when she wasn't telling him anything? Did she have something to hide? Or was she just embarrassed? The man wasn't her boyfriend. "Who is he?"

She waved her hands again, a poor disguise for her inner turmoil. "Nobody. I just wanted to apologize, and also to thank you for what you did. Even though it didn't seem like I was appreciative, I was, okay?"

"Okay." Had fear compelled her to retaliate against Lincoln that day? She may have been afraid of what the man would have done had she not taken his side. "If there's anything I can do to help, just let me know. I'm right next door."

She smiled. "Yeah. I know." She met his gaze awhile longer.

This was a lot different than the first time they'd met. And the most they'd ever spoken.

An uncomfortable silence passed. She glanced down his body, checking him out, and then grew serious.

Maddie nudged Lincoln's hand, and he pet her head.

"Your leg is better," Remy said.

The first time he'd met her he'd been on crutches. "Yes."

"Did you break it?"

She hadn't taken the time to ask before. She hadn't

taken the time to make conversation at all. "No." He hesitated, wondering if he should say. "Actually, I was shot."

She went a little still and then asked, "How? Why?"

He contemplated not telling her. But he wondered if he told her, would she open up to him about the man named Wade? "A friend of mine got into some trouble, and I got in the way." He grinned. "I can't seem to stay away from trouble."

She caught his meaning, that he'd gotten into her trouble. "Must be some trouble."

"At the risk of sounding like I played a role in an action movie, my friend came to me for help, and things fell apart. My sister was here at the time, and an arms dealer tried to kidnap her to use against my friend. I was shot, and my friend saved my sister. The dealer's in prison now." He didn't get into the rest of the story, how Braden McCrae and Arizona had unraveled the mystery, which had included the kidnapping of Braden's sister and stepsister and attempts to steal weapons technology from the company where Braden worked.

"An arms dealer, huh? What are you, some kind of Homeland Security agent?"

"No. I teach martial arts." He left out the other detail that he was also a bail enforcement agent. He didn't know why. It was just a feeling. It was also something he didn't really share with many people.

"I have a tough guy for a neighbor," she teased, but he could tell she liked it. He wasn't a cop, but he wasn't afraid of bad guys. He enjoyed solving the mystery of tracking the fugitives and, even more, the satisfaction of bringing them in.

"And who do *I* have for a neighbor?" he deliberately asked.

Between them, Maddie sat patiently, her head moving from one to the other as they spoke.

"I just got a job at a microchip corporation. I'm an HR assistant."

A human-resources assistant? He'd recently learned the house next door was a rental. Where had she gotten the money to afford it? This wasn't the most expensive neighborhood in Denver, but it was pushing the million-dollar mark. She may have gotten a deal on hers since it was in need of renovation, but still. How much did an HR assistant make? It couldn't be that much. Plus she had a loaded Audi Q5 Prestige in her garage. Pricey for an HR assistant.

His curiosity grew. "Where did you move from?"

A flicker of reluctance crossed her pretty eyes. "California. Near L.A."

Vague. "What brought you here?"

The reluctance he'd seen was gone now, and in its place was a brick wall. She shrugged. "I don't have any family. It was time for a change. I've always liked it here."

"No family?" Not even a sister or an aunt?

"No." Her head lowered. "My mother raised me, and I never knew my dad. My mother died in a car accident a few years ago."

"I'm sorry to hear that. You must have had a tough time."

"I learned to take care of myself. Mom had life insurance. That helped. I used some of it to go to college."

College? Her eyes flashed to his when she realized her slip. She hadn't meant to tell him that. "I have an English degree. What can you do with that, right?" She half laughed.

Although she quipped, he could see she was lying.

"When did you graduate?" He kept a light tone. People relaxed more when all they were doing was answering harmless questions.

"Six years ago. You?"

"I didn't go to college."

"Just martial arts school, huh?"

"Yes. And I love to read."

A firecracker of a smile burst on her face. "Me, too. Biographies, mostly."

Something in common. "Mysteries for me. Some nonfiction."

"Do you have a family?"

She must know he did. She'd seen his mother stop by. The way she asked said it was important to her. Family.

"I have a huge family," he stated hesitantly. "There are eight of us, and our parents live in California. Most of the time."

"I see a limo drive up every once in a while."

"That's my mom. Dad sometimes comes with her." He watched her process that. His parents had money.

"Ivy." She nodded. "I didn't piece it together until now." She glanced around his house. "You live modestly for someone who has such wealthy and well-known parents."

She was completely guileless as she made the observation. Nothing changed other than the wonder of discovery. She didn't become flirtatious as most women did, thinking they'd struck gold. He could recognize the shift immediately. Flirting went into overdrive. Efforts to impress, to latch on to him became nauseating. But not with this woman.

"What's it like being the son of a famous movie producer?"

"I'm not the one who's famous, so most of the time

it's like being part of any other normal family." And he preferred it that way. "The press can get annoying."

"I can't imagine." A moment passed, and they shared a look. "Well. We should get going." She looked down at Maddie, who still sat patiently. "You're never this good with me. What's gotten into you?"

Maddie lifted her paw and rested it on her leg.

Remy laughed and shook her head. "I hope you don't mind her coming over here all the time. I haven't been able to get someone over to fix my gate."

"Like I said, I could fix it for you, except then I wouldn't get visits from Maddie." He pet the dog's head, and she stood to come closer for more attention.

Still smiling, Remy moved toward the door and patted her leg. "Come on, Maddie. Ready for dinner?"

The promise of dinner brought Maddie following her out the door.

His curiosity grew over his new neighbor. She didn't have any visitors and kept to herself. Lincoln was social with all the neighbors. They all loved having him nearby and frequently invited him to barbecues and dinners and holiday parties. Remy had too much to hide. At least it appeared that way.

Remy Lang realized she was still smiling after she went back to her house to feed Maddie. Drat. That wasn't in the plan. She had too much to lose to risk engaging in a relationship with a martial arts instructor. Her neighbor. Her big, strong neighbor who'd come to her rescue. She had to admit, having a man like that next door had made her feel safe. But it was foolish to feel that way. She couldn't share her past—particularly Wade Nelson's role in it—with anyone. Her survival depended on it.

Wade was not what she'd expected. When this all had started, she'd thought she could depend on him to help her, but she could not. Since then, she had taken matters into her own hands. She was close to resolving everything. Soon, she'd have her life back. If Wade didn't ruin it for her first. He'd caught on to what she was doing, and now he was angry. That was why he'd hit her. And Lincoln had seen it. That scared her more than anything. What would Wade do? He knew too much about her. She'd trusted the wrong man. And now Lincoln had gotten involved.

Sitting on her off-white Broyhill sofa, she turned on the big-screen television. Maddie came into the room, licking her mouth and hopping up onto the sofa beside her, smelling like dog food. Remy loved that.

The dog curled up beside her and lifted her head to gaze up at her. Talk about a heartbreaker.

"Oh, yeah, Maddie girl, you're my dog again. Your new boyfriend isn't here, and now I'm all you've got."

Maddie blinked and then slung a paw over her leg.

Smiling, full of good feelings, Remy draped her arm over the dog and lifted the remote with the other.

Maddie's ears perked up and her eyes zeroed in on the front door. Remy's pulse shot into action. Had the dog heard something? She looked toward the front door and then the kitchen and the back door. No one was there.

Maddie jumped down from the sofa, hair rising all along her back. She growled.

Remy stood and headed for the kitchen, where she kept a gun. At the threshold, Wade emerged from the garage, thwarting her with his own gun in hand. Shoulder-length hair, tall and muscular, he had an intimidating presence, a hoodlum presence.

Had he been waiting in there? How had he gotten in? He must have entered while she'd been at Lincoln's and hidden in the garage. She'd left the front door unlocked.

"Put the dog outside," he said.

Beside her, Maddie growled again.

When she didn't move, Wade aimed the gun at Maddie. Remy smothered a sharp indrawn breath. Frozen, frantically undecided over what to do, she could only stare at the weapon. Should she go for Wade's gun while it was aimed away from her, or do as he said?

All her life she'd made sure she took care of herself, that she didn't have to depend on anyone else. She was master and commander of her present moment and future. A gun aimed at her dog changed that. She was at Wade's mercy. That went against everything she was. And made her mad.

"I'll kill the damn thing," Wade said.

She'd do anything to keep her dog safe. In charge again, she went to the back door and slid it open. "Come on, Maddie."

The dog glanced at her, and then Wade.

Wade stepped forward.

Maddie barked and moved closer to Remy, protecting her. Remy stepped outside, and the dog did, too. Remy was tempted to run.

Wade appearing at the open door aiming the gun stopped her. Maybe Maddie would go next door or her barking would alert Lincoln.

She reentered the house and closed the door before Maddie could follow. Her heart wrenched with the sound of frenzied barking.

"In the living room," Wade ordered her.

Afraid Wade would do something about the barking, she did as he said. But as soon as she made it to the living room and faced Wade, Maddie's barking stopped. She was running next door.

"You've been sneaking around again," Wade said, stepping close to her with dangerous eyes.

Had he seen her? When?

"What were you doing at my store three days ago?" he asked.

"What are you talking about?" She played ignorance, the same as she'd done the last time he'd come accusing her of spying on him and his friends. That time she'd followed him when he'd met some men she hadn't recognized. Nothing had been exchanged, but she suspected he'd gone to discuss one of his illegal gun deals, deals that he expected her to execute for him.

He leaned in to bring his face close to hers, the gun at his side as though he didn't think he needed it to keep her under control. "You know damn well what I'm talking about. You're supposed to be working with me, not against me."

"If working with you means breaking the law, I'll pass."

With a smirk, Wade straightened. "You've already done that. And if you don't start doing what I tell you, the cops are going to find out."

Because he'd tell them. Soon, he wouldn't be able to threaten her like this. Soon, she'd be able to call the cops herself and have *him* arrested. But for now, she had to be patient.

Remy spotted Lincoln at the back door. She'd left it unlocked for him, hoping he'd retrace Maddie's path. Sure enough, he had. Wade's back was to him. Careful not to shift her eyes, she used her peripheral vision to watch Lincoln enter.

"I'm only going to ask you once more," Wade said.

Before he could repeat the question, Lincoln put the barrel of his pistol against the back of Wade's neck. "Put the gun down."

While Wade's face morphed into deep, angry lines, Remy stepped back. He crouched and put the gun on the floor, rising with his hands away from his body, palms up.

"Step away from it," Lincoln commanded next.

With an evil glare at her, Wade did as he was told.

Remy knelt for the gun as the two men faced each other.

"Why do you keep harassing Remy?" Lincoln asked.

When Wade didn't answer, he searched the man's pocket until he found a wallet. One-handed, he flipped it open and found a driver's license. Shaking it free, he let the wallet drop and read the name. Wade Nelson.

"Is this address current?" he asked.

"Go to hell."

Lincoln studied the license. "Why are you here?"

"Just let him go," Remy said.

"Why don't you ask *her* why I'm here?" Wade said.

"I'm asking you."

Remy had a sick feeling that Lincoln was asking Wade because he suspected she was hiding something, and he had a better chance of finding out what that was with him. Remy could only wait and hope Wade didn't reveal anything.

"How much do you know about her?" Wade asked.

Lincoln backed up, still holding his gun. "Why did you come here? What do you want from her?"

Wade glanced at Remy, smug with the knowledge that he could expose her. She hated him for that. Lording it over her.

"You'll have to get that from her," he finally said.

He wasn't going to tell him anything. Remy inwardly sagged with relief. Revealing certain things he knew would do damage to himself, too. If Wade ratted her out now, she'd never cooperate with him.

"Get out of here, then," Lincoln said.

He was letting Wade go without pressing him for answers. But why had he looked at the driver's license? What could he learn from that?

Wade picked up his wallet.

Lincoln handed him his license. "If I see you here again, I'll send you on an ambulance ride." Taking the gun from Remy, he removed the clip before handing it to Wade.

He took it, and furious eyes turned to Remy. "You're going to regret this."

Not if she could help it. She was in a race against time now.

Wade yanked the door open and slammed it as he left.

Lincoln turned to her. "What was that all about?" Beating her was enough, but threatening her with a gun took it to a new level.

She didn't say anything, just imagined what his reaction might be if she did, if she told him everything. Confiding in someone would be refreshing. But she could trust no one with that. Not anymore.

"Why is he threatening you?" he asked.

"Where's Maddie?" she asked instead of answering.

His mouth pressed together ever so slightly, disappointedly perhaps, but his eyes gave nothing away. "I left her at my house."

"I'll go and get her." She started for the back door.

"Remy."

Spinning to face him, she said, "Don't ask questions,

Lincoln. Number one, I barely know you, and number two, I can't tell anyone about Wade."

"Why not?" He approached, his strong, confident strides making her wish she could trust him. And more.

As he came to a stop, she almost gave in. But good sense intervened and she turned again, this time going out the door.

"What kind of trouble are you in?" he asked from behind her.

She went through the broken gate and opened his backyard gate.

"I can help you," he said.

Could he? Against Wade? Maybe, if that was all it entailed. But it was far more dangerous than that. No. No one could help her. As always, she had to take care of herself. She could depend on no one else. Besides, if Lincoln knew how she'd crossed paths with Wade, he might change his mind about helping her. And she could not risk that.

Chapter 2

The next afternoon, Lincoln settled down on his sofa with a turkey sandwich and a football game. A bark at the back door was his daily signal to get back up. Maddie stood on the other side of the sliding-glass door, beyond the nose smudges he'd given up cleaning. A toy was on the step between her paws, her tail wagging excitedly.

He opened the door. "You're early."

She trotted past him, going to the pantry. Facing him, she sat, tail wiggling away.

He chuckled and gave her the requisite treat.

When she finished, she jumped up onto the sofa with him, curled up with her head on his leg. He rubbed her ears and watched her eyes slide closed.

Any minute Remy would be here to get her. He was looking forward to it. More conversation. Picking through her secrets. Why he was inclined to involve himself in those secrets put him in check. People with secrets had a tendency to lie. What did he want from her? Her mystery or her body? Her body might not be worth the mystery. She might be the kind of person he hunted for bail jumping. He hadn't called the cops because he still wasn't sure she fit into that category.

After a while, it dawned on him that Remy wasn't coming over. Standing, he went to the front door and opened it. No sign of Wade's car. Remy's house was quiet.

Where was she?

He glanced back at Maddie, who still lay on the sofa, content as could be. If Remy was in trouble, the trouble had come after Maddie had left.

Something wasn't right. Going to the closet near the door, he opened the small safe he kept there and retrieved his pistol. Maddie jumped off the couch and was ready by the door.

"No. You stay here." He left her inside and hurried to the broken gate.

Moving slowly toward the back door, which was left open as it had been last night, he heard a crash inside.

"Where is it?" a man's voice growled.

More crashing.

Lincoln peered through the open door. Remy sat on her sofa, one man standing off to the side aiming a gun. The other swiped items off the shelf, searching for something. Both were in suits, as though they'd been on their way to dinner when they'd stopped by here. The one aiming the gun at Remy was slightly heavyset with a receding hairline in an otherwise thick head of hair, the other muscular with dark, curly hair.

They must have just arrived, or Maddie wouldn't have come over to his house, and if she'd known they were there, she'd have been more agitated. Entering the house, he quickly moved out of sight into the kitchen, and then put his back to the wall separating the kitchen from the living room. At the edge of the wall, he emerged into sight and fired at the man pointing a gun at Remy, taking out his knee. The heavier man went down as his partner charged. Pivoting, Lincoln blocked the swing of the other man's hand just in time. They sparred a few more times before Lincoln caught him open and rammed his fist into his larynx. As the man choked for air, Lincoln kicked him off his feet and kept him there with the sure aim of his gun.

Checking on Remy, he saw the heavier man held his bleeding knee, and she had picked up his gun. She was resourceful, and he was glad she could overcome fear.

Lincoln turned back to the curly-haired man. "Who are you?"

The man didn't answer. Lincoln hadn't expected him to, but he hoped to at least glean some idea of why they were here.

"What are you looking for?" he asked.

Still the man didn't respond, merely looked up at him, waiting for a bullet. He wasn't going to get one. Lincoln didn't kill that way. He'd let the law do its job.

"Lincoln!" Remy called, but her warning was too late.

A third man rushed into the room from behind Lincoln and grabbed Remy before he could react. The third man hooked an arm around her neck and pressed a gun to her head. Another suit. Dark, short-shaved hair, pale-gray eyes.

Two more men entered from the back door, both in suits, one taller than the other by just a couple inches, both lean in form, one blond and the other brunette.

"Drop your gun," the man holding Remy said against her ear.

Remy's eyes closed briefly, her renewed fear palpable. She knew these men, especially the one who had her. She dropped the gun she held, tossing it out of reach of the man still at Lincoln's feet.

"You, too," the man said to Lincoln.

Lincoln was outnumbered and outgunned, but he controlled his fear. Best to wait for his next opportunity. Whatever they were looking for, Remy had it. They had time, but probably not much.

"Give your gun to my friend," the man holding Remy said calmly.

After flipping on the safety, Lincoln gave the curly-haired man his gun. The man took it and stood.

"Search the house," the one holding Remy said. "And make it quick." He was the lead thug. He exuded a false sense of power that stemmed from his gun and the team he had with him.

The man shot in the knee stumbled to his feet, and one of the tall, lean men helped him out the door. The other two began to tear apart Remy's house—the curly-haired man and the other tall, lean man. A few minutes later, both came out from the hallway, one of them carrying a manila envelope.

Lincoln checked Remy. Her eyes met his before she blinked long and slow, full of dread.

One of the men handed the dark-haired one the envelope, and took over with a gun at Remy's head.

"Take care of them," the dark-haired man said. "Then meet me at the OneDefense store."

"Yes, sir," the man with the gun at Remy's head said.

The other jabbed Lincoln with his gun. "Try anything and my friend here will shoot her."

He believed him. Remy's frightened eyes met his. These two were going to kill them. He winked at her. She had no idea what he was capable of, and humor could disarm fear. The best news was that dark-haired bastard had left only two of his men in charge of the task.

She eyed him quizzically as they were forced outside. He imagined her thoughts. How could he joke at a time like this? They were about to be killed, and he was winking at her.

He grinned, glancing from her to the man behind him. That man gave him a shove, a reaction to Lincoln's smirk.

Remy mouthed, "Stop it." He was well aware of the danger, but succumbing to hopelessness would do them no good.

Outside, he searched for signs that anyone would see them being taken. No cars drove by. No one stood in lit windows. The two armed men were careful. They checked first before guiding them to a parked SUV. It hadn't been there when he'd gone over to Remy's house.

Remy was shoved into the back, and he was led to the front passenger seat. He wouldn't risk her being shot by trying anything just yet.

The man drove toward the foothills, turning off on a two-lane highway and then off onto a dirt road that led to open space near the foothills west of Denver. It was dark. Even darker near the trees, where the driver stopped.

He could hear Remy's breathing.

"Get out," the driver said, "or she dies."

He highly doubted they'd off her in the car and leave all that evidence, but Lincoln indulged the man. Remy looked at him wide-eyed, as though she couldn't believe how calm he was and how easily he did as he was told.

He got out and waited for the man in the backseat to do the same, forcing Remy to get out after him. The driver got out, too, and Lincoln saw that he'd left the keys in the ignition. That would come in handy in a few minutes.

When Remy left the car, he hit the backseat man's gun hand at the same time he grabbed Remy by the arm and tugged her down. She fell onto her hip. Lincoln used his foot to knock the backseat man's wrist. The gun fired and dropped from his grasp. Fisting a handful of the man's hair, Lincoln rammed the man's head down against the top edge of the car door, then drove his knee into the man's sternum.

He grunted in pain while Lincoln retrieved the gun and used it to bash the back of the man's head. The man went down as gunfire from the other side of the car sent bullets through the windshield.

Staying low, making sure Remy was still protected, Lincoln waited for the driver to reach the front fender of the SUV and then fired, hitting the shoulder of his gun arm. The gun dropped. Tactically moving in on the opportunity, Lincoln charged for the man. Around the front of the car, he knelt and picked up the gun, his gun. The driver sat on the ground grimacing, blood oozing from the gunshot wound.

"Get in!" he yelled to Remy.

She did, while he aimed both pistols at the fallen man and ran around him to the driver's side, getting in and then reversed the vehicle enough so he could spin it around. The back passenger door flapped wildly before slamming shut. Bullets hit the side and back of the car as they raced away.

Remy's breathing eased from frantic to just trying to keep up with her heart. She was scared.

"First time they've ever come after you?" he asked.

She nodded.

"Who are they?"

Swallowing, she glanced over fretfully and didn't answer.

A man who wasn't her boyfriend was threatening her, and now a group of strange men dressed in suits had just tried to kill her. Why?

"What was in the envelope?" he asked.

She kept her face forward. She still didn't reply.

Sighing, Lincoln drove back to town. "I'm taking us to the police, then."

"No!" She sat ramrod straight in her seat, eyes bright with renewed adrenaline, her hand tight on the door handle and the other clenched in a fist.

"No?" he replied mockingly.

"No. I can't go to the police."

Can't go to the police? "Whenever I hear people say that, it usually means they're in trouble with the law."

A few strained breaths passed before she said, "I haven't done anything wrong."

"Good. Then let's go tell the police about all of this. And while we're there, you'll tell them what was in the envelope."

She leaned her head back against the seat and closed her eyes. "I'm dead. They won't stop until they find me." She lifted her head. "And you now."

"Why me?" Would they assume he knew what she'd done? Or had his mere presence at Remy's house been enough? He'd seen them take the envelope.

Her head fell back against the seat again.

"If I'm in danger, then you should tell me everything you know," he said. "I'm better equipped to deal with matters that way. You're an HR assistant…or so you say."

Her head came up once more. "What's that supposed to mean?"

He didn't answer. But his silence was enough for her. He glanced over and saw her shrewdly assessing him, picking up on the accuracy of his suspicion. She may even be a little awed. He didn't let her in on the fact that his investigative ability was part of his job.

"What makes you better equipped than me? You're a martial arts instructor, not a cop."

Again, he didn't respond, just kept driving.

After a while, she asked, "Where is my dog?"

"She's safe. At my house."

"Take me home first. Then we can call the police."

Was she only trying to buy time? Would going home be a diversion? He wasn't letting her out of his sight until he knew why a bunch of criminals were about to come after him.

Remy gripped the door handle of the SUV as Lincoln drove down the street toward their homes. There was a marked police car in the street and another that was unmarked parked in her driveway.

"What are they doing here?" She'd planned to escape Lincoln, take Maddie and make a run for it, but now she was trapped.

Lincoln didn't respond. He was probably as stumped as her. How could they have found out about their abduction so fast?

"Keep driving," she said. "Don't stop."

"What?"

"Please. I can't talk to them." Oh, God, what would she do? She couldn't be arrested.

"Why not?"

His sharp tone said enough. She must sound like a real fugitive.

He drove to a stop in front of the house.

Remy saw two detectives at the door. One was in tan slacks with a purple dress shirt and tie, and the other wore dark blue slacks with a white dress shirt and tie. The officers were still in the police car, but as soon as they spotted her, they began to get out.

"No." The whisper emerged before she caught it.

"Why are you afraid of the police?" Lincoln asked.

She couldn't answer. Her life could be over in a matter of minutes. All that would be left was rotting in prison.

"You don't understand." Shaking, fumbling with the door handle, she opened the SUV door and got out.

Lincoln came around the SUV, studying her intently. "Make me understand."

She stared at him, numb with all-consuming fear. Stark. Terrifying.

"Ms. Lang?" the detective in the purple shirt called, leaving the front porch to approach. He was in his thirties, younger than his partner, taller and thinner, too.

Remy heard her own breathing, hating her weakness, helpless to be strong when the consequences were so great. She was innocent, but no one would believe her.

"Remy?" Lincoln took her hand.

She focused on his blue eyes.

"It'll be okay."

Her heart did a flip from the unexpected kindness, kindness she hadn't had in more than two months. But he couldn't possibly know it would be okay.

"We'll put them off for now."

Because he wanted to know what she was hiding, why men would not only try to kill her, they'd now want him dead right along with her. She owed him the truth. There was no refuting that. But the consequences were unforgiving if he didn't believe her.

"Come on."

Keeping her hand, he led her away from the SUV to the waiting detectives and officers. Did they know? Had Wade told them?

She tightened her grip on Lincoln's powerful and steady hand. Walking toward the detectives made her knees weak. Lincoln hooked her arm with his and supported her on her death walk. She was seldom like this. There was very little she allowed to rock her. She was a strong woman, but going to jail for crimes she hadn't committed threatened to break her.

"Ms. Lang?" the purple-shirted detective repeated.

"Yes," Lincoln said. "This is Remy Lang."

"Who are you?"

"Why don't we go in and talk?" he suggested.

The detective passed a studied gaze over Remy and then nodded. They went inside; the officers waited outside. In case she ran?

Lincoln guided Remy to the sofa and sat beside her, a stranger and yet someone she could rely on.

The older detective sat in the chair adjacent to the sofa, and the taller one took out a pen and notebook and remained standing.

After the tall detective introduced himself as Baker and his partner Henderson, he asked, "How well do you know a Mr. Wade Nelson?"

She squeezed Lincoln's hand, only then realizing she held it again.

"Not well. I met him two months ago."

"How did you meet?" Baker asked.

Her heart was beating so hard, and her mouth went dry. "I…" This was rapidly going downhill. "Why are you asking me about Wade?"

The detective paused, scrutinizing her. "He was murdered last night."

Remy covered her mouth with her free hand. Shock ripped away anything else she'd suspected. Murdered…

"How? Who?" They were here questioning her. Did they think…

"How did you meet Mr. Nelson?" Henderson asked from the chair.

She had to lie about that. She was a terrible liar, but she had to now. "I ran into him…at a coffee shop."

"Which one?"

She gave them the name of one near Wade's gun store. He went there almost every morning.

"When was the last time you saw him?" Baker asked.

Remy hesitated.

"He came to her house around six o'clock last night," Lincoln said. "He was threatening her."

"Was that the last time you saw him?" the detective asked her.

"Yes." The lie left her numb with dread.

He studied her a moment longer. "Why was he threatening you?"

Remy tried to subdue her shaking but sensed Lincoln picking up on it. "He…h-he must be angry that I broke up with him."

"You were seeing each other?"

Lincoln was watching her as closely as the detectives.

The lies were terrible and getting worse. "Yes. Not

seriously, though. Just…seeing each other once in a while."

The detectives shared a look, and then Henderson said, "We have a witness who says they saw you meet him last night."

Remy's heart flew. Panic engulfed her. She was afraid her breathing gave her away.

"One of Mr. Nelson's managers said he'd been coming to see you a lot lately, and he was on the phone with him when you arrived at his home at 8:30 p.m. He said Mr. Nelson told him he had to go because you'd shown up."

"I did go and see him. I tried to convince him to stop threatening me."

"For not seeing him anymore." Baker spoke with a hint of cynicism. He didn't believe her.

She didn't respond.

"Why did you lie about the last time you saw him?" Henderson asked.

"I…forgot I went to see him last night."

"You forgot?"

Remy swallowed the constricting fear tightening her throat. "Yes."

"What time did you leave?" Baker asked.

"I wasn't there long." Thank God that was the truth. "Thirty minutes, maybe."

"And where did you go after that?" Henderson asked.

"Home."

"Can anyone confirm that for you?" Baker asked.

She glanced over at Lincoln, who met her look and said nothing. He hadn't seen her come home. No one had. Looking back at Henderson, she reluctantly said, "Probably not." She hadn't stopped anywhere on the way home. The only person who could confirm the time she left was dead.

Baker closed his notebook.

Henderson stood. "We'll be in touch."

After the detectives left, Remy changed into jeans and an azure-blue boat-necked T-shirt and rejoined him in her living room. It was after seven o'clock. Late but not that late. Lincoln had felt and seen her trembling when the detectives had questioned her. If she preferred to be alone, he wasn't picking up on that. But he wasn't picking up on a willingness not to, either.

"I need to get my dog," she said, folding her arms in front of her, uncomfortable.

He wondered what had her uncomfortable, the detectives or being alone with him. Maybe that was it. She didn't want to be alone, but she didn't want to be alone with *him*.

"Right." He led her out of her house, making sure she locked her door, and then ushered her over to his.

Something dug deep into him to ensure no one who dared to come after them again would harm her. It was a strong instinct, one he could not ignore despite her fear of the law. Those detectives had to have known she wasn't telling the complete truth. So why was he so intent on protecting her? He needed answers. His life was in danger right along with hers now. Wasn't that enough of a reason? He couldn't leave her to her own defenses. If those men were going to go after both of them, it made more sense to stick together.

He shut the door as Maddie bounded to Remy for her trademark exuberant greeting, stuffed burger gently clamped between her jaws, pushing up her furry, whiskery, white cheeks.

"Come on, girl," Remy said.

She was going to leave. Sleep next door. Alone.

"Wait." Lincoln stepped in her way. "You shouldn't be alone right now."

"What?" One of her hands went to her stomach, not out of dread; Lincoln was beginning to suspect she couldn't keep her hands still.

"If those men come back, it's best if you're with me. I have a guest room."

Gaze unwavering, she lowered her hand and hooked her thumbs on the belt loops of her jeans. She didn't argue. How could she? If she slept alone tonight, she might end up dead.

But the nervous fidgeting, the inability to stay still, revealed her discomfort. Was she wondering if he'd press her for information? He would. But not just yet. He wanted her relaxed when he asked her the questions he had.

"I'll start dinner. We can go back to your place later so you can pack a bag." Locking the door, he walked into the kitchen, Maddie on his heels after her ears perked with the sound of the word *dinner*.

Taking his gun out of the front of his jeans, he set it on the counter. Remy was slower to follow. She eyed the gun and then watched him get some things out of the refrigerator.

"Why do you own a gun?" she asked.

"It's legal." He wasn't ready to tell her more about himself. Keep her guessing for now. He needed her to do the talking first.

He started a skillet of hamburger going and began cutting up peppers and onions.

"What are you making?"

"'Even the Kids Love It' casserole."

"A kid recipe?" She grinned wide, his relaxation strategy already going to work. "Are you a good cook?"

"I wouldn't go that far." He chuckled at the idea. Him, a good cook. Ha! "Casseroles are easy, and they taste good. My sister is a real pro at making them for me. She doesn't know it, though."

"Which of the eight is she?"

"Arizona. The youngest." He smiled his fondness. It had been a while since she'd come over to play a board game with him.

"I can see you're close. Are you that way with all your brothers and sisters?"

"No. Arizona and I are the closest, even though we're the farthest apart in age. When she was a kid, I was the one she always came to when she was being bullied and, later, when she was older, when the press crawled a little too close."

"Tough big brother, huh?"

"She's always needed watching over."

"Protective." She mulled that over awhile, making him wonder what she was thinking. Was being protective a good thing or a bad thing to her? She struck him as very independent. Women like that didn't appreciate being treated like a helpless damsel in distress.

Lincoln didn't see it that way. Men were typically physically stronger than women. They *could* protect them.

"Arizona thinks she can do more than she actually can, or maybe it's more than she *has* to do."

"She goes above and beyond?"

"She lost a fiancé several years ago. He was kidnapped and killed, and she had a hard time getting over it." He went to the sink to wash his hands. "Now she wants to start up an adventure organization for victimized people. Sort of like fear therapy."

Remy moved farther into the kitchen toward the refrigerator. "That's commendable. She sounds like a very brave woman."

"*Brave* is a good word for her. And she's got a good man in her life to keep her out of trouble. I don't have to watch her so closely." He grinned as he dried his hands with a paper towel.

"Good man? What is that?" Beginning to feel at home, she opened the refrigerator and took out a bottle of water. "Want one?"

"Sure."

Dodging Maddie, whose nose was to the floor looking for fallen scraps, she opened the cap for him and set it by the cutting board he'd just taken out of the cabinet.

Leaning against the counter beside him, she asked, "What's in a kid's casserole?"

He moved to a lower cabinet and took out a kettle, greeted by Maddie's cold, wet nose. "Noodles, peppers and onions, corn, burger, lots of cheese and some special ingredients." Straightening, he filled the kettle with water.

"Secret ingredients?"

Putting the kettle on the stove and turning the burner to high, he went to the pantry and took out a can of cream-of-chicken soup and one of nacho sauce, holding them up for her inspection.

She laughed. "Okay, so you can't cook."

"Can you?"

"When I'm forced."

Chuckling at their similarity, he dumped the onions and peppers into the burger and, after a few minutes, the noodles into the now-boiling water. When the onions and peppers were tender, he mixed everything together and put it into a casserole dish. A little cheese on top and into the oven.

Next, he went to the garage to get food for Maddie.

"You have dog food, too?" Remy watched him pour food into one of two bowls beside the refrigerator. There was already water there.

"I bought it just in case." In case she needed someone to watch her dog. In case Wade proved to be too much brawn for her to handle. In case Maddie became a permanent resident in his house....

Maddie inspected the bowl of food. Unlike with her treats, she ate slowly. Munching away, looking around and up at them with the wag of her tail then going down for another dainty bite.

Remy smiled at Lincoln and then drank some water. She was relaxed, the way he wanted her to be. Now they could talk.

"Who's Wade Nelson?" he asked.

Lowering the bottle of water, her smile faded, soft eyes guarded now. But she didn't appear surprised by his question. She must have expected him to bring it up eventually.

When she didn't say anything, he said, "I'll find out whether you tell me or not." He'd seen the man's driver's license, and he had a really good memory.

After a yielding sigh, she put the bottle of water on the kitchen counter. "He runs a OneDefense store here in Denver."

"He sells guns?"

She folded her arms as though chilled. "Retail. Yes. OneDefense Corporation has lots of stores around the country."

"I've heard of them. Why was he threatening you?"

She'd already said she couldn't tell him. But he wasn't going to let up until she did. As she met his eyes, she must have realized that.

"I've been watching him. I've suspected for a while that he was dealing in illegal gun sales, and I've been trying to gather evidence against him."

"Why?"

"I want him out of my life."

"Why is he in your life?"

Her eyes were steady on his. She was a crafty woman, strong and self-sufficient, but he suspected she wasn't always that way. She was in survival mode. And she didn't want to answer him.

"When I met him I didn't know the kind of man he was."

The kind involved in illegal gun sales? How had she gotten herself involved with someone like that? "How did you meet him?" It hadn't been at the coffee shop. Like the detectives, he could tell she lied about that.

Her clear, beautiful green eyes stared up at him. Whatever had her tongue-tied was worse than anything that had occurred since she'd moved in. More dangerous than Wade's fists. This was as dangerous as the dark-haired man who'd come to her house for the envelope.

She put her hands on the edge of the counter. It made her breasts rise a little, drawing his attention there. He was afraid when his eyes lifted they held too much heat. But when he saw an answer in hers, he didn't stop it.

Stepping closer, he bent to bring his face right above hers and asked, "What was in the envelope?" His voice was gruff, unintentionally so.

She drew in a breath and began to sidle away. He

stopped her with his arms, putting his hands on the counter and caging her.

Her gaze lowered to his mouth, as though the sound of his voice lulled her. Then she lifted her eyes. "Not enough. Just some paperwork from Wade's store showing some missing inventory. Wade caught me before I could trace the illegal sales."

"You were going to try to find out where the sales went?"

"I want to know the entire operation. Who's involved. Sellers. Buyers."

"Why not leave it up to the ATF? They could have gone in and done an inspection."

She turned her head aside, avoiding him as much as she could while trapped by his arms. The sound of Maddie eating had a calming effect.

Not calming enough. Remy wasn't answering him.

Cupping her chin gently, he brought her head facing him again, looking into her eyes.

She closed hers. When she opened them, she began. "OneDefense has fifty-some odd stores around the country. I want to know which of them are involved."

Still hedging. "How did you meet Wade?"

She licked her lips and pursed them before they dropped open, sultry without even trying. "I can't tell you."

"You said yourself—they're going to come after me now. I have a right to know."

She didn't reply, but seemed to struggle with how.

"Who sent those men to your house?" he helped her out by asking, his voice lower and deeper than he intended. He was too aware of her physically.

Those crystalline green eyes softened. "Why do you think someone sent them?"

"The dark-haired man was in charge of getting the envelope, but he isn't at the top."

She angled her head, brow going a little lower. "How do you know that?"

"I'm a good judge of character. Who sent them, Remy?"

She blinked slowly, in resignation. "Tristan Coulter. He's an account manager at OneDefense. Their headquarters are in California, but there are several retail stores all over the country. Wade runs the one in Denver."

At last, progress. "Did you meet him before or after you met Wade?"

"Before." Now her voice had dropped, sultry heat building between them.

"Is that how you met Wade?"

Slowly she shook her head, her gaze going to his mouth before rising back to his eyes. "A friend of mine told me Wade was someone I could trust."

He moved closer. "Who's your friend?"

"Someone who worked at OneDefense." She sounded breathless.

"Who?"

Her mouth pressed closed, signaling he'd reached a point where she'd stop talking. He was okay with that. He had enough to go on for now. Another determination took over.

Pressing his body to hers, he slid his hand to the back of her neck so that he could satisfy an intensifying curiosity of how her mouth would feel against his. When her hands glided up his arms to his shoulders, he deepened the caress. Full. Warm. She fit him well. They kissed well together. He touched her tongue with his. Only their tongues were in contact for a brief moment, and then he kissed her fully again.

She made a sound that transported him into an eddy of fevered passion.

Chapter 3

The repeated ring of the doorbell followed by an abrupt opening of the front door jolted Lincoln out of the kiss. While Remy's breath caught, he grabbed his gun and moved to the edge of the kitchen entry.

A file of people entered his house. Mom. Dad. Autumn. Jonas. Savanna. His mother noticed the gun and barely faltered. Blond hair in a bob and wearing jeans and a white T-shirt, she looked years younger than she was. He flipped the safety on his gun as Arizona brought in the rear, Braden McCrae and his son along with her.

"Lincoln Ivy, what are you doing with that?" his mother asked, carrying two grocery bags. Tall and lanky behind her, russet-colored hair unruly as usual, Dad held three more. Jackson Ivy taking some downtime from big movie business.

He chuckled when he saw the gun. "You look like you belong on one of my sets."

Great. One of Mother's impromptu family gatherings was about to descend upon him. Camille Ivy made a job out of Home and Family, and the hour of day didn't matter.

"It's after eight, Mom."

"It took us a while to put this all together. Brandie, Macon and Riana couldn't make it." She walked past him as though that were a normal explanation.

His youngest brother and Number Five of the siblings rarely attended family get-togethers. "Macon still in rehab?"

"Don't start with that." His mother stopped short when Remy appeared in the kitchen entry, hands in the front pockets of her jeans. "Who's this?"

"My neighbor. Remy Lang."

Remy looked uncomfortable as she awkwardly took one of the bags from his mother, and they introduced themselves.

"Ah, the neighbor," his dad's deep voice boomed. He approached Remy with the three bags. "We've heard all about you." He leaned in toward her. "It's the reason Lincoln's mother dragged us all here." He winked back at Lincoln and his mother.

"Oh." Flustered, Remy carried the bag into the kitchen, Mom trailing behind, already asking questions.

It had to have been Arizona who'd started them all talking.

Refined and slender in a silky tan pantsuit, Autumn brushed long, light red strands of shiny hair behind one ear as she kissed Lincoln's cheek. "Hi, oldest brother."

It had been a while since he'd seen her. "Hi, second oldest."

She laughed.

Savanna stood behind Autumn; Number Six of the Ivy Eight had darker hair, with barely a reddish tint, and was taller. Her eyes were strong and happy today, but Lincoln knew she had her moments when she still struggled with heartache over her last relationship. Autumn hadn't succumbed to that disease yet. It would take a strong man to make her commit. She had striking beauty like Savanna and an even more striking mind. The Ivys were all attractive in their own way, befitting the offspring of a famous producer.

Jonas showed up to all the family gatherings because he never exerted himself on anything that didn't involve workouts or women. Few knew he was capable of more. He just hadn't found his way yet. It was hard when you were the son of a wealthy man. No one in this family had to work for a living.

"Is your divorce final yet?" Lincoln asked, shaking Jonas's hand.

"Last month."

That was his third.

"I'm staying away from women for a while."

Lincoln didn't believe that. Except there was something different about his brother today. A fire in his eyes that Lincoln hadn't seen before. He looked thinner than the last time he'd seen him. "Still working out?"

Obsessively. Twice a day.

"I bought a Trek Madone. Still hunting down bail jumpers?"

Jonas was riding a bicycle? Trimming down. Lincoln had always thought he'd gotten too muscular, like a bodybuilder.

"Are you going to race?"

"No, I just like it."

Weight lifting had defined him once. Lincoln had never thought that was all there was to Jonas. He was glad to see his brother finally growing out of that shell. Maybe it had been his last marriage. He'd seemed to love the woman, but it had been obvious to many that all she'd wanted from him was his Ivy name. She must have been disappointed when the entertainment media hadn't painted her in a favorable light. Just another of Jonas's whimsical and meaningless marriages. It wouldn't last. And it hadn't.

He hugged Arizona. "Thanks for telling Mom about Remy."

She laughed a little and leaned back from the hug. "Can't keep a secret like that."

Like what? All he'd done was notice her. But Arizona had seen that.

"After I get Aiden settled, I'll get a game of Clue ready," Arizona said. "It's my turn to kick your butt."

As Lincoln marveled over her motherly instincts, Braden gave him a man hug, a few quick pats on his back, and Aiden was mesmerized by the television that Arizona had turned to a cartoon network.

Lincoln headed toward the kitchen, where his parents had taken the groceries and Jonas and Savanna had followed. His father's laughter joined Autumn's. Already his mother was well on her way to exploding his kitchen.

"There's a casserole in the oven," he said, half joking.

"Savanna is taking care of that," his mother called from the stove, missing his sarcasm.

Savanna had removed the casserole and had found a container she was now dumping it into without ado.

"What's for dinner?" he asked, seeing Remy's deer-in-headlights stare from the other side of the kitchen island, Autumn at her side. She white knuckled the back of an island stool.

This wasn't exactly how he'd thought meeting his family would go. He wouldn't have thought she'd meet them at all.

Arizona entered the kitchen carrying the game, Braden behind her. Now the gang was assembled. It grew loud in the room. Braden stopped to talk to Lincoln's parents. Arizona gave him a shove, propelling him toward the table. He went there, seeing Autumn and Savanna engaging Remy in conversation. She still seemed awkward, disliking the loss of control. If she could, she'd bolt out the front door. Why did being surrounded by his family do that to her?

Jonas took a seat at the island and listened to his sisters and Remy, pretty soon joining the conversation. Something about positive thinking. Savanna was a motivational speaker.

Lincoln sat across from Arizona.

"The neighbor, huh?" Arizona wiggled her eyebrows at him as she put three cards into an envelope. "Remy, wasn't it?"

He shouldn't have told her Remy's name. "Her dog keeps coming over." Lincoln looked down at Maddie, who'd put her head on his thigh, the whites of her brown eyes flashing as she gazed up at him, tail wagging.

"Look at that. She loves you," Arizona marveled. "Does the neighbor come with her?"

"She follows shortly thereafter."

"I knew you were more interested than you would admit."

"I'm not that interested." He glanced over at Remy to make sure she couldn't hear them. She answered questions from Savanna and Autumn on her job as a human-resource assistant while Jonas listened. Her vague replies made him wonder if that was why she was so tense. She didn't like being asked personal questions. What was she hiding?

"Yeah, right," Arizona said.

"She's got a lot going on in her life," he argued. Abusive men and bullets. "Too complicated for me."

"What do you mean, complicated? All women are complicated."

"No, I mean *complicated.*" He told her about Wade, leaving out their kidnapping.

"He threatened her?" She handed him some playing cards.

"And then he was murdered. The police came by to talk to her."

She drew a sharp breath. "Murdered?" She glanced over at Remy. "Do you think she did it?"

"No. Be quiet." He glanced around the kitchen. Mom and Dad were still busy preparing dinner, and Remy was listening to Jonas tell her about one of his rides.

"Why did the police question her?" she whispered.

"She was probably the last one to see him alive."

"Why was he murdered?"

Braden joined them beside the table. "Someone was murdered?"

Tall and broad, he had short, dark brown hair and green eyes that had sobered. When he sat on the chair beside Lincoln, Maddie went over to investigate.

Lincoln told him about Tristan. "I haven't had a chance to check him out yet."

"Do you need help?" Braden asked. "I owe you after all."

"No need. This time I can avoid involving more

people than necessary." Lincoln looked pointedly at Arizona.

"If you need help, we can help you," she said.

"Me, not you," Braden told her.

"Neither one of you. I do this for a living." No way was Lincoln allowing them to get involved.

Arizona smiled her awareness of his determination. "Remy is in good hands with you." She picked up a game piece. "I'm Professor Plum."

He took it from her. "You were Plum last time. I'm Plum. You be Mrs. Peacock."

Braden sat down next to Arizona. "I'll play, too."

"Did she rope you into these games, too?" Lincoln asked.

"She makes them fun." He leaned over and kissed her, making his sister radiate love.

Lincoln didn't press them on what kind of fun they had when they played board games. He was pretty sure they rarely finished them.

Checking on Remy again, he wondered if she was in good hands. Was she safe with him? He wasn't so sure. Tristan wasn't your average thug. And depending on what Lincoln learned about him, this could be more dangerous than he'd imagined so far. Too dangerous, even for him.

Remy watched Lincoln playing a game with his sister and her husband. She'd seen the way he looked at her and didn't have to guess what the three were talking about. His freedom of communication was both admirable and disturbing. She wasn't sure she wanted his family knowing the police had questioned her in connection to a murder.

Lincoln's dad finished making chili for the chili dogs

they'd decided to make tonight. Remy wasn't sure how that was better than Lincoln's casserole.

"Do you do this a lot?" she asked Autumn. Savanna and Jonas had moved over to the table to watch the game going on there.

"Have family parties?" Autumn looked around. Jackson Ivy swung Camille around for a dance in front of the giant pan of steaming chili, humming a tune, both of them smiling at each other. Jonas gave a shout as Lincoln found the murder weapon in the library, and everyone else laughed, except Arizona, who shouted, "I knew I should have made you let me be the professor!"

"Yeah. Mom loves to keep in touch," Autumn said.

And could afford to fly in and out whenever the whim took her.

"She descends randomly. Last month it was Savanna's house in Pagosa Springs. Savanna wasn't happy about it. For a motivational speaker, she sure is morose."

Remy looked over at the woman. She seemed to be enjoying this party, but Remy had seen the hint of sadness earlier when they'd talked briefly.

"Samúð," Autumn said, the foreign language sounding beautiful on her rich, sultry voice.

She'd been slipping in words like that ever since she'd gotten here.

"What is sa-moo?" Remy asked.

"Icelandic for *pity*. I wish I could snap her out of it." Autumn continued to watch her sister.

"You know languages?"

"Several. That's what I do for a living. I'm an independent contractor for now."

"Really?" Remy glanced around the crowd of people who didn't have to do anything to earn a living but did. There had been a time when she had worked hard to earn an above-average income. She was nowhere near the wealth surrounding her, but she'd managed to work her way to a comfortable living. That was before she'd met Wade.

"You all seem so normal, and then…" She looked back at Lincoln's dad, who'd released his wife to stir the chili.

"Yeah. It was always important to Mom that we be raised as normally as possible. We were spanked and grounded just like other Americans, trust me. My parents believe that discipline is necessary no matter what walk of life you come from."

Remy nodded. "I can see that." She turned to Autumn. "You have an amazing family."

"What about yours? Do you have family here?"

Family…

Remy contemplated avoiding that piece of conversation, putting her hands on the back of the kitchen island stool. "My mother died three years ago."

"Oh, I'm so sorry. That must have been hard on your family."

"It was just the two of us." Remy was too aware of the stark contrast between this family gathering and those she'd grown up with.

"No grandparents?"

"My grandfather died when my mother was an infant, and my grandmother never remarried. My mother was an only child like me. I never had a chance to meet my grandmother. She died when my mother was eighteen."

"What about your dad?"

"He left before I was born. I guess single motherhood runs in the family." She smiled past her difficulty in talking about her father. Many times she'd gotten curious about who he was and had always stopped taking action to try to find him. He obviously hadn't been interested in her, so why should she bother tracking him down? Still, the curiosity had taken root. Seeing her mother die alone hadn't helped. Her mother had loved the father of her child, and like her own mother, had never remarried.

"Well, if you wind up in this family, you'll probably wish you were back in the days you were an only child." Autumn breathed a laugh.

How would she end up in this family? Why had Autumn said that? Remy looked over her shoulder at Lincoln and caught him staring, intent blue eyes and sexy, messy blond hair. His arm was resting on the table, biceps round and strong.

"He keeps looking at you like that."

Remy dropped her hands from the back of the chair, uncomfortable.

"Are you two seeing each other?" Autumn asked.

"Oh, no. We're just neighbors, and Maddie loves him."

At the sound of her name, Maddie trotted over and sat, lifting a white paw, looking up with sweet eyes. Then a low growl began, puffing her whiskery cheeks, building into a soft, communicative bark.

Autumn laughed. "I was going to ask who Maddie was." She knelt and pet the dog. "No introductions necessary. Hello, Maddie." The dog shifted her butt so that she could put her paw on Autumn's leg now.

"What a sweet dog."

Remy shook her head as Maddie's gaze moved to her, as though saying, "She likes me more than you." "You don't know the half of it."

"Food's on," Camille said.

Remy surmised that Lincoln kept paper products on hand for events such as this. He had a big pantry full of them.

"Here you go, honey." Camille handed Remy a plate and took one herself. "Let's fill up."

Oh, no. Did she mean to sit by her? Remy had no other choice than to precede the woman to the spread on the counter by the stove. She put a dog on a bun and covered it with chili, followed by a few fries.

Just as she'd feared, Camille led her into the dining room off Lincoln's living room, where someone had lengthened the table and added a few chairs, and sat beside her.

Camille ate a few bites before using her fork as a conversational pointer. "You know," she said, "Lincoln is my oldest."

"Yes, he told me." She ate a fry.

That news seemed to give Camille pause. "You two have been getting close."

"Oh, no." Why did everyone think that?

"Lincoln isn't exactly an open book. Especially after Miranda."

Remy sensed his mother testing her. Did she know about Miranda? "Who is that?"

"His girlfriend. He was going to marry her. He's never told me that, but I know."

"What happened?"

Camille abandoned her fork, and sadness sobered her eyes. "They were on vacation in New York, walking down a busy street when a drive-by shooting took place. The shooter was targeting someone else, but she was in the way. It was completely random."

The violence of it caught Remy unprepared. Lincoln

seemed to attract that kind of mayhem. And now Remy had dragged him into her mess.

"That's horrible."

"He still thinks there's something he could have done. It happened more than seven years ago, and still he can't let it go." Camille shook her head with lingering sadness. "It's the reason he became a bounty hunter."

Remy went still. Bounty hunter? "I thought he taught martial arts."

"He does. But he hunts bail jumpers, too."

Lincoln entered the room with his plate, joining the rest of his family at the table and sitting on the other side, two chairs down from his mother. He caught her look and eyed his mother, clearly picking up on the somberness of their talk and not liking it.

And didn't it just figure that he was a bounty hunter? If Remy could, she'd get up and run out of here and keep running. Her dog and fear of Tristan stopped her. Maddie sat beside her, begging for food with just a look and a string of drool hanging indecorously from her whisker-peppered cheek. She had to find a safe place for Maddie while she cleared her name.

Lincoln shut down his computer, simmering over what he'd just learned from his internet search. It hadn't taken long.

His family had finally left after midnight, and after he took Remy over to her house for a bag of clothes and toiletries, she'd gone to bed and he'd sneaked into his office. He'd still been annoyed after trying to get his mother to tell him what she and Remy had discussed at dinner. His mother had feigned ignorance on her way out the door, claiming she had only tried to get to know his new girlfriend. Remy wasn't his girlfriend. Nor would she ever be after what he'd just read.

Now he understood why she was so reluctant to talk to police. She was wanted for murder in Newport Beach, California. And he was drawn into the trouble.

Lincoln was furious.

Not caring about her privacy, he went down the hall and opened the guest room door. She stood beside the bed, covers in hand, ready to climb in. Freezing when she saw him, she stared, unconcerned with the spaghetti-strap, knee-length nightie she wore. Right now, neither was he.

"We aren't going to sleep until you tell me about Kirby Clark. And make sure you don't leave out the reason why you tell everyone your name is Remy Lang."

A couple webpages had revealed that. Clark's murder was all over the news, and so were pictures of a striking look-alike to Remy Lang, known in Newport Beach, California as Sabrina Tierney, top HR executive for OneDefense Corporation. A far cry from the assistant she was now. He'd stopped reading then. He wanted to hear it from her. Better yet, he'd rely on some strategic friends for better intel.

At last she gathered her wits and straightened.

"I didn't kill him," she said. "Tristan Coulter is trying to frame me for his murder."

"Why?" His patience had already worn thin, and he struggled to hang on to what was left of it now.

"I was a friend of Kirby's."

He stepped forward. She stayed on the other side of the bed. "You're going to have to do better than that."

Ramrod straight and still, she didn't respond. Why would she? She'd assumed a false identity to escape the trouble that had chased her away from California.

"What kind of friend was Clark to you?" he said to help her open up.

Several seconds slid into the past before she turned and sat on the bed.

He went there and sat beside her, partly to let her know he wasn't leaving until he had answers, and partly as a supportive gesture. He had no idea where the latter came from. The woman had lied to him. But he wanted her to tell him the truth.

"I met him at a conference," she finally said. "We struck up a friendship after that. He wanted more. An opening came up at OneDefense, and he helped me get the job."

"What conference?"

Again, she hesitated. "It was a gun show."

A gun show. "You like guns?"

"I've taken up an interest recently." She sounded almost sarcastic.

"What's recent?"

"Over the past two years. But I've target practiced before that."

She didn't strike him as the type to have an NRA membership. "Did you know about the job when you went to the gun show?"

"No. The gun show was a few weeks before the job became available."

"And you suddenly took an interest in a job at OneDefense? Didn't you already have a job?"

"I worked for an insurance company that wasn't paying well. Certainly not as well as OneDefense. And…"

And what? Had she known about the illegal gun sales? Had her allegiance with Kirby primed her to get in on the profits?

"Did you ever become romantically involved with Clark?"

Her eyes blinked. "As I said, he wanted more. I didn't."

He'd seen from pictures that Kirby Clark was an attractive man. Divorced. Available. Had she used him to get in on the gun sales? She claimed to be trying to gather evidence against Tristan. That much must be true. Lincoln had seen the envelope, and Tristan *was* trying to kill her. But that didn't mean she didn't have her own agenda where the gun sales were concerned. And she had developed an interest in guns before she'd met Kirby.

"Why was he murdered?" he asked.

That upset her. She averted her head and again didn't reply immediately.

"We had plans to go for drinks and dinner one night. I was early getting to his office." She looked up at him, and he saw the truth in her eyes. "Tristan was there. He was trying to convince Kirby to join him in his illegal operation. I couldn't tell if Kirby was seriously considering it or if he was playing along to keep Tristan under control. Tristan saw me in the doorway. There were still a lot of people in the office building, so he didn't do anything right away. He pulled me into Kirby's office and closed the door. That's when he told Kirby he thought they should get rid of me. Kirby argued with him, and eventually we were able to get out of the building."

She lowered her head, tears springing to her eyes. "We were sure Tristan would try to kill me. We went for a quick dinner to make plans. He gave me Wade's name and told me to leave California. When he drove me home, Tristan was waiting inside my house. He had a gun."

Wiping away a tear, she took a pillow from the bed and hugged it, then slowly turned to look at him, cheek resting on the pillow. "Tristan found a knife in my kitchen and tried to stab me. Kirby stopped him. He and Tristan fought, and Kirby was stabbed. Tristan forced me to handle the knife. He was wearing gloves. He never used his gun and took the knife with him when he left. The police found it in a Dumpster near my house. As Kirby lay there dying, he told me to go as we'd planned. I called for help for him and did as he suggested. Now I wish I never had."

Because going to Wade had led to more trouble. Lincoln reached over and touched her back, rubbing gently. "Did Wade help you the way Kirby said he would?"

"At first. He arranged a false ID for me. But he held that over my head, tried to get me to start buying guns through his store so that he could sell them illegally on the street. He was getting greedy. I refused, and he began to get violent. Then he discovered I was gathering information on him. Most of the money he made from the illegal gun sales went to Tristan. Tristan is running the operation."

"Why was Wade killed?" Lincoln asked, although he already had a pretty good idea.

"He knew about Kirby, that Tristan was the one who murdered him. I told him. He must have threatened to go to the police."

Because Wade wanted more money out of the gun operation. So Tristan had killed him. If what Sabrina was saying was true, she hadn't known Wade was in on the gun sales until after she'd gone to him for help.

Lincoln believed her. She was telling him the truth.

But there were some things she was keeping from him, such as why she'd gone to the gun show. Why would someone who worked for an insurance company take interest in firearms? He supposed it was possible. Lots of people had hobbies outside of work they didn't share. But other aspects of Sabrina's personality didn't fit the profile of a gun enthusiast. Her femininity. Her relationship with her dog. Hell, the dog itself. Although a hunting breed, Maddie was no hunter.

Perhaps she'd known about OneDefense, taken an interest in the company and planned to get a job there. What drove her? What was she after? To expose Tristan? Or use what she had on him to get what she wanted? What could that be? Money? Or was meeting Kirby innocent?

Now that Tristan had thwarted her efforts to clear her name, what would she do? What would *they* do? It was time for him to take charge.

"Go pack a bigger bag. We're going to California," he said.

"What? No. The police are looking for me there."

"They're going to be looking for you here, too. If they haven't pieced together Kirby's murder and your false name yet, they will very soon."

"How do you know that?"

"They'll recognize you in photographs, for one."

The rest would be simple logic. How could she be Sabrina Tierney, wanted for questioning in one murder investigation, and Remy Lang, a person of interest in another? Both in different states. Of course, it would appear she'd run from one only to land herself in trouble with another.

He watched her lower her head as she drew the same

conclusion. The only way to clear her name was to expose Tristan. And how would they do that when she was continually being linked to murders?

Chapter 4

Sajal Kapoor whistled as he pushed his blue janitorial cart along the polished floor of a wide hallway at OneDefense Corporation. He'd grab himself a soda before heading up to the executive and management offices to finish up his night. He was more anxious than usual to leave. His wife worked part-time at a bank. Their schedules worked well for their son and daughter, ages ten and fourteen. Sajal took them to school in the mornings and his wife picked them up. But he was always eager to get home to see her. His wife and kids were his world. He was a simple man and, frankly, was glad there were people like the ones who ran this company. He preferred his undemanding job over that life. He put in his forty hours and went home. His weekends were devoted to his family, not work.

Things sure had turned out different than his dad had always taught him. Left out of those teachings was the reality that a man had to sacrifice a family life if he wanted to make a lot of money. That wasn't something Sajal had the slightest desire to do.

His parents had moved to the United States before he was born and raised him to believe this was a country where dreams came true. This gun company wasn't his idea of a dream, but it gave his family health insurance and a roof over all their heads. His wife's income went for food and clothing, and his income covered the rest. They even managed to save a small amount each month.

Hearing Enrique and Jasper at the espresso machine, a smile perked up Sajal. Tuesday night at ten o'clock in Newport Beach, California just got a little brighter. Jasper always wore jean overalls. He was OneDefense's senior electrician. Enrique was one of four handymen. Leaving his cart near the long cafeteria island, he went to the two.

"Sajal," Enrique greeted in his Spanish accent.

"Good morning," Sajal said with a slight Indian accent he'd gotten from his parents, who still spoke their native language frequently. They hadn't mastered English as well as Sajal had. Growing up here was different than immigrating.

Jasper handed him an espresso. He took it with a nod of appreciation and sipped.

"We were just talking about Kirby Clark," Jasper said. "I heard on the news this morning that there's still no sign of Sabrina Tierney."

The entire company had been abuzz over Kirby's murder. And why wouldn't they? It wasn't every day a man was murdered at your place of employment.

First, a rumor had spread that Kirby and the head of HR had been having an affair, then he'd turned up dead and the woman had disappeared.

"You think she did it?" Jasper asked.

"I heard another woman who was seeing Mr. Clark showed up last Tuesday asking questions about Sabrina," Enrique said. "The two didn't know about each other. He was bangin' them both. And you will not believe this...the other woman is married!" Enrique's eyes popped wide open, and a big, white, toothy smile formed on his face. He was loving the gossip.

"Explains why he kept her a secret," Jasper said.

Sajal wasn't so sure all of this gossip was accurate. "Sabrina's assistant said Sabrina and Kirby were just friends. They went to lunch and dinner a lot but didn't sleep together."

"That's what they'd want you to believe." Jasper finished his espresso. "I think Sabrina found out about the other woman and killed him."

Sabrina Tierney had always been kind to Sajal. She'd worked long hours and had usually been in her office when he'd come by to empty her trash, one of the last things he did before leaving for the night. She'd hand him the trash can and ask him how his family was doing. She even remembered their names. It was rare when someone at that level acknowledged him so genuinely. No, that woman had a good heart. He didn't care what the news said. She didn't kill Kirby. He may not be the brightest man on Earth, but he had a good sense about people, and Sabrina had never given him a bad feeling.

"Have you ever met her dog?" Sajal asked.

Both Enrique and Jasper looked at him without answering, mystified over his question, in such contrast to the scandal.

"No owner of a dog like that could be a killer," he continued. "She brought her in sometimes, when she worked real late." Which had been often. "That dog would jump up on me and try to lick my face off. Always had a stuffed toy to show me, too." He wondered what had happened to her and Sabrina.

"You really don't think it was her?" Jasper asked.

Sajal shrugged. "I'm no detective, but it just doesn't seem that way to me."

After a bit, Jasper said, "You think you know people, and they end up getting arrested for murder. It happens."

Enrique nodded. "Yeah. The quiet neighbor. Teachers molesting students. Priests." He nodded again. "Yeah. Sabrina seems nice, but she could have murdered him."

"Who else could it have been?" Jasper asked.

"The married woman," Sajal said.

The two mulled that over.

"She was pretty upset when she came here," Enrique said. "I didn't hear her talking to Tristan, but I did see her leave. She was crying." His accent drew out the last word.

"The news said the knife used to kill Kirby was found in a Dumpster near Sabrina's house. Her prints were on it," Jasper said.

"Of course they were," Sajal argued. "It was her knife. It came from her kitchen. Anyone could have put it there."

"Like the secret woman," Enrique said.

Or someone else. Sajal thought there was more going on than any of them knew. If Kirby's murder would ever be solved, he'd bet they'd all be surprised by the outcome. But it was nothing the three of them would solve over espresso. And Sajal had a wife to go home to.

"Well, I should get going. My wife said she'd wait up for me tonight. I don't want to be late."

"Ah," Enrique teased. "Sajal's gonna get lucky tonight." His accent accentuated *lucky tonight*. It sometimes annoyed Sajal.

Jasper said nothing, his face turning somber. He'd recently finalized his divorce, and he wasn't the one who'd wanted it. His wife had declared she'd grown beyond what their relationship could give her. Jasper hadn't known until after she'd served him that she'd met another man. He was devastated. Sajal was concerned his friend and coworker wouldn't be able to overcome it and move on.

Enrique, on the other hand, had yet to be married. "Someday you'll understand." Sajal finished his espresso and threw out the small cup. Then he gave Jasper a pat on his shoulder. "Try to distract yourself with your work. If you're going to think of her, think of the good times and don't regret."

Jasper's sorrow lifted just a little. "You always know what to say, Sajal." He checked his cell phone. "Too bad it isn't as easy as it sounds."

Turning, Sajal went to his cart. "See you both tomorrow."

"Have fun tonight," Enrique said, drawing out *tonight*.

Without responding, he kept his annoyance to himself and left the cafeteria. He pushed his cart toward the executive and management offices. He cleaned those last since the executives and managers were always the last to leave at night.

Thinking of Maeve, Sajal finished the executive offices and headed for the storage closet down the hall for more supplies. He'd clean the managers' offices and then he'd be finished. A man passed him in the hall as he unlocked the door. Sajal glanced at him, but the man paid him no heed. Tension deepened otherwise shallow wrinkles on his brow and around his mouth. He was perhaps in his early fifties. His strides were long and purposeful. He wasn't a tall man. Average. In pretty good shape, with only a slight protrusion in the stomach area. He had green eyes and fine, medium brown hair that had yet to go gray.

The man reached Tristan Coulter's office and pushed the door open without knocking.

"We need to talk." The man intended to close the door behind him, Sajal thought, but it stopped an inch or so from doing so completely.

Any other office, Sajal would have moved on out of respect for privacy. But this was Tristan's office, the very one visited by Kirby's secret lover. Sajal wasn't one to give in to gossip, but he found himself curious nonetheless. He dallied in the supply closet, which was directly across the hall from Tristan's office. He didn't understand Tristan's job. As account manager, he was part of customer service and had a team of representatives who reported to him.

"The chief came to see me this afternoon," the visitor said.

Sajal heard Tristan's chair move as though he leaned back against it. He didn't know what kind of man Tristan was, but he'd heard rumors that he had a bad temper, that most of those who reported to him didn't like him and even feared him.

"Have a seat, Archer. Calm down and tell me what's got you in such a lather."

"Don't patronize me. It's easy for you to sit behind that desk and tell me to calm down. This whole thing is blowing up, and I want nothing more to do with it."

"Sit down, Archer."

"You son of a—"

"Sit down!" Tristan shouted.

Archer must have gone to sit down. Sajal leaned to peer through the open supply-closet door. The windows on each side of the door to Tristan's office had blinds on the inside that were closed. He could see a sliver of the back of Archer's head through the barely open office door. He had gone to sit in front of Tristan's desk. Sajal couldn't see Tristan. His chair was blocked by the door.

"He suspects something," Archer said. "He asked me why I was so convinced Sabrina Tierney killed Kirby when the crime scene suggests there were more than two people involved. Fibers were found that aren't linked to either Kirby or Sabrina. He knows there was a third person there, Tristan. I can't keep insisting Sabrina Tierney is my primary suspect. Nobody will believe me."

Tristan remained silent for a beat or two. "What fibers were found?"

"Clothing. A green cotton fiber."

Tristan didn't say anything at first. "That doesn't mean anything. Fibers alone can't convict someone. You have to be able to prove someone committed the crime. Let the chief speculate. Tell him you'll look into it."

"I did. But he asked why I hadn't yet."

"What did you tell him?"

"That I missed it. He looked at me funny and told me to report to him after I finished checking it out."

"So check it out. It won't lead anywhere."

"How can you be so sure?"

"Because you won't let it lead anywhere." Tristan paused. "Right?"

Archer now paused.

Sajal heard Tristan move. Archer stood from the chair, and Sajal saw Tristan's hand go to his back.

"You worry too much," Tristan said. "This will all work out. You'll see."

"I should have never listened to you."

"You had no other choice. You did the right thing, Archer. Now, go home and relax. Tomorrow you can check into the fiber and report it to the chief. He'll forget all about it then, and all of this will be a thing of the past." He guided Archer to the door.

Sajal turned his back and pretended to be busy in the supply closet. He put some window cleaner into his cart. When he emerged from the closet, Archer was gone, and Tristan stood in his now-open doorway, slightly graying hair belying his sixty years. He was in shape and looked younger than he was. Sajal only knew his age because one of the administrative assistants had told him.

"Oh," Sajal said. "Mr. Coulter. Working late tonight?"

"How long have you been in there?" Tristan asked.

Sajal shrugged. "Not long. Just restocking for tomorrow."

Tristan merely studied him, picking him apart. Sajal could feel him wondering if he'd heard any of the conversation between him and Archer.

"Did you see the man that was just here?"

"I heard someone leave your office, but I didn't see anyone, no. Is there a problem?"

"No." Tristan's lined mouth turned down in false nonchalance. "No problem."

Sajal pushed his cart down the hall, eager to get away. "Have a nice evening, sir."

"You, too.... I didn't catch your name."

Sajal stopped, his heart jumping into apprehensive beats. "Sajal Kapoor, sir."

"Mr. Kapoor. You have a good evening, as well."

Sajal smiled. "Thank you. I will." He was certain this would be the one and only time Tristan Coulter would remember a low-level employee's name.

Sajal shut the door after arriving home and saw his wife come to greet him. "How was your day?" Maeve asked, kissing him when he leaned down. She usually waited up for him. She had the day off tomorrow so he didn't feel too badly about keeping her up past her bedtime.

"Strange." Straightening, he looked into her brown eyes and noticed that she'd done her hair and wore one of her favorite sundresses that smoothed her slightly overweight frame. "You look beautiful."

She beamed, her subtly crooked teeth flashing. "What was strange about today?" She turned and led him into the kitchen.

He didn't really want to talk about it. "Let me get comfortable."

"Meet you in here."

It smelled wonderful. He walked down the hall of their three-bedroom ranch and called, "Where are the kids?"

"At Mom's for the night. She's taking them to school in the morning."

They really had the night to themselves, then. Sajal changed into shorts and a Yosemite National Park T-shirt and went into the kitchen where his wife was stirring spaghetti sauce. She made it with sausage and lots of tomatoes, just the way they both loved it. Spaghetti was the first dinner they'd had together. He'd taken her to a local place, not a chain. And when she'd ordered spaghetti, he'd known he'd met his soul mate.

He leaned over her shoulder and kissed her behind her ear.

After she giggled softly, she asked, "What was strange about today?"

Sighing, still not wanting to talk about it but compelled to share with his wife, he answered, "I heard a conversation that disturbed me today."

As her mouth opened to probe, he shushed her and held his finger up, pressing it to her lips. He saw her eyes register his concern.

"Sajal." She swatted his hand away.

Now her brow lowered, and those lovely eyes admonished. She knew something was amiss. He almost smiled. Worry kept it at bay. He loved her so much. Strong, beautiful woman.

"My darling." He kissed her cheek.

She pushed his chest. "You tell me now!"

He stepped back, adoring her, calmed by her. "I love you even when you're mad."

She poked him with her finger, not hard enough to hurt, just demanding.

"I heard Tristan talking tonight to a man I don't know. It was about Kirby Clark's murder."

Her hand flattened on his chest. "You're worried. What did they say? Tell me all."

He didn't want to.

"Sajal…"

He sighed again, this time with more reluctance. "Maeve. It is work."

"Work? The CEO was murdered, Sajal. Now, you tell me what you heard."

He contemplated refusing. Would he put her in danger if he did as she asked?

"Sajal…?"

He knew that tone. There was no getting around answering her. "I heard Tristan talking in his office tonight." His wife turned the burner to simmer. The water for the noodles was just beginning to boil, and the smell of baking French bread began to fill the house. "A man came to see him. He called him Archer. They talked about Kirby Clark's murder, about evidence Archer was concerned would come to light."

"Evidence?" Maeve put noodles into the water.

"Fiber evidence. Archer must be a detective because he mentioned his chief."

"And this Archer person is hiding evidence?" Maeve faced him, grave confusion and worry filling her eyes. "What does Tristan have to do with it? Why is he involved?"

"That I don't know. He was supporting Archer, who seemed afraid he'd be caught."

"Why? Does he know who killed Kirby?"

"Oh, I definitely think he does."

"Do you think it was Tristan?"

The way Tristan had spoken made Sajal say no. He was supportive of Archer. But then, Tristan was known for his ruthless ways, his fearlessness. In business, he was successful. He'd probably worked his way up to the executive ranks.

"What were you doing outside his office?" she asked.

"I was in one of the supply closets. It was across the hall."

"Did they see you?"

"Tristan did. He asked how long I'd been there. I pretended not to be aware that he and Archer had talked."

His wife's eyes searched his face. She was worried. He didn't like seeing her that way. "Did he believe you?"

Sajal replayed the exchange in his mind and had to answer honestly. "I don't know."

Chapter 5

Lincoln believed her.

Sabrina leaned against the window frame of their Newport Beach hotel, gazing out at the city lights and darkness beyond where the ocean began. They'd left Denver this afternoon, as soon as Lincoln had been able to make flight arrangements. Maddie was at his house and Arizona was going to dog-sit.

His trust had shifted something in her, something too warm, something she rarely had the privilege of feeling.

Turning from the window, she watched him pore over the papers that had been waiting for him in an envelope when they'd arrived at the hotel. He sat at the dining table in the top-floor, spacious suite, more like an apartment. His blond hair hung in uncombed spikes over his forehead, neatly trimmed over his ears and at his nape. His shoulders sloped down to strong arms resting on the table. She'd stayed in nice hotel rooms before, but not this nice.

Lincoln's long fingers holding the paper recaptured her attention. Clean and masculine, they made her imagine naughty things. She'd blame his trust in her. Growing up without a father and seeing her mother so lonely had impressed upon her greatly the importance of choosing well in a man. Sabrina had dated a lot. Most of them never went beyond meeting once for coffee. That was because she'd gotten so good at recognizing a waste of time when she encountered one. Lincoln didn't resemble any of them. So why was she going down this path? Lincoln wasn't a prospect.

She wandered over to the table. She was spending a lot of time with him, that was all. Her radar was fuzzy. Maybe that was because she wasn't dating him. Theirs was a chance encounter. She hadn't studied him or looked for key flaws or asked him the list of questions she asked every man she took an interest in.

"How old are you?" she asked. Blurted, more like. It was the next thought she'd had after the last.

His blue eyes lifted. And, oh, were they blue.

"Forty-two. You?" One brow lifted higher than the other and his head cocked a little. He probably wondered why she'd asked.

"Thirty-six." He didn't look forty-two. She didn't look her age, either.

He put the paper down and leaned back against the chair. "My mother didn't tell you that?"

"No. She said you were a bounty hunter." She sat on the chair beside him.

The reason why he'd become a bounty hunter hung between them. He knew his mother had told her.

"Is she the reason you aren't married?" She didn't have to explain it wasn't his mother she was talking about.

"Do I have to have a reason?"

"Everybody has a reason."

He glanced down at her ring finger. "What's yours?"

"I haven't met anyone worth the risk."

She watched him wonder why marriage was a risk to her.

"That's an interesting way of putting it," he said. "Did someone break your heart?"

"Everyone gets their heart broken." She didn't want to bring up Chet, the man she'd seen before OneDefense had come into her life.

"Who broke yours?" he asked.

She tapped her fingertips on the table, seeing the challenge in his impossibly gorgeous eyes. Why were they talking about this? Oh, yeah, because she was the one who'd started it. "An insurance executive who neglected to tell me that he was married."

He winced. "He lied? Sorry."

She was glad he wasn't teasing. There was nothing humorous about that experience, especially since she'd always been so careful.

"His name was Chet. We weren't engaged," she said, tapping her fingers some more. "And it couldn't have been as bad as it must have been for you to see that woman shot and killed. If anyone's sorry, it's me."

He looked down at her fingers, which she stilled with a caught smile.

"Nervous?" he asked.

"No." She couldn't hold still. And her curiosity was to blame.

"Bored?"

She laughed once. "No." With him? Never.

He lifted the paper again, but Sabrina wasn't finished with this conversation.

"What was she like?" she asked.

He looked up from the paper with a stone mask keeping deeper emotions at bay. "I'd rather not talk about that."

It had happened so long ago, and still he closed the door on the pain. His mother's worry was more than validated. Would he never get past the grief? He probably felt guilty, too. He hadn't been able to save Miranda. She'd been shot and he'd walked away. And now he was a bounty hunter because of it. He chased bail jumpers, criminals who shot people like the woman he'd loved. He kept them from running free. He made sure they faced the justice they deserved.

"Have you been with anyone since then?" she pressed.

"A few. Not many. That isn't important to me right now."

He was forty-two. Would it ever be important? She grew apprehensive over her feelings, or those she might have for him if she continued to allow her curiosity to seek answers.

"Were any of them relationships?" she couldn't help asking.

He stared at her. "Why are you asking me these questions?"

She lowered her eyes, unable to voice the truth.

"I did see one woman for a few months."

Only one had lasted months? "What happened?" Had she gotten too close?

"It ended up not working out."

"How did you meet her?" She should really stop this feeding of her curiosity. What about him lured her? She took in his masculine body and handsome face. Aside from that....

"I just ran into her one day. We were waiting in line at a deli and struck up a conversation. I met her for coffee after that."

He got a faraway look, remembering.

"It must have been special," she said.

"It was, more than I anticipated. If I'd have known…" He put down the page he held.

Something must have happened that day, something he didn't feel good about. "Were you seeing someone else at the time?"

It was a moment before he answered, seeming surprised that she'd guessed. Most men who weren't monogamous hid it better than he did.

"I wouldn't put it that way," he said.

"But you did meet someone."

"It wasn't intentional. I didn't get a chance to tell Rayna before she saw me with the other woman."

"It sounds like you cheated on her." Funny, he hadn't seemed like a jerk when she'd first met him.

He remained calm. "No. You don't understand. It wasn't serious, at least that's what I thought at the time. I didn't mean to hurt her. When I met the other woman, I realized that Rayna wasn't right for me. I was going to stop seeing her."

But Rayna had seen him with the other woman before he could. Sabrina's disgust must have shown because he sighed in exasperation and said, "I didn't know she had feelings for me already. We'd only dated a few times. We never even had sex. If I'd have known she was getting too serious, I would have broken things off with her sooner, but she never told me."

She was probably afraid to. She'd probably known he didn't feel the same, since he still wasn't over his lost love.

Sabrina realized how deliberately aloof he was regarding relationships. His distance was his armor against love, against venturing into what he'd had with the dead woman.

"I didn't mean to hurt her," Lincoln insisted, sounding as though it was important she believe him.

"Were you always like this?" she asked.

He looked confused. "Like what?"

"Open to meeting other women when you're dating someone else?"

"I wasn't open to it," he said angrily. "I didn't plan on meeting someone else."

And he and Rayna hadn't been serious. He hadn't intended to hurt her and wouldn't have cheated on her. But his avoidance of serious relationships was a defense mechanism. "You must have really loved her."

"I said I don't want to talk about Miranda."

"You need to." She'd never met anyone who needed to talk more than this man did. Didn't he see how screwy his philosophy on women had become?

No, he couldn't possibly, or he wouldn't believe dating other women while seeing another was okay by anyone's standards. Whether it was discussed or not. Maybe that poor woman had seen what Sabrina now saw—that he was operating on a broken heart that was fed by guilt. She'd taken a chance on him that he'd find love again, with her.

And look what that risk had gotten her. Her very own broken heart.

When Sabrina realized she was in danger of falling into the same trap, she went cold inside. Some day she could be that woman, walking up to a restaurant patio or into a coffee shop or wherever, seeing the man she'd taken a chance to love with another woman.

She was glad he believed that she hadn't murdered Kirby, but that was as far as her feelings would go with him from now on. If there was one thing Sabrina was good at, it was shutting down a man who didn't meet her requirements. And number one on that list was being trustworthy. Lincoln might be trustworthy when he fell in love again, but would he ever allow himself to be that vulnerable?

Trustworthy. Faithful. Committed. Those were her three top requirements.

Number one: debatable. She couldn't trust Lincoln based on his history.

Number two: debatable. That depended on where the line was drawn. He denied being open to meeting other women, but he had met someone and been open to seeing more of her, regardless of his status with Rayna.

Number three: absolutely not. Check, "No." Lincoln was not a committer.

She shook her finger at him casually. "Just for the record, nothing is ever going to happen between you and me. When all of this is over, we go back to being neighbors. I'll get my gate fixed. I don't want Maddie going over to your place anymore."

He sat there looking at her, confused again. "Why are you so mad?"

"I'm not mad. I'm just making sure you understand that I'm not interested in anything remotely romantic with you."

After a moment, he answered, "All right. I can respect that. I'm just curious about one thing."

She lifted an eyebrow.

"What are you so afraid of?"

"Me?" He was the one with the commitment problem. "Are you afraid if I kiss you again, you'll like it?"

Yes. "I don't get involved with any man who's afraid of commitment." *And hung up on another woman.*

"I'm not afraid."

Yeah, right. "Then tell me about Miranda."

"What's wrong with kissing?" he challenged. "What's wrong with doing more if we feel like it?"

He was deliberately evading her. "I'm not interested," she said.

"You were yesterday."

She couldn't deny that. "And when it gets too serious? What then?" It was the "what then" that she wasn't interested in.

That stopped him. Standing up, he walked across the room and stood at the window.

Exactly what she thought. He'd run. He was running even now, getting up and walking away like that. "One more for the record." Tapping her fingers on the table, she waited for him to turn and face her. "You were interested, too. When we kissed. But that's as far as it goes."

He didn't respond, and that told her all she needed to know. He agreed. They had chemistry, but taking it further wasn't an option—at least it didn't seem like one.

Picking up the papers to stop her tapping fingers, she began to read; Lincoln and his commitment phobia were officially not her concern anymore. Clearing her name was her sole purpose. She began to register what she was reading and grew absorbed.

"Where did you get this?" she asked.

Striding over to the table, he leaned down, braced by one hand, brow still low after being forced to face the degree of their chemistry. It gave her slight pause. He must feel that he was more interested than expected. She had to steer temptation away from that carrot.

The paper was an extensive background on Tristan

Coulter. He'd grown up poor. Both his mother and his father were dead. His stepmother was alive and ran a pastry shop somewhere in L.A. They were estranged. Tristan never went to see her. Didn't help her financially. He had a sister and a half brother who lived in California. There was nothing in the report about them, not even their names. Divorced twice. Married to a much younger woman now and lived in a very nice, pricey-looking house. There was a picture of it. His job as an account manager paid pretty well, but Sabrina didn't think it paid that well. She stared at the picture of a smiling Tristan, all charisma, handsome for his age of sixty, healthy, his hair just beginning to get gray, but his eyes were beady and calculating. How long had he been involved in illegal gun sales?

"No arrest record?" she asked.

"None. But if you read further, you'll see that he was in and out of trouble through school, recurrently with two other boys who are now dead."

She looked up at him.

"Car accident, they called it."

Sabrina was glad she didn't have to pretend to be Remy anymore. They'd spent much of the day trying to figure out a way to spy on Tristan, but the security was too tight at OneDefense, and it was pointless to sit outside his home when he was at work all day.

By midafternoon, overcast, they had given up for the day and were on their way back to the hotel. Or so Lincoln thought.

"Take the next exit," Sabrina said to him.

He glanced over at her in confusion. Leaned back in the driver's seat of their Mercedes rental, his long, jean-clad thighs slightly parted in a relaxed pose, flat stomach covered by a soft and loose sage-green button-up short-sleeved shirt, chest stretching the material in all the right places, he was a dream. A clean-shaven gentleman with a daring streak.

"Just do it," she said, thinking she sounded a little too aroused.

He'd done his fair share of checking her out. She wore a white-and-teal sundress that really flattered her figure. She'd told herself this morning that she hadn't packed it for him.

He took the exit. "Something else you're keeping secret?"

That ruined her glow. Wishing she didn't have to take him along, she only instructed him where to drive. She hadn't told him about Bonnie Edwards for a reason. Bonnie was the only living person who knew her, really knew her. Having no family anymore, her long-time friend was all she had left. Sabrina cherished her. That close bond was what drew her here. She hadn't been able to contact Bonnie until now.

Checking behind them, she made sure no one followed. Lincoln noticed. She doubted there was anything he wouldn't notice. Calm and collected, he drove where she indicated. They reached the gated community where Bonnie lived with her husband, an attorney who helped pursue lawsuits against supposed "patent infringements." Despite his questionable employment, he was actually a nice man. He also treated Bonnie like a princess.

At a pale brown stucco and white-trimmed house with a three-car garage and panel of windows in the front, Sabrina told Lincoln to stop.

"Who lives here?" he demanded.

"A friend." She got out before he could say more and

walked up to the front door. She hadn't called. Bonnie had a busy schedule of taking care of kids, going to the spa, shopping or volunteering at the Orange County Humane Society, but it was late enough now that she was probably home.

She rang the bell, Lincoln standing beside her, not happy with her secretiveness.

Bonnie answered the door. A redhead like Sabrina, her straight hair was cut short. Her green eyes were darker than Sabrina's, and she was shorter by about two inches. She wore jeans and a blue rayon blouse, feet bare to reveal freshly painted toenails. It must have been a nail day.

"Oh," Bonnie breathed. "Sabrina, my God." Bonnie opened her arms, and they hugged briefly and not too close. "I've been so worried about you. Why didn't you call me? I've been going out of my mind wondering where you were and if you were all right."

"I know, I'm sorry." Sabrina leaned back. "This is the soonest I could manage. I didn't want to put you in any danger."

With her hands still on each of Sabrina's biceps, Bonnie nodded grimly. "It's terrible about Kirby. Come in." She moved aside, taking in Lincoln.

Sabrina introduced him as her neighbor who was helping her in her situation. That only marginally placated her curiosity.

"Sabrina didn't tell me about you," Lincoln said.

Bonnie led them through the square, marble, ornately trimmed entry with closed doors on each side and an archway ahead, through which was a large living room and kitchen area.

"Sabrina and I have known each other since we were kids," she said as she led them into a great room. A woman waited there, wearing a maroon blouse and tan pants.

"Will you bring us some tea, Ms. Pearl?" Bonnie asked courteously of the woman.

Ms. Pearl gave a slight bow and went to do her bidding.

Bonnie had an embarrassed way of doling out orders or exerting the affluence money gave her. She was of humble roots, like Sabrina. They'd grown up in the same neighborhood. She'd met her husband in college, and they'd fallen in love. If her husband's success had changed any of that foundation, Sabrina couldn't see it.

"How's the trolling business?" Sabrina asked. She always teased Bonnie over that.

Bonnie's face sort of fell. "Dwight isn't happy. He's looking for another job, but no reputable firm wants to hire him. He got this job right out of college, remember?"

She did. "He'll find something." She was relieved he was trying to get away from that kind of business, thwarting innovation instead of promoting it as was the real intention of patents to begin with.

No sounds of children came from other parts of the house. "Kids not home?"

"They have music lessons after school today. I have to pick them up in an hour."

They'd have just enough time. Sabrina didn't want to stay long in case Tristan's men caught up with them.

Bonnie sat on the sofa, Sabrina beside her. Lincoln remained standing, his gaze going over every inch of Bonnie's house.

A pitcher of tea arrived with three glasses filled with ice. Ms. Pearl put the tray on a long, wide coffee table that held books on tropical places where Bonnie and her husband had no doubt visited.

"So tell me everything. What's happened to you?" Bonnie said, eyeing Lincoln again. "I've only heard what's in the news. And I know you didn't kill Kirby."

"It's Tristan. He's selling guns illegally at some of OneDefense's stores." She told her all about Tristan killing Kirby and the reason she had to flee to Denver.

Bonnie's eyes rounded and her mouth dropped open. "Oh, you poor thing. Well, at least you aren't alone. You have Lincoln here."

"Yes." Sabrina didn't fall for the lead-in that let her know Bonnie was fishing for more details on Lincoln. He was handsome enough to qualify as potential boyfriend material.

"Have you gotten anything on Tristan?"

"Not yet." Unfortunately, what she had gotten, she'd lost.

"I thought there was something off-color about him. You said Kirby didn't trust him, either."

She looked at Lincoln, who patiently waited. "No, he didn't."

"You talked about it?" Bonnie asked.

"Not really." She sipped her tea. "It was more of a feeling."

"I didn't know you were that close," Bonnie said, more leading in to what she wasn't asking directly. "If you'd have had more time, I bet something would have happened between the two of you."

"I don't think so." Bonnie didn't understand, and Sabrina wasn't going to enlighten her right now.

"Why not? He was attractive enough. A little older than you, but attractive."

Kirby had been seven years older than her. "Nothing was going on between us. I liked him. He was nice, that's all."

Bonnie searched her face, not buying it. Sabrina shared many things with her friend, but not that. Not Kirby.

Bonnie glanced at Lincoln as though biting her tongue because of his presence, uncertain of Sabrina's relationship with him and forever a loyal friend. Sabrina didn't give her trust to just anyone. Bonnie was genuine all the way through and definitely someone Sabrina trusted.

"When you said you were going to work for OneDefense, I wondered if it was a bad idea," Bonnie said. "You had it made at Pacific Life. Why did you leave? You didn't have to."

Lincoln wandered over, seemingly casual, but Sabrina wasn't fooled. "Yes. Why did you leave Pacific Life?" he asked.

"I told you," Sabrina said to Bonnie. "It was more money and I needed a change."

"That was right after you met Kirby." Bonnie didn't believe her.

"That isn't why I took the job."

"Wasn't it?"

Sabrina stared down her friend, who passed a look at Lincoln, clearly certain he was the reason Sabrina wasn't being forthright. Then she turned back to Sabrina and reached over to squeeze her hand. "I'm so sorry, Sabrina. You've not had the best luck when it comes to men."

Sabrina slipped her hand free of Bonnie's, a reaction she saw Lincoln notice. She appreciated Bonnie's concern and affection; she just wasn't prepared to handle it right now.

Bonnie didn't press anymore. They'd catch up later, when Lincoln wasn't around. "The police came to talk to me," she said. "That's how I found out you were missing."

"I'm sorry I put you through that."

Before Bonnie could respond, Lincoln asked, "Why did they come to question you?"

"They wanted to know if I knew where Sabrina was. Of course, I didn't. They asked about your relationship with Kirby." She hesitated. "I told them what I thought."

That he and Sabrina were involved.

"I told them you didn't kill him, too," Bonnie quickly added, clasping her hands on her knees. "They asked how you met him and why you took the job at OneDefense. They confirmed that Kirby fired the previous VP of HR just days before he hired you. They seemed pretty sure he did it deliberately because of his relationship with you. And then they told me about Kirby's lover."

Sabrina sat straighter. "Kirby was seeing someone?"

Bonnie hesitated, not expecting Sabrina's reaction. "You didn't know?"

"No. How would I? Do you think he would have told me?" Anger ignited and burned. How could she have been fooled—again? What was it with her and cheating men? She looked up at Lincoln, who was still watching her.

"She's married, which was probably why he kept her a secret. And get this—after the police came here asking questions, I heard on the news that a woman went missing. It's the same woman Kirby was seeing."

Sabrina couldn't control the sensation of betrayal that gripped her. Kirby had been a charismatic, ambitious man. Type-A personality, but kindhearted. Enjoyed the finer things in life, but could wear flannel and watch movies all day. She hadn't loved him. Not yet. She had held back, waiting. Was he someone she could open up to? She hadn't felt she'd known him well enough. In the end, he'd not only led her to Wade, he'd been having an affair with a married woman the whole time he'd been pursuing her. Somehow that was worse.

Why did his betrayal hurt her when she hadn't loved him? It must be the dishonesty. After watching deceit tear her mother apart, the injustice of it had stuck with her. That was why she was so careful about the men she chose to see. But being careful didn't seem to do any good.

"What was the woman's name?" Lincoln asked, ever the cool head. Kirby's lover going missing was pretty significant.

"Tory," Bonnie said. "Tory Von something. Von Every." She turned to Sabrina, who saw her concern. "Sorry. I thought you knew. The police seemed to think you had a motive to kill him."

And what other motive could there have been other than jealousy? She was furious with Kirby for lying to her, but he hadn't deserved to die for it.

She swatted the air with her hand, perfecting a blasé attitude. "Oh, stop. Why does everyone think I was seeing Kirby? Seriously, we were just friends." But he had wanted more, and hadn't been honest about Tory.

When Bonnie looked at her funny once again, Sabrina checked on Lincoln. As she suspected, he'd noticed the change in Bonnie. Now he wondered why her closest friend had thought what everyone at OneDefense had. Sabrina wasn't ready to get into that. Lincoln believed her, but her relationship with Kirby, however brief it had been, was too personal. And too complicated.

Seeing that Bonnie's awareness of Lincoln stopped her from questioning her further, Sabrina stood up and turned her back on both of them. She could hear Bonnie's silent question: Why was she claiming she and Kirby hadn't been involved romantically? And why did it bother her so much that he'd lied to her? Going over to a bookshelf, she inspected the framed photographs mixed among books there. It always warmed her immeasurably to see the picture of them just after college.

Lincoln appeared beside her. She looked up at him, at his eyes she was beginning to love so much, the knowledge in them. There was speculation, too. He wasn't stupid. He knew there was something she wasn't saying.

When he put his hand on her shoulder and gently squeezed, a gesture of reassurance, she was taken aback. Rather than suspicion, she received understanding from him. Was he trying to get her to talk? Or was he sincerely by her side?

The look in his eyes made her yearn for the latter. Anxiety over how much he'd probe kept her from falling for it. She could not tell anyone about her relationship with Kirby, not in any great detail.

"Oh. I almost forgot. Someone came to see me last week," Bonnie said, effectively stopping Lincoln from starting any kind of interrogation.

Sabrina fully expected one to come, however. She faced Bonnie. "Who?"

"He said his name was Pasquale." She stood and went to the kitchen, where her purse hung from the back of a kitchen-island chair. Digging inside, she procured a business card. "He was looking for you." She walked over to Sabrina, who was stunned into motionlessness.

She took the card. Pasquale Manco's OneDefense business card. The Italian she'd met once. Kirby had introduced him as OneDefense's vice president of domestic sales, and a friend.

"What did he want?" she asked.

Lincoln remained quiet, keeping his observations to himself for now.

"He didn't say. Just said that if I ever saw you to give you that card and tell you to contact him."

"How did he know to come to you?" Sabrina asked.

"Kirby. He said Kirby talked of you often, and said once that you had no family except for a close friend. Me."

Sabrina had talked of Bonnie with Kirby. She'd told him a lot of things, things that, in retrospect, perhaps she shouldn't have. There was that trust issue again. Why was it so hard for her to pick out men who were trustworthy? Kirby had seemed to be that kind of man. How could she have determined he wasn't sooner than she had?

Thinking about the time they'd spent together, she couldn't come up with a single example. She'd never suspected he was having an affair with a married woman, and she'd never suspected that Wade was crooked.

Sabrina met Lincoln's patient eyes and contemplated figuring out a way to meet Pasquale by herself. What did he know?

Chapter 6

Sabrina was agitated after they left Bonnie's house. Lincoln figured she'd try to ditch him if she could. That was why he wasn't letting her out of his sight. He took her to an internet café, where he looked up information on Pasquale Manco. Sabrina sipped on a latte, her clear, pretty eyes watching him, while he watched her with sexual desire he tried to smother. It was chilly, the overcast sky darker than before and promising rain. Lincoln closed his session on the computer.

"Well? Is he a pedophile?" she asked. When he looked up to acknowledge her, she said, "Drug addict? Thief?"

Recognizing her teasing, he stood and went to her. Close. "No."

She didn't move, even though she had to feel crowded. "He's got no criminal record. You can go ahead and call him."

Pulling out her phone, she used the card Bonnie had given her and pressed the numbers on her smartphone, then turned on the speaker.

"Yes?" Pasquale answered.

"Mr. Manco?"

"Who is this?" he queried in accented English.

"Sabrina Tierney." There need be no further introduction.

Lincoln waited out his lengthy pause.

At last, he said quickly, "We need to meet, but we must be very careful. I have obligations tonight and an early meeting tomorrow that will last most of the day, and a dinner with a client tomorrow night. I can meet you the following day. Can you be at my home by 7:00 a.m.? I should not be missed at work, and in case I am being watched, I should adhere to my schedule."

"Are you being followed?" Sabrina asked. And was his phone being tapped?

"I do not believe so. I have searched for listening devices as well and have found none. Can you come to my home?"

Lincoln gave Sabrina a nod.

"Of course," she said.

They'd meet at midnight if he had something important to tell them.

Pasquale gave her the address, which Lincoln wrote down. "Please ensure you are not followed. I risk much by speaking with you."

"We won't be followed."

She disconnected and went with Lincoln outside. Thunder rolled with the imminent threat of rain. In the rental, Lincoln began to drive.

"What does Pasquale know about you and Kirby?" he asked.

She turned her head toward him, picking up on where he was going with this. He'd tried to get her to talk after they'd left Bonnie's, but she hadn't budged. It looked as if she wasn't going to now, either. She didn't reply.

He asked the same question he'd asked after leaving Bonnie's. "If Kirby wasn't the reason you took the job, what was? And don't tell me it was because of the money." That was what she'd said before.

"It was," she said nonchalantly, or a good imitation of it.

"Omitting the truth is enough, Sabrina. You don't have to lie on top of it." He rarely lost patience, but he was close to losing it now. He saw her notice.

"I'm not lying. Kirby offered me a lot more money than my other job was paying me. It was an offer I couldn't refuse."

That he believed. "Then that was one reason you took the job. What was the other?"

She turned her head forward and again didn't reply. At least that was better than lying. Whatever she had to hide must be pretty important to her. Pretty illegal. Pretty dangerous....

"You got me drawn into this. I need to know everything you do."

"I didn't draw you into anything."

No, he'd been a good Samaritan and gone to her aid. Now an illegal gun dealer would like to see his life end as much as he'd like to see Sabrina's.

"If Kirby wasn't your lover, who was he to you?" She had to give him something.

"A friend."

Something more than that, her standard answer. Friends, not lovers. It started to rain, big drops splattering on the windshield. "Did you know he was going to be at the gun show?"

"No."

"But you hoped someone like him would be," he surmised. "Someone from OneDefense?"

She said nothing, confirming what he already suspected. Going to that gun show had been no coincidence.

The violent lurch of the steering wheel and the drag of the rental car to the right interrupted his thoughts. They'd just gotten a flat tire.

With a soft, startled inhale from Sabrina, he pulled over to the side of the road. The rain had picked up, more big drops connecting on the windshield. That would make for an inconvenient tire change.

Popping the trunk, he climbed out and hurried to the back, ignoring the uncomfortable pelting of rain. Traffic passed in both directions, splashing water but avoiding them. Sabrina appeared at his side, surprising him. A lot of women would stay in the car.

Lifting the stowage well cover, he discovered it void of a spare tire. No spare? In a Mercedes? Had the car come from the factory that way or had the rental agency neglected to replace it? It didn't matter. They had a flat, it was raining and they had no way of fixing either.

The rain gathered intensity as a torrent unleashed.

"Well, we could go to the beach for a while," Sabrina called into the din.

Was she joking?

With her mouth crooked and her eyes playful, her hair getting drenched along with her clothes, she began to do hot things to him. Yes, she was joking.

"No?" she teased. "What do you want to do while we wait for the car to be fixed?" Stepping back and planting her legs a bit wider, she gave a grand sweep of her arm as rain dripped from her chin and hands. "Can't get any wetter than this."

Interpreting her meaning much differently than she'd intended, he laughed and then put his hand on her back. "Come on, we'll go somewhere dry to call the rental company."

Jogging across the street, they headed for a strip mall with Haute Cakes Café in the middle. Under an archway, they reached the courtyard. No patrons sitting outside today. Lincoln opened the door for Sabrina, and, dripping wet, they entered.

A woman at one of the smaller tables inside looked up, her yellow Lab doing the same from where it sat docilely beside her.

Sabrina cooed and knelt to pet the dog, who began licking her wet face.

"You're making me miss my Maddie." Sabrina stood, smiling a hello at the woman, who beamed pride over her dog.

"They let me bring her in until it stops raining," the woman said.

The restaurant allowed dogs on the patio

"Lucky dog," Sabrina said.

The outer walls were all glass, and the café was open, giving the feel of still being outside in the torrential rain.

Lincoln followed a hostess to a table. "Arizona is taking good care of Maddie."

"I know. I just miss her."

"It hasn't been that long since you last saw her."

When she turned back to send him a "really?" look, he understood. Maddie was adorable enough to miss in a very short period of time.

Sitting across from her, he called the rental company. A representative told him someone would be sent with a new tire. With any luck, by the time they finished here, the car would be ready. He figured it would take at least an hour.

They had a little time to kill. He sat back and looked at Sabrina; her hair was wet, but she was still beautiful. He tried to minimize how her silly side appealed to him, her easy way of dealing with the rain. She was a brave woman. Independent.

She looked back at him, and soon they were both sort of grinning at each other. New attraction flared, smoking hot. He busied himself with checking out the restaurant and what he could see of the patio. Nothing unusual. No one noticed them.

"Why martial arts?"

Sabrina's question brought him back to her. This was beginning to feel like a date.

"What made you start teaching it?" she amended.

Was she trying to get to know him better? He wanted to get to know her. In an intimate way. "It was just a natural progression. I started doing it as a kid and it stuck."

"What do you teach?"

"Karate and kickboxing mostly. I started working out with kickboxing and then got into karate." He enjoyed it; that was how he'd gotten into it. "Why human resources?"

"I went to college right after high school. Who knows what they want to do with their life at that age?" When she smiled at the self-criticism, he saw a deeper part of her, one he sensed she rarely revealed. "I picked business administration because it was broad. It applies to all types of companies. But it's dry as hell."

She laughed. "I'm good at what I do, but come on. It's not space travel."

He chuckled at her funny humility. "What would you do now? If you could start over?"

She leaned back, her head tipping dreamily and eyes roaming the restaurant. She captivated him.

"Probably go back to college for a different degree. I love anything to do with history. Artifacts. Doesn't matter what kind. Each one has a story to tell. Where they came from. The people who created them or used them. It's fascinating."

Why was he so into her? From the moment he'd seen her move in next door, he'd been physically attracted; now it was her mind that had him entranced, a woman who was a person of interest in two murder cases and was hiding something.

His phone rang. It was the rental car company. Their rental was ready. That hadn't taken long. He was a little disappointed.

"Time to go," he said.

Neither of them moved to leave. They'd still be together but not like this, on a date. He couldn't figure out why he liked that so much. He wasn't known to be a soft guy. Sabrina softened him, though.

Finally, he stood.

Sabrina did, too, seeming as disappointed as him. He held the door for her. It was still raining outside, but not as hard as before. Under the overhang of the roof, she stopped and looked into the rain.

"Do we have to?" she asked.

"You didn't have a problem with it before." He let the door close behind him.

"That was before we sat down in there." And talked. Connected.

She faced him. "You know, one of my favorite things to do is go to museums."

Why was she talking about this? Was it just for something to say? Something to cover up what was really going on here? This burning curiosity of each other?

"Not institutions," she said, stepping toward him. "Although I still love those. I like them specialized. Private."

"Private is good," he said. Some privacy would be nice right now.

"Historic houses. Local history. I could spend hours doing just that."

He could spend hours naked with her. As he continued to look at her, she grew aware of how sexual his thoughts had become and she got uncomfortable. She fidgeted, shifting her feet, rubbing the back of her neck and avoiding his eyes. He hadn't meant to make her feel that way. He was flattered that she felt free enough to talk to him that way.

How many chances had she had to share the things she loved with people? He didn't think there were many, judging by her excitement now and the way she hadn't wanted to leave the table in the middle of talking. But why did she feel she could share it with him?

When she started to turn away, he looped his arm around her waist and pulled her against him. "I think it's great that you have such a passion for private museums."

The O of her mouth and wide, startled eyes made him want to kiss her. Her body felt hot. Her hands were on his chest, and her breasts were in slight contact along with them.

"My mother collects antiques and donates them to private museums across the country," he said. "I know of a few in Colorado I could take you to."

Her stunned look smoothed into warm delight, and he questioned the wisdom of making future plans that involved her. Making her happy overrode any adherence to that warning. And as she relaxed in his arms, sort of melted there against his chest, doubt scattered. As he continued to look into her eyes, she responded with a sultry droop of her eyes. Unable to resist, he dipped his head and kissed her.

Her indrawn breath and sliding of hands up his chest made him ignore her warning not to do this again. She wanted him to. Angling his head, he kissed her more deeply, holding her tighter. This was different than the last kiss, a lot more urgent, rampant with passion.

He backed her up against the trunk of a palm tree that sprang up from a square in the patio, not caring about the rain. Sabrina didn't, either. She gave back what he initiated, even digging her fingers into his hair. Her breathing was ragged. So was his. He wanted to take her back to the hotel.

The sound of footsteps broke the spell. Lincoln lifted his head and stared down at her.

"Sabrina Tierney?" a man asked from behind him.

Sabrina instantly tensed.

Lincoln turned to see two uniformed cops standing there in the rain. Someone had recognized her in the restaurant and called the police. If he'd have been paying attention, he might have been able to get them away from here in time. But being with Sabrina, talking to her, had lowered his guard.

Assaulting a police officer was sort of out of the question, but if he didn't do something, Sabrina might be arrested. Him, too.

"Are you Sabrina Tierney?" the officer repeated.

"No. I'm Remy Lang."

"The police in Denver told us you were living there under that name. Sir, would you step away from her?"

Normally the one chasing bail jumpers, Lincoln couldn't believe he was about to become the one chased.

Turning toward the officers, he kept his body between them and Sabrina and then moved forward. Giving the first officer a shove that sent him falling into the other one, he grabbed Sabrina's hand and ran for the archway.

"Stop!" one of the officers yelled.

Sabrina pulled her hand from his and ran beside him. They dodged traffic crossing the street. Sabrina ran around to the other side of the rental as he got in. The tire was fixed and another car was running behind them, a man from the rental company inside.

Lincoln raced out into the street as Sabrina slammed her car door shut. He veered around a corner, seeing the officers not far behind in their marked car, lights flashing.

He swore.

"I'm sorry," Sabrina said beside him, sounding earnest.

She hadn't meant for him to become embroiled in her mess. But now not only were gunrunners after him, so was the law.

"We have to get rid of this car." He raced around another turn and swerved to avoid an oncoming car. The police car had to nearly stop to avoid a collision with the same car. Lincoln gave the Mercedes full throttle. It was fast, but cop cars were made for this. Chasing lawbreakers.

Another turn brought him into a neighborhood full of mature landscaping. Passing a moving truck, Sabrina screamed as he veered back into the right lane and narrowly avoided a head-on with a car. Turning again, he began to gain distance from the police car. Before the cop car came into view, he turned onto another street and then found a long driveway and parked.

"Come on." He grabbed the duffel bag he'd made sure was in the rental for this very purpose.

Taking out two lightweight jackets, he handed her one. "Put it on."

She did, and they got out, walking down the sidewalk together. Lincoln saw a motor home parked in a driveway ahead. Glancing back, seeing no sign of the cop car, he went to the camper and tested the door. Locked, of course.

There were no other cars in the driveway. Going to the garage, he peered into a window. No one appeared to be home. He'd rather not do any damage to the motor home. Going to the backyard, he took out some tools and made quick work of unlocking the back patio door, hoping none of the neighbors were watching.

Inside, Sabrina followed him while he searched the house for keys and found them right there in the kitchen, hanging from a cute key holder.

Back outside, he and Sabrina got into the motor home, dumping his duffel bag on the floor between the two seats. Then he backed out of the driveway. As he drove down the street, the police car passed through the intersection ahead. Going the opposite direction, he kept close vigil on the rearview mirror outside the driver's-side door. When no sign of the police appeared, he began to look for a shopping mall. After that, it'd be a place to stay the night. Having a mobile hotel room helped.

Now that the immediate danger of being arrested had passed, the memory of kissing her filtered into its place. His desire for her was escalating. Normally he didn't have a problem with attraction to the opposite sex, but something about her triggered caution. What was stopping him from taking her to bed? Her resistance, for one, but there was something else. It felt good with her. He couldn't recall a time when it had felt better. Miranda...

He stopped the thoughts from coming. Mourning her death had eased over the past year or two, but it was still there. He'd never rushed himself to get over her. He figured it would come in time, and that time was not now. Maybe that was what bothered him. He wasn't finished grieving. But that didn't mean he couldn't explore relationships with other women. Why was Sabrina different?

Sabrina couldn't stop staring at Lincoln. She wasn't one to reduce herself to hero worship, but Lincoln had been her hero today. Not only had he surprised her about the museums his mother donated to, he'd actually run from police with her.

Like her, he'd changed into dry clothes, drool worthy in faded jeans as he sifted through all the clothes they'd bought before coming to this off-the-beaten-path campground. The RV was fairly new, with two pullouts that opened the tan-and-cream-colored space. She sat at the bench-style table, and he stood at the couch nestled in a pullout. They couldn't go back to the hotel. The campground host hadn't asked for identification. Only money and a name. How he'd known this place would be so ideal, she couldn't guess. Maybe it was part luck.

As he removed price tags and filled the second duffel bag he'd purchased, she watched how his biceps moved. Kissing him still had her drugged from its potency. Somewhere in the recesses of her mind hovered the warning that this was exactly what she'd intended to avoid. Was she headed for the same fate as that woman who'd fallen for him, only to see him out with someone else?

Standing, she went to the refrigerator and removed the steaks. They'd also stopped at the grocery store to stock up on food. Taking those, along with a paper plate, she found a long cooking fork and left the RV to start dinner. She'd already made a salad.

Activity buzzed in the campground. It was still light outside. Children were having fun in a small playground, swinging, driving toy trucks through a sandbox, running on a patch of grass. The smell of barbecues and campfire smoke permeated the air. The family next to them sat around their fire pit; kids—a boy of about twelve and a girl of about eight—held metal skewers for roasting marshmallows.

Seeing families like that always gave her a strange feeling. She had never been part of that, which didn't upset her. Being raised by a single mother and being an only child had been the only life she'd known growing up. And her mother had been loving and supportive. She'd had no disadvantage being raised that way. If anything, it had been better than being raised by a father who didn't love her mother. And clearly, her father hadn't loved her mother. Sabrina was sure she hadn't missed anything as a result of his bolting.

The family in the site next to theirs stirred her curiosity, however. Sometimes that happened. She'd see families together and be drawn into them, observing them as she was now. Being part of a unit would be nice, but if she wound up raising a child on her own, that would be fine, also. She'd never put many boundaries on what she expected out of life. Mainly she just wanted to be happy, and as long as men weren't lying to her and breaking her heart, she'd be fine.

The RV door opened and Lincoln stepped out.

Him, for example. He was beginning to be someone who was capable of breaking her heart. Worse, she'd never lost control with a man the way she had in that moment. Kissing him had been the center of her universe, the only thing that mattered. She'd had to kiss him, and would have kept kissing him if those policemen hadn't arrived.

She turned back to the grill. The steaks didn't take long. Lincoln brought out the salad and plates and dressing. She forked the steaks onto the plates and sat across from him, listening to the father talk to the daughter at the site beside them.

"Daddy?" her tiny voice queried sweetly.

"Yes, Pookie?"

"Can we go to Disneyland again tomorrow?"

The man chuckled. "We'll see."

Sabrina noticed Lincoln watching her and resumed eating her meal.

"We should have gotten some wood for a fire of our own," she said.

"Why don't you come join us?"

Sabrina saw the woman from the other site smiling over at them. She'd heard her comment about the wood.

"Let's go." Lincoln said, standing.

They were finished with dinner anyway, and it was too early to go to bed. She wasn't looking forward to sleeping in the RV with Lincoln tonight. Even though she knew the danger of letting herself fall for him, having sex with him would probably feel great.

After taking all the dishes into the camper, Sabrina

followed Lincoln over to the fire of the other campsite. The woman stood and gave introductions. She had long, straight, blond hair and wore jeans with a wine-tour T-shirt. Both the kids were blond, too. The boy was busy burning four marshmallows. Tiffany and Brad. Their parents were Gabriel and Amber. They'd come here to take the kids to Disneyland and the San Diego Zoo and were heading home the day after tomorrow.

When Lincoln introduced himself, Amber smiled and said, "We recognized you. We were trying to figure out a way to invite you over." She turned to Sabrina. "Then you made that comment about the wood."

They'd recognized Lincoln as Jackson Ivy's son. Some people really paid attention to entertainment news. He didn't seem to mind the attention. Maybe he was accustomed to it.

"Gabriel and I saw your dad's latest movie and loved it. *The Last Planet.* We love the action he puts into his movies."

Lincoln nodded politely. It must get tiresome when he encountered people this way.

"That was a cool movie!" the young boy exclaimed. "They had to escape seven-hundred-mile-per-hour winds in order to go back to their planet."

Sounded far-fetched but probably very entertaining.

Tiffany snuggled closer to her father, besieged by bashfulness at the moment. Gabriel put his arm around her and kissed the top of her head.

"Have you ever thought about acting?" Amber asked.

Lincoln scoffed with a laugh. "Never."

"You're all so famous. Your mother with all her fantastic parties. And eight kids! Two is a handful, but I suppose money helps. Were you raised by a nanny?"

"My mother had help, but she was very active in raising us. So was my dad, despite how busy he was."

The woman looked awed. "An all-American family. They don't print that in the press." She laughed. "I recently read something about Autumn. She's a fascinating woman. And she must be so smart to know all those languages."

"Yes, she did well in school and college."

"But not so well with men if the tabloids are right."

"They're usually not," he said.

"So she didn't break up with Deangelo Calabrese?"

Sabrina saw Lincoln struggle with that. Deangelo was a rising star on a new hit mystery television series. "She did break up with him."

"The article said some of the men she's been with say she's too high maintenance."

"Autumn is an independent woman. Some men can't handle that about her. She's busy with her career and travels all over the world doing translations. She's just not ready to settle down."

"What about Macon? How is he doing?"

"He's out of rehab. I just saw him. He's doing really well."

Didn't Amber know she was asking very personal questions? Sabrina supposed that didn't matter when a family such as the Ivys was constantly in the spotlight. Frankly, it amazed Sabrina that Lincoln was being so nice. He was a good man.

"I never read anything about you," Amber said. "There was something a long time ago about a woman who was killed."

"Amber," her husband admonished. "That's not courteous."

Amber's face crumbled. "Sorry. When I saw you pull

in next to us I just got so excited. It's not every day that an ordinary family like ours gets to spend an evening with someone famous."

"It's all right," Lincoln said kindly. "It happens a lot."

Sabrina marveled over his patience. She couldn't say if she'd be as understanding. His seemed to have no limit. She took in his biceps and chest in that green shirt again. No limit on sex appeal, either.

She noticed Amber checking the both of them out, full of speculation.

"Are you two married?" She looked down at Sabrina's bare ring finger.

"No," Sabrina answered. "We're neighbors."

"Oh." She contemplated them both one at a time before focusing only on Lincoln, the famous one. "You must be close if you decided to drive to California to vacation together." Her eyes became teasing. "Is she your girlfriend?"

"Yes," he said, shocking Sabrina.

Then she realized he couldn't tell the truth, that they were on the run from dangerous criminals and had stolen the RV to get away from police.

"Oh, how romantic! You're neighbors and now you're in love." Amber smiled at them with delight.

The word bounced around in Sabrina's mind. They weren't in love, but what if they were?

Lincoln reached over and took her hand, making sparks fly as he looked at her as though he really did love her.

"Yes, we fell pretty hard for each other," he murmured. "I took one look at her when she first moved in and was hooked."

"Ooh," Amber cooed.

Part truth rang in what Lincoln said, keeping the

sparks electric. She could almost believe he meant every word.

"How did you actually meet?" Amber asked.

"Her dog kept coming over to my house," Lincoln said.

Sabrina finally recovered enough to pitch in with the ruse. "My yellow Lab fell in love with him first."

Amber laughed softly. "Where is the dog?"

Oops. Sabrina scrambled for an answer.

"We flew here and rented the RV. My sister is watching her."

Amber leaned contentedly back on her camp chair, lost in celebrity titillation.

"You're pretty," the little girl said to Sabrina.

She'd shed some of her shyness and sat away from her father, who presently was cooking a marshmallow for her.

"Thank you," Sabrina said. "So are you."

The girl giggled and ducked her head behind her father's arm.

"It's time for bed, Pookie," her father said. "Eat the marshmallow and go get into your jammies."

The girl sullenly took the marshmallow, waving the metal stick in the air to cool it.

"We should head back." Lincoln stood, extending his hand to Sabrina, who took it as though she was his girlfriend.

"Thanks for coming over. See you in the morning," Amber beamed. "I can't wait to tell all my friends that I stayed the night next to Lincoln Ivy and his new girlfriend."

Sabrina waved and kept her hand in Lincoln's all the way back to their camper. Climbing the stairs, she faced him as he shut the door. "You must get so sick of that."

"It's all right. Most people don't understand that growing up with someone famous isn't all that different from growing up with an unknown."

How would he know? "Your family may be different than others that are famous." All she'd observed so far was that his parents were very family oriented. The fame didn't change that.

"I'm not the one who's famous. My dad is. He's the one who has to live it every day."

"Okay, you don't live it every day, but people still recognize you."

"True. Harmless enough. If I had to live it every day, I might be less accommodating."

Smiling from the warmth his attitude gave her, she got busy cleaning the kitchen. They'd just left everything in the sink when they'd gone over to the other camper. Not that there was much. Just some cooking utensils and the salad bowl.

Lincoln turned on the small flat-screen television that was hanging in the corner above the table. But instead of watching it, he gazed at Sabrina. She first sensed his attention, then saw it. Pretending to be girlfriend and boyfriend had stirred him up, too.

She dried the utensils and then the salad bowl. Reaching up to the top shelf of the cabinet, she struggled to put the bowl back where she'd found it.

Lincoln came up behind her, sending sizzling tingles all over her body. Putting one hand on her hip, he took the clean salad dish with his other and set it on top of three different bowls. Standing close behind her, she lowered his hand. Unbearable, exquisite heat fueled desire. Acute awareness of his hands on her hips consumed her. His fingers touched her abdomen. What if they moved down? His breath tickled the skin of her temple. He was looking at her. Where? Her breasts? The V of the sundress didn't reveal much, but maybe he could see more from his current vantage point.

The idea of him aroused by her made her tip her head back. His blue eyes smoldered with passion. Seeing hers, they flared with greater intensity. This inexplicable fire rapidly spread and grew. He brought his lips down to her neck. The soft brush of them sent her pulse flying. It simply felt too good to stop, just like what had happened at the café. She'd been startled that he'd drawn her against him, but the exchange and the undeniable chemistry had turned her into a malleable pool of desire. Just like now.

She reached up and sank her fingers into his hair, and put her other hand on one of his at her waist. His mouth kissed along her jaw. She tipped her head more, seeking. His mouth touched hers, tongue parting her lips and moving in. She sucked in a needy breath. His free hand glided up her stomach and curved over her breast.

Breathing faster now, his kiss hardened. His hand caressed her breast. His other moved up, hers still on top of it, and he felt her other breast, his hand kneading gently. Then his hands moved down, bending to reach the hem of her sundress. Sabrina braced her hand on the countertop as he kissed her, and she felt his hand on her upper thigh. His fingers brushed her underwear, then slipped in through the top and parted her. When he found her wet, he groaned and breathed heavy, lifting away from her mouth.

While his fingers rubbed slowly up and down the length of her opening, his eyes drilled sexual fire into hers. Craning her neck to see him, she closed her eyes as sensation overwhelmed her. He was going to make her come.

"Lincoln," she breathed. "Oh." He had an expert touch. So gentle. The friction just right over that magical cluster of nerves.

"Yes."

Tingles swelled, broaching mindless eruption.

He sank his finger inside of her and used his thumb to continue stimulating her. She instantly cried out and a deep orgasm crashed upon her.

While she was still held captured by sensation, he turned her in the corner of the RV's kitchen area. She put her arms around him as he pressed his body to hers, pinning her deliciously to the cabinets. She felt the hard length of him. He'd lifted the hem of her sundress again. The ridge behind the material of his jeans rubbed against her soft, moist underwear.

When he began to unfasten his jeans, Sabrina's world settled. He'd just made her come. She'd let him. She'd loved it....

"Stop." She gripped his wrist, stilling him before he pulled his underwear down, and then hers.

This could not go any further

Seeing his passion clamoring for release, she felt an urge to give back what he'd just given her. But to do that, she'd either have to please him orally or let him make love to her. Her stomach flopped. The excitement grew unbearable.

She pushed his chest.

He stepped back and refastened his jeans, not saying anything, not getting angry. But the fiery passion had vanished from his eyes. He stared at her a moment, a sort of confused intensity overcoming him. Then, turning, he left her there and went into the bathroom. Moments later, she heard the shower.

With her hand above her breasts on her chest, calming her breathing, she felt an awkward mix of relief and attraction. The man never got mad. While that magnetized her, she also had to remember that he had a commitment issue. And after kissing him twice, she didn't think she could sleep with him and not fall in love.

Chapter 7

Sajal emerged from the men's restroom off the lobby and saw the security guard yawn at the reception desk. The visitor sign-in book was on the top counter. After overhearing Tristan talk to Archer, Sajal had noticed men watching him, men he didn't know. Tristan had stopped by and spoken with him once, too. The undercurrents were ominous. Sajal was afraid for his family. Whatever Tristan and Archer had been talking about, it wasn't something Tristan wanted to get out.

"You look like you could use some coffee," Sajal said to the guard. He needed to take a look at that visitor log.

The man looked up and grunted tiredly. "Already had two cups."

Stopping at the desk, Sajal put his hand on the visitor log. "I brewed a fresh pot in the break room."

"Thanks." The guard made no move to get up and go get a cup of coffee.

"Slow night?"

The guard grunted again, bored and tired. "You have no idea."

"Yeah, for me, too." Sajal turned to his cart and pretended to straighten some cleaning chemical containers.

Another guard appeared through the locked doors leading to the rest of OneDefense Corporation. "I smell coffee."

"Fresh pot in there," the guard behind the reception desk said, yawning again.

"Awesome. I'd love a cup." The second guard passed the desk and went to the break room through an open door off the lobby.

The guard behind the desk stood. Stretching with another yawn, he walked away from the desk. "Maybe another cup would help."

Finally.

Sajal quickly opened the visitor log and flipped pages back to the date that Enrique said Kirby's lover had come to see Tristan. Finding the day, he scrolled down with his forefinger until he found the name of a woman who'd written Tristan's name as the person she'd come to see. There were no other visitors for Tristan that day. This had to be the woman Enrique had mentioned.

Tory Von Every.

He closed the book and pushed his cart away from the desk just as the guards left the break room with cups of coffee in hand. He went to the facilities warehouse at the back end of the building, where his desk was, and parked his cart.

Leaving the warehouse, he made his way toward the back door and walked across the parking lot to his seven-year-old white Ford pickup truck. Someone smoking inside another car caught his eye. A man. He didn't appear to be looking at Sajal. What was he waiting there for?

Sajal got into his truck and drove out of the lot. The car followed. He drove home as on any other night, shaken to see that the car followed.

When he pulled into his driveway, the other car drove by.

Inside, the house was quiet. He went to the front window and peered out. The car was gone and didn't return.

Finding Tory Von Every hadn't been easy. She wasn't listed in any directory, but she had a Facebook page that revealed her husband's name, whose LinkedIn page revealed his employer.

Sajal walked into the lobby of the Balboa Bay Club & Resort, located on the waterfront of the Newport Beach harbor. Trimmed in white, the granite-topped reception desk awaited guests at the end of beige-and-brown offset tiles. A huge painting of sailboats under puffs of clouds in a blue sky took up the entire wall behind the desk. Two clerks worked today, one finishing up with a guest, the other smiling as he saw Sajal approach.

"Can I help you?" the clerk asked, short black hair combed back from his young face, brown eyes innocent of life's rude awakenings.

"I am here to speak with Mr. Von Every." Gordon Von Every was the hotel's guest-services manager. Sajal gave the clerk his name.

"Is there a problem, sir?"

"No. This is a personal visit."

"One moment, please." The clerk picked up a telephone and spoke briefly to someone. Then to Sajal said, "Please, wait over there."

Sajal went to a seating area but didn't sit. Fifteen

minutes later, a man in a black suit and tie appeared. He looked to be in his mid-to-late thirties, had a slightly receding hairline and pale blue eyes that didn't smile with his mouth.

"Mr. Kapoor?" He extended his hand, probably being nice because he had to for his job, but Sajal could sense him wondering why he was here.

"Yes. Thank you for seeing me." He glanced around. "Is there somewhere we can talk?"

"I'm sorry. What is this about? Do I know you? Have you stayed with us before?"

"No, to both questions." He hesitated bringing up the subject of his purpose here, but didn't see a way of avoiding that. "This is about your wife and her relationship with Kirby Clark."

The man went still, his cordial facade falling away. "Are you a policeman?"

Sajal shook his head. "I work for OneDefense Corporation. I'm actually looking for your wife, Tory."

"Tory? You must not have heard. She's been missing since last Wednesday."

The day after she'd gone to see Tristan. Sajal recovered from his shock. "Where was she last seen?"

"Why are you here? What do you do for OneDefense?"

"I'm a janitor." He didn't feel comfortable telling him what he'd heard Tristan and Archer saying.

Gordon's gaze studied Sajal's face and then his entire body. "You're a janitor? What are you? Undercover or something?"

Undercover? What did he mean? "No. I'm a janitor."

"What are you doing here, asking me about my wife?"

Sajal hesitated. People walked past them and around

the seating area. The elevator bell dinged. Dishes clanged from the hotel restaurant.

"I don't think Sabrina Tierney killed Kirby Clark," Sajal finally said, keeping his voice down. "As a janitor, you hear things. People talk without thinking."

"You heard someone talk? Who?"

A man sat on the sofa near them. Sajal moved a few steps away, in the middle of the lobby. Gordon followed, standing before him again.

"Your wife went to see Tristan the day before she disappeared."

Gordon didn't appear shocked by that. "She complained about Tristan. She thought he killed Kirby." He didn't sound as though he cared one way or the other.

"Did you know she was having an affair with Kirby?"

Now the man went rigid, rage and hurt chilling his eyes. "Yes. I reported her missing, but I don't care if she never comes back."

Gordon's wife was missing. She was the one Sajal needed to talk to. He feared what Tristan would do, feared he didn't believe Sajal had heard nothing. But Tory was gone. Had Tristan murdered her? Would he murder Sajal if he discovered too much?

"I've got to go." Sajal walked away.

"Wait."

But Sajal kept going.

Outside, he got into his pickup truck. He'd carry on as usual now. He wouldn't try to solve the mystery of Kirby's murder. He was a janitor, not a detective.

That night, Sajal walked down the hall and peered into his teenage daughter's room. Isadora was buried under covers. He found just enough of her cheek to give her a soft kiss, careful not to disturb her. Next he checked on his son. Payne had kicked most of the covers off his body. Sajal kissed the boy on his cheek, too, then made his way to his bedroom where Maeve was curled up on her side. He left his jeans and long-sleeved button-up shirt on and went back down the hall, hungry for dinner.

Heating up the plate of food his wife had left for him, he turned on the small television in the kitchen.

"Sajal Kapoor?"

Sajal spun around to see a man dressed all in black standing in the threshold of his kitchen. He held a gun in his gloved hand.

"Let's go for a ride, shall we?"

His wife's face flashed to his mind, sharp and piercing him with love, along with fear and an animal instinct to protect her and their kids. They were still sleeping. He'd just checked on them. They were safe for now.

Not wanting his family hurt, he preceded the man out the door without a fight. Two more were waiting in a car parked in his driveway, one in the driver's seat, the other in the back.

The man forcing him along opened the door and pushed him. Sajal got in, seeing the man in the back also held a gun. The other one sat in the passenger seat and the driver pulled out into the street.

"Where are you taking me?" Sajal asked.

No one answered.

Sitting back, tense and waiting to be shot and terrified for his family, Sajal endured the twenty-minute drive in agony. Then at last the driver pulled into an alley in a dangerous suburb of L.A. A bum slept on cardboard. Lights from a small upper-level window glowed. The car stopped in front of a metal door.

"Out." The man beside him jabbed his ribs with the gun.

Sajal tried to slow his frightened pulse as he exited. The sound of a siren offered no solace, since it was responding to a call that wouldn't bring him rescue. The bum didn't stir.

The man in black opened the building door, and Sajal was treated to another jab as he was ushered inside. A back room to what might have once been a business that opened to the street in front, it was now dirty and junk filled. Missing patches of drywall revealed a glimpse of the dark storefront. A man sat at a card table.

Tristan.

Two of the men stood near the door while the jab-happy man told him to sit down. Sajal sat before Tristan, who looked comfortable and unafraid in his suit and tie, deceptively sophisticated.

"Sajal Kapoor," Tristan said.

Just as he'd predicted, Tristan had remembered his name. He didn't respond.

"The janitor who went to see Gordon Von Every today."

Sajal waited for the sick surprise to pass. How had Tristan learned that? He had been careful not to be followed, but he must have been. He looked back at the two by the door, at the driver, and wondered if he'd been the one to follow him. He must have deliberately fooled him.

Sajal should have known better. He was no detective.

"What did you talk about?"

"It wasn't him I was looking for. I was looking for his wife." He decided it was best to stick with the truth.

"Tory, who the police are looking for."

Sajal nodded.

"Why did you want to talk to her?"

"I heard a rumor that she came to OneDefense to see you, to ask you about Kirby."

"She did come to see me. She was angry, accusing me of killing him."

"So you killed her instead?" he couldn't resist saying.

"I thought you didn't hear me talking to Archer in my office."

Sajal said nothing. Tristan hadn't brought him here to have a conversation. Why force him at gunpoint if he had good intentions? It didn't matter what Sajal revealed. He was a dead man if he couldn't get away.

"Is Archer afraid of you?" Sajal asked.

"For a janitor, you're awfully inquisitive."

Archer had teamed up with a powerful man, a man who had at least three henchmen, but more than likely had more than that. How had a businessman such as him found them? How had he fallen so far off a decent path? He was a manager at OneDefense. He made good money, more than Sajal, anyway. When had it become less than enough?

"What did you hear, Mr. Kapoor?"

"I heard nothing. I only heard the rumor about Tory Von Every."

Tristan contemplated him awhile. "I don't believe you."

Standing, he gave a nod to the man behind Sajal. The two by the door escorted Tristan outside. The metal door banged shut.

Sajal had to act fast. He moved the chair back and swung his arm around as he stood. Catching the man off guard, he knocked his aim away as the man pulled the trigger. The explosion would be sure to attract attention.

Before the man could fire again, Sajal grabbed his

wrist and squeezed. Sajal was a big man, bigger than this one. He easily pushed him back against the wall, drywall breaking away and falling to expose brick behind it. Sajal banged the man's wrist against the hard surface until the gun fell.

Kicking the gun away, he punched the man and then went to pick up the gun. Aiming it at the man, he knocked him on the head. As the man slumped, disoriented, he backed toward the front of the store.

In the other room, Sajal turned and ran. The front door required a key. He frantically searched around and quickly settled on a barstool covered in dust along with several others. There were booths up here, too. It must have been a restaurant at one point.

Tucking the gun into his jeans, he lifted one of the stools and threw it through the window. Glass shattered and fell. Jumping through the opening, he caught a glimpse behind him. The man staggered into the storefront.

Sajal ran down the street, seeing a yellow cab heading toward him. He veered into the street and waved the taxi to a stop. Climbing in, he gave the driver his home address. The man who'd chased him stood on the sidewalk, watching him pass. The car was still in the alley, but the bum was gone.

Isadora Kapoor walked beside her friend, Candra, a tall, thin, long-haired blond girl she'd been friends with since fifth grade. Candra hadn't been this loud and obnoxious before this year. It was as if she'd turned fourteen and became a different person. Right now, she ended a call from her new boyfriend with an embarrassing, "See you later, baby."

Rubio Sanchez was a big Hispanic kid who was near

to flunking out of school. He'd already been arrested for underage drinking. His brother got in trouble for giving him the booze. What did Candra like about him? She'd gone to a party with him last weekend and told Isadora all about how much fun she'd had. Isadora had asked her if she'd tried alcohol, and Candra had said no. She'd been afraid to. Her parents would be livid.

"He asked me to go with him to another party," Candra said. "A bonfire." She beamed.

That would be like camping out. Isadora's family had never gone camping. That was one thing Isadora envied some of her other friends for doing. Sleeping in a tent. Fishing. Marshmallows and chocolate around a fire. How exciting!

"Are you going to go?" Isadora asked.

Candra flipped her hair as she looked over at her. "If I can sneak out of the house. You should go with me."

Temptation and instant fear hit her at once. "No way. My dad comes home from work late. He'd know I was gone."

"Rubio asked if you'd be there. He said Darius would be there."

Darius was Rubio's best friend, a blond-haired, blue-eyed boy who was just as near to flunking out of school as Rubio. Candra kept trying to fix her up with him.

"It would be so fun if all four of us could hang out together," Candra said.

At a party where there'd be alcohol and Rubio would smoke cigarettes. That part she didn't like, but the party idea did sound fun.

"My parents won't let me date until I'm sixteen."

"They don't have to know. Everybody dates now. Your parents are in an ice age."

Isadora saw her house up the street and walked a little faster. She was torn over the things Candra wanted her to do. It seemed exciting, and lots of other kids did go to parties and try alcohol and cigarettes. But should she?

"Come on, Isadora. Wait until your dad gets home and then sneak out. We'll meet you there. It's not far from here. You can ride your bike.

Riding her bike late at night would be daring, for sure.

"I'll try to sneak out," she heard herself say. Why was she agreeing? Even as she did, she felt her stomach knot against it. What if she got in trouble? Her parents would be so mad.

Reaching her driveway, she saw her dad's truck there. He never came home at this time. Why wasn't he at work?

"Hey, your dad is already home," Candra said, smiling. "You should be able to sneak out now. He'll go to bed early tonight, probably."

"Maybe."

"Call me, okay?" Candra kept walking down the sidewalk, her house just a few down from here. "Darius is cute. You'd like him."

Isadora went to the front door. Opening it and stepping inside, she heard her parents talking in their bedroom in low, urgent tones. Putting her backpack down, she walked down the hall and would have gone into her bedroom if not for what she heard her mom say.

"Go to the police, Sajal."

What were they talking about? Was it the reason her dad was home so early?

"No, Maeve. You shouldn't have called them this morning."

"What was I supposed to do? You didn't come home last night."

"Archer Latoya is a detective. I can't go to the police, and I can't stay here and put you in danger."

Isadora moved to the edge of the bedroom door.

"But you said the chief of police was questioning Archer. That means he's suspicious. You could go talk to him." Her mom sounded afraid. What had happened?

"I need a little time," her dad said. "Please. I have to do this."

"If you disappear, you may never be able to come back. I might never see you again."

What did her mother mean? Was her dad going away? Why? Was he in trouble?

"I will. I promise. I will find a way."

"Sajal. I'm frightened."

"If I'm not here, you'll be safe. Nothing in this world is more important to me than you and the kids. I need to know you're all safe."

"How do you know that by staying away from us we'll be safe?"

"Tristan will think I'm running scared. It's me he's after, not you or the kids. He'll be looking for me. I don't want him to look here."

Why did her father think they'd be in that much danger? Her mother was afraid. She could hear it in her voice. That scared Isadora, too.

"Don't be afraid," her dad said. "I'll take care of this. You'll see."

"Promise me you'll be okay."

"Nothing will keep me away from you and our kids. You're my life. I'll do anything to keep us together."

"I believe you."

Isadora heard her parents embrace and kiss.

"You're a good and honest man, Sajal. I'm so happy to be your wife."

"I love you."

"I love you, too."

Nothing like this had ever happened to them. Her dad was talking about going away to keep them safe… from what?

Chapter 8

Pasquale Manco lived in a Newport Bay Towers penthouse that overlooked the Balboa Peninsula. Standing in the elevator, Lincoln had his gun ready, tucked out of sight in the back waistband of his jeans and covered by the hem of his short-sleeved charcoal-colored ripstop camp shirt. After the night before last, he'd vowed to enforce rigid control over his physical reaction to her.

She'd been quiet and withdrawn ever since. They'd spent yesterday avoiding each other, a challenge in a small RV. But they'd given each other space. He needed time to sort out his feelings. The last time a kiss had felt like that, he'd been in love and Miranda had been alive. That was what had pulled his mood down. After the shower he'd taken to cool his desire, he'd been unable to stop ruminating over her. It was always painful thinking of her, but last night had been one of the worst, as fresh as the days following her death. Not being able to go back and change history always tortured him, wondering what might have been had they not been in New York that day.

Having a strange woman do what Miranda had done to him unsettled him. He still couldn't explain why. He wouldn't turn love away if it ever came his way again, but the possibility of it with Sabrina didn't jibe. Was it her secrets?

No, it was the way she made him think about Miranda, the way she made him feel the same as he had back then. Except now he wondered if these feelings that drove him out of control were stronger than they had been back then. Was that why he felt so down thinking about Miranda? Did he feel guilty?

Sabrina bumped into him as he stepped off the elevator and into the hall, one of her soft breasts pressed against his arm.

"Sorry." She seemed and sounded awkward.

He ignored it as he found the apartment. He had his own fair share of disconcertment regarding this chemistry that had sparked out of nowhere, from seeing her for the first time, to kissing her, and then the other night. He didn't think it had been that urgent with Miranda. Yeah, disconcerting. Plenty of time had gone by since her death, but he couldn't shake the sense of betrayal, that he was doing the betraying.

Sabrina rang the doorbell, and seconds later, Pasquale opened the door. "Are you certain you were not followed?" he asked, his voice colored by a soft accent.

"Yes," Lincoln said.

Peering into the hallway in both directions, he invited them in and shut the door.

Inside the spacious penthouse, Lincoln followed

Sabrina past a wide hallway with three white doors and a desk on one side. Dark blue and off-white mosaic rugs covered a white slate floor in the living room and dining area. Tan and dark blue sofas and chairs sat before a fireplace with a seventy-five-inch television mounted above. Adjacent to the dining area was a kitchen with mahogany cabinets and gold granite countertops. Straight ahead, patio doors offered a view of the bay and dock filled with sailboats and yachts. The balcony looked to run the length of the penthouse. Despite the small space, the price tag of a place like this was probably around two million. His vice president salary at OneDefense must be impressive. He was in sales, so maybe he worked on commission, as well.

Between the living room and dining area, Pasquale faced them and said to Sabrina, "Tristan does not know that Kirby and I were friends."

If he did, what would he do? If he found out Lincoln and Sabrina had come to see him, he'd take an interest, that was for sure.

"We won't tell anyone we were here today," Sabrina assured him.

"I would not have given Bonnie my card if I wasn't sure about doing this," he responded. "But, thank you."

Lincoln walked over to the patio window and peered outside while he waited for Pasquale to start talking. The dock below was quiet. Not many were out at this time of morning. He saw no one suspicious.

"Kirby told me he was beginning to worry about Tristan," he said. "He said Tristan was becoming aggressive in his work, targeting deals that were questionable. He was always operating beyond his title, manager of customer accounts, but behaving more like Kirby's equal. In fact, Kirby had to put him in his place on several occasions. Tristan spoke out of turn and made business decisions on certain deals without consulting the executive staff."

Lincoln turned, wondering how much Kirby had told him of Tristan's deals.

"Kirby told me much of Tristan's unruliness, but I could see that there was something he was not saying." Pasquale paused to gather his emotions. "It was three days later that he was killed, and police began looking for you." He looked at Sabrina as he said the last.

He'd obviously not believed Sabrina had killed Kirby or he would never have given Bonnie his card to try to reach out to her. Kirby hadn't trusted Tristan, so neither did Pasquale. But Kirby hadn't told him about the illegal gun sales.

"Kirby must have known something. I also believe you know what that something is," he said to Sabrina.

"I was beginning to discover that when Wade Nelson was killed," she answered.

"The Denver store manager." Pasquale nodded. "I heard of that. Did you also know that the owner of the Orange County OneDefense store has gone missing?"

Another store manager had gone missing.

Sabrina glanced briefly at Lincoln in shock and then said to Pasquale. "No. We didn't know that."

"Cesar Castillo. His wife runs a small market near Muscle Beach," Pasquale provided, and Lincoln made a mental note of the information.

"There is also a janitor who was reported missing yesterday. I heard it on the news this morning. Sajal Kapoor cleans the managers' offices at OneDefense. Tristan's office."

"He's missing, too?" Sabrina asked.

"Appears to be."

"Do you think he may have discovered something?" Lincoln asked.

"Discovered something. Overheard something. Yes. I believe he has, and I am hoping he is not dead."

"Have you spoken with his family?" Sabrina asked.

Pasquale shook his head. He fell into silent thought, and Lincoln got the impression that he was about to say something that might be difficult for them to hear. Or maybe just Sabrina, judging by the way he looked at her. "There is someone else who's gone missing."

It took Sabrina a few seconds, but then she caught on and snapped, "I know about Kirby's affair."

"I'm sorry," Pasquale said.

Sabrina lifted her hand to stop him.

"He loved her," Pasquale continued, "but after he met you, that relationship began to change."

Sabrina lowered her hand, waiting for Pasquale to go on. Lincoln did, too.

"He had been seeing her for five years. She was like a drug he could not stop using. She would promise him she would leave her husband, but she never did. She had young children, you see. A boy and a girl. They are young teenagers now. Tory could not leave because of them. That is what she told Kirby. It made her seem honorable. But Tory Von Every was not an honorable woman. I tried to convince Kirby of this, but his addiction was too severe. Tory enjoyed enticing a man of Kirby's status. It is my opinion that it was the scandal she craved. Having Kirby and her husband thrilled her. If Kirby was aware of that, he refused to admit it to me. When she wanted him, he obliged her."

Lincoln watched as Sabrina listened, absorbing it all and on the fence as to which side she leaned. Was she still angry with Kirby for lying about his lover, or offended over how unfeeling that woman had been toward him?

"But you must believe me when I say you were beginning to change that."

"Kirby and I weren't seeing each other that way."

"Not yet," Pasquale said. "I saw the two of you together. Kirby was going to pursue you. He told me so."

"Without ending it with Tory?"

"Perhaps not immediately. He could not refuse her. But given time, and the heart of a good woman, that would come naturally. Tory did not have much to offer him when you talk of a future life. You did. Kirby was not a fool. Tory had sex to offer. You had more than that. You had a heart."

Tension stiffened Sabrina's body. Lincoln was fascinated to watch her reaction to this revelation. She may claim nothing had been happening between her and Kirby, but she felt something for the man.

"Kirby would have wanted you to know the truth," Pasquale said.

That had been the main reason Pasquale had sought her out. For his friend. To make sure the woman he was growing to love knew the truth.

Sabrina turned away, obviously struggling to process what Pasquale had said. Sex drew certain men away from the women they loved. Would sex have continued to draw Kirby away from Sabrina? Lincoln sensed her wondering that.

"What do all of those people know about Tristan?" she finally asked.

Assuming Tristan was behind the murders and the missing people. And Lincoln never assumed anything. Not until he had all the facts.

"He's selling guns illegally through the stores," Lincoln said.

Pasquale didn't appear surprised. "I suspected as much. Tory, the janitor and the two store managers must have discovered his activities."

"Or refused to do as he demanded," Sabrina put in.

"It's not enough," Lincoln said. "Selling a few guns on the street is illegal and he could go to jail for it, but to kill to keep from having to quit?"

"He must be branching out to other sales," Sabrina said.

Bigger sales. The missing inventory Sabrina had found was good evidence, but there was more. What kind of clients did he have?

"That's what worries me," Pasquale said. "Kirby must have discovered his activities."

"He may have been in on them." Sabrina told him everything they knew, including what she'd heard Kirby and Tristan talking about that day in Kirby's office, and Tristan catching her listening.

"I don't believe it," Pasquale said. "Kirby would have never done something like that."

"Maybe he was trying to stop Tristan," Lincoln said.

"He would have told me."

"Would he have?" Lincoln challenged. "And put you in danger?"

With a sigh, Pasquale lowered his head. "Perhaps not."

After a moment, Lincoln moved to Sabrina and took her hand. "We shouldn't stay any longer." He looked at Pasquale, who nodded his agreement.

"If I hear anything more, I'll contact you," Pasquale said.

"Thank you," Sabrina said, and turned with Lincoln's guidance.

When they were outside and out of hearing range from Pasquale, Lincoln decided to try to get her to open up.

"Were you working with Kirby to expose Tristan?" he asked.

"No. I didn't know what Tristan was up to until that day I heard them talking."

He believed her. She may not tell him anything about her relationship with Kirby, but she hadn't known Tristan was dirty when she'd taken the job at OneDefense. If she hadn't been after Tristan for his illegal gun operation, what had she been doing? What other reason could she have had to get involved? He didn't want her around when he found out. Whatever she was hiding, she'd do everything she could to keep it from him. At least, that was his hunch. And any secret was no good in Lincoln's opinion.

They reached the street and started walking toward the new white Cadillac CTS-V rental Lincoln had arranged with one of his special passports.

He'd get answers to all of his questions. And he'd start with the lead detective of Kirby's murder case. But first he had to make sure Sabrina stayed put for an hour or two.

Back at the RV, Lincoln waited until Sabrina was settled in for the night. Right now she was in the bathroom washing her face. He'd just finished on his computer and had received the email he'd been waiting for. He'd asked a friend from the Denver police department to help him dig up information on the Kirby Clark murder case, someone who'd keep his digging secret. He'd come through with a contact who was willing to talk to Lincoln.

Sabrina appeared in the narrow hall in a two-piece black-and-white pajama set, ready to climb into bed. Hair in a ponytail, she had him fighting an urge to grab hold of it and do something naughty with her. Sitting at the kitchen table, he watched her glance his way before leaving the bathroom and going into the bedroom in the back of the RV. He'd occupied the pullout couch last night, and would do the same tonight—after he finished with the detective. But first he had to be sure Sabrina wouldn't try to follow him.

Hearing her climb onto the bed, he stood and went to his duffel bag. Finding the spare pistol he kept in there, he made his way down the hall. Keeping Sabrina safe was his top priority, but he couldn't take her with him, and he couldn't risk her following.

Leaving her here was tougher than he thought, though. The idea of something happening to her, of her getting hurt, or worse, agitated him. Moreover, why that agitated him troubled him.

In the doorway of the small room, he saw her notice he was fully dressed. She held a book in her hands and lowered it to her lap, angling her head in curiosity.

"Going somewhere?" she asked. Then she saw the gun in his left hand. "What are you doing with that?" Her finger pointed to the gun at his side.

He went to the bed and sat down, resting his pistol on his thigh.

"You're acting strange," she said.

Was he? Was his worry showing? That was so uncharacteristic of him. "I have to leave for a while."

"Leave? Now?" She looked down at the gun. "Where are you going at this hour?" It was after ten o'clock.

"I'm going to talk to an officer about Kirby's murder case." For obvious reasons, she could not go with him. At least he hoped she'd see it that way. "I need you to stay here."

Seeing her register who he was going to meet, he thought she'd agree. But then she set the book aside and threw the covers off her. "I'll go with you."

He stopped her with his hand around her wrist. "No."

"No?" She began to catch on that there was more to this than she suspected. "You can take me with you. I can wait in the car."

He shook his head and repeated, "I need you to stay here."

"Why? The officer doesn't need to know I'm in the car."

"He might see you." Surely she saw the possibility of that. Besides that, he planned on breaking into the house afterward. Things might get dicey.

Turning her wrist, he put the gun on her palm. She took hold of it and he let go of her.

Now he'd have to go. Leave her. She'd be alone, vulnerable to Tristan. Too many people had gone missing or been killed already. If Sabrina were the next victim...

"Why are you acting so strange?" Sabrina asked.

Lincoln berated himself for letting his anxiety get the best of him. "How am I acting strange?"

Her gaze roamed over his face, down his torso and back up again. "You're...tense, and...secretive."

He'd have to watch that. "Stay here, Sabrina."

He attempted to stand, but she took hold of his wrist and stopped him. "What did you find out?"

"Nothing yet."

The confusion cleared from her face. "You're afraid of what you might find out from the detective."

He didn't respond. Let her think that.

"I thought you believed me."

"I do believe you." About certain things.

The hurt in her eyes made him slip his wrist free. "Do you know how to use that gun?"

She inspected the pistol in her hand, appearing comfortable holding the weapon. "I'll manage."

He nodded and should have been on his way by now, but something he couldn't control kept his feet still.

Seeing his reluctance, Sabrina rose from the bed. "I'll be all right."

Her perceptiveness almost bothered him more than leaving her alone. *Turn. Go.* An inner voice still had logic, but he couldn't move.

She stepped toward him, putting her hands on his chest and giving him another reason for his difficulty. He could feel her heat.

Going up on her toes, Sabrina pressed her lips to his. If she'd planned to diffuse his tension, she'd succeeded, temporarily. He held her head in his hands and kissed her with more purpose. She met the flare-up of passion.

Finally, he lifted his head. "Promise me you won't go anywhere."

"I promise." Her voice was deep and sexy from the kiss. He toyed with the idea of being late for his meeting.

"Do you mean it?" he asked, sticking to business.

Once again, her keen perceptiveness keyed in on his worry. "I'll be all right, Lincoln."

He wasn't so sure. "If anything happens to you…" He verbalized the thought. Miranda's face tormented him as it always did, lifeless and dotted with blood after she'd been shot. The weeks and months following that tragedy had been the worst of his life. He didn't need a similar incident to add to his memories.

"I'm not Miranda," Sabrina said.

The sting of her insight punched right where it counted.

"I have to go." Uncomfortable with the comparison, thinking that losing Sabrina might be worse than Miranda, he left the RV, slamming the door behind him. Was Sabrina deliberately trying to get him to talk about her? His beautiful Miranda, with her dancing brown eyes and silky, shiny, thick chocolate-brown hair.

It disturbed him that curly red hair and green eyes replaced the vision, green eyes that had looked at him with such selfless commiseration. She cared how much Miranda's death had hurt him. Despite how she protected herself, despite her extreme reaction to his meeting that woman and Rayna catching him, she cared. She had trust issues with men, and for a good reason, after her experiences. He would think she'd withdraw in the face of a man's emotion over another woman. Instead, she'd reached out to him.

He struggled with how that warmed him, how it opened a crevasse in his heart that had closed after Miranda had been shot. Lincoln hadn't felt the way he had for Miranda since her death, and he wasn't sure he wanted to now.

He drove faster than he should to the 24/7 diner where he'd been instructed to meet. The flat-roofed, neon-cluttered, windowed building stood on a corner of an old neighborhood. There wasn't much traffic. Thirty years ago it might have been a booming business. Now it just looked tired and near extinction.

With his hand on the door, he was about to go inside when someone called his name.

"Lincoln Ivy?"

Lincoln turned. A thin, six-foot man with dark, short

hair and intense brown eyes stood inside the open car door. He'd been sitting in the vehicle waiting for him.

"Yes?"

"I'm Cash Whitney. Would you care to join me?" He gestured at his car, a shiny, new, black Subaru Tribeca.

Glad he'd come armed, he walked to the passenger side and got in.

Cash didn't drive away, but he kept his eyes on their surroundings even as he spoke. "We have to keep this short."

Lincoln agreed and waited for him to say what he could.

"I won't ask you where Sabrina is," he surprised him by saying. "I was one of the officers who responded to the call the night Kirby Clark was murdered. I'm not convinced she did it."

"What makes you say that?"

He hesitated, glancing his way and then at their surroundings again, through the windshield, through the driver's-side window. "I know what evidence was gathered, and some of it has recently gone missing."

"What kind of evidence is missing?"

Cash's hands gripped the steering wheel even though he wasn't driving anywhere. After a moment, he turned his head toward him.

"I met you tonight as a favor to a friend. We're capable of handling this without your help. Just tell your girlfriend to lay low for a while. We'll have it cleared up soon. That's all I meant to share with you."

This had been a waste of time if that was all he'd come to say. "What kind of evidence?"

Cash looked straight ahead.

"I might be able to help," Lincoln said.

"Your friend in Denver said you were a bounty hunter."

"I am. And I'm good at what I do." He had experience digging for information. That was how he found jumpers. He tracked them down and brought them back to jail. He didn't have to track Tristan down, but he'd dig up all the information he needed on him to have him arrested.

He watched Cash digest that. And after a while, he finally said, "Clothing fibers. Whoever took them must know they could place more than one person at the crime scene."

"Tristan Coulter?"

The officer looked perplexed. Lincoln told him about the missing inventory at Wade's store. If Sabrina hadn't been a suspect in the murder, she wouldn't have run and could have told police what she knew.

"You have no idea what this means to the investigation," Cash said. "Archer Latoya is the lead investigator on the case, and he's Tristan Coulter's half brother."

The news detonated in Lincoln. Latoya being the lead was no surprise, but Tristan being his brother? Boom.

"I discovered that when I did some research on OneDefense. I checked all the backgrounds of the executive and upper-management staff, people who might have worked with Kirby. I thought it was interesting and maybe a little peculiar that the lead investigator was closely related to someone Kirby worked with."

"Did you check into Latoya?" Lincoln asked.

And Cash nodded. "I checked into both of them. They come from a broken home. There were some domestic-abuse records but no charges. Archer's background checks out. So does Tristan's. I couldn't find anything on either one of them to suggest they'd turn criminal." He faced ahead and then looked back at Lincoln. "There was one thing, though."

Lincoln braced himself.

"Archer Latoya paid off a significant amount of debt last year. To the tune of about fifty thousand. A lot of money on a detective's salary, and he didn't have it in his bank account. Someone gave it to him. It was a transfer from an account in Grand Cayman. Untraceable. The transaction looks legal. Life must have improved considerably for him. His wife got half the savings in their divorce, and he'd bought her share of the house. The divorce coincided with the payoffs."

"Do you think Tristan could have given him the money?" Had he helped his half brother through a difficult divorce?

"If he's involved in illegal gun sales? Yeah, it's not only possible, it's feasible."

"But the family was broken. Are Tristan and Archer close?"

"I've never seen Tristan around the station, and Archer never talks about him. I'm not his best friend but I've asked around. They both live here in Newport Beach. The mother doesn't live far from here. Brea. I stopped by and talked with her. It wasn't a long talk. She hasn't seen either son for years."

Lincoln liked the man. He was proactive and resourceful, unruffled and always thinking. He'd have to thank his friend in Denver. He'd taken time to find the right contact for him.

"Can you give me an address on Archer Latoya?" he asked.

Cash pulled out a small notebook from the compartment between the seats. Flipping to the right page, he handed the pad to Lincoln. Lincoln read the address and committed it to memory.

"I've already talked to him," Cash said.

"I figured you had."

The cop half grinned. "I won't tell you not to go meet him."

"Thanks."

"Be careful."

"Let's stay in touch."

Cash nodded. "I'll let you know if I learn anything new, and you do the same. Just be sure no one finds out we're talking. Accusing a member of law enforcement of murder won't go over lightly. We have to be sure."

Lincoln opened the passenger door. "We will be."

Parking far enough away, Lincoln lifted a small laptop from the seat next to him where he'd put it. Next came a compact leather tool case—a very special tool case. Taking the case with him, he left the rental and walked down the street. He saw the single-car garage door open at Archer Latoya's white two-story house. That made it easier to break in. He was hoping Archer went to bed early. It was after ten o'clock now, and the street was dark and void of activity. The houses beside this one were close together, blinds and draperies were closed and no one was at the windows.

He entered the garage, passing a black Honda Accord. Trying the inner garage door, he found it unlocked and stepped inside. The door opened to a laundry room. Through that, he saw part of a living room where a portion of one wall had been removed to open up the view from the kitchen. A flat-screen TV hung on the wall, playing a crime series. A man reclined on a sofa, his feet up on an ottoman, three beer cans on the side table along with a pile of magazines and a dusty lamp.

Quietly, Lincoln approached. Archer Latoya's eyes were closed and he snored. He'd planned to install a transmitter if Latoya had been sleeping, and then wake him up to have a conversation. He was sleeping pretty soundly. The beer probably helped. Leaving him there, Lincoln decided to install the transmitter. He found an electrical outlet in the hall toward the garage and knelt. Checking on Archer, still hearing him snore, he opened the tool case and removed a small transmitter with wires springing from it.

Using the tiny tools, he connected the transmitter inside the electrical outlet and then put the cover back on. The entire process took less than five minutes.

Closing the tool case, he tucked it into the waistband of his jeans and took his pistol from its holster under his shirt. Going to the couch, he stood before Archer, who hadn't stirred.

"Archer Latoya?" Lincoln said.

The man snored loud once and then slumped back into deep sleep.

Lincoln nudged him with his pistol on his temple.

The man's green eyes fluttered open, bloodshot from drinking, and then he blinked rapidly when he saw Lincoln standing there with a gun. Scrambling to sit up straighter, he looked from the gun to Lincoln's face, sleep and alcohol slowing down his processing time. At fifty-one or so, he was in fairly good shape, not tall but average, lean except for his stomach, and still had all his brown hair.

"What are you doing?" he finally asked.

"I'm here to talk to you about Sabrina Tierney," Lincoln answered.

The man breathed heavily, unable to overcome the shock of waking to find a stranger with a gun in his house. "Who are you?"

"That's not important. What's important is that you tell me why you're allowing Tristan Coulter to set Sabrina up for the murder of Kirby Clark." It was a stab in the dark, but he needed to find out where this man's loyalty weighed heavier—with Tristan, or with the law.

The man stared at him. Cat and mouse. The detective in him began to resurface, no longer startled out of deep sleep or afraid.

"Tristan Coulter has nothing to do with the investigation," he said.

Not exactly true. "You and I both know Sabrina didn't kill Kirby Clark, so why are you trying to pin her with it?" Lincoln leaned down and patted the man to make sure he wasn't armed, and then moved around the ottoman to sit beside him, keeping the aim of his gun on him. Sitting beside him may relax him more.

When Archer didn't respond, Lincoln asked, "How did you pay off all your debt last year?"

The detective in him registered what he'd said. "Someone has connections." Meaning Lincoln. "What area of law enforcement are you in?" Then recognition slowly dawned in his eyes. "You're that movie producer's son. Police tried to arrest Sabrina at Haute Cakes Café, but you ran with her. I was briefed this afternoon." Archer leaned back and smiled. "The producer's son is a cop?"

"No. I'm not a cop. Why are you helping Tristan?"

"I'm not helping him. If you aren't a cop, then what do you do?"

"I think you are helping him. What I need to know is why."

Both of them were deliberately avoiding answering questions.

"I could always look it up on the internet," Archer said. "There's probably plenty of information about you there." With Jackson Ivy as a father.

"Not while I'm pointing this gun at you," Lincoln said.

Archer glanced down at the gun Lincoln held casually, and then back up at him, hesitating, reluctant to believe he wasn't in any real danger.

"Are you in on Tristan's illegal gun operation?" Lincoln asked.

"What illegal gun operation?"

The way he asked almost seemed as though he were fishing for how much Lincoln knew. "The one I plan to expose."

More hesitation rendered Archer silent, and his teetering on whether he was in danger or not leaned more toward not. Lincoln was becoming certain that the debt was at least part of what motivated him to hide evidence.

"Did Tristan use the money he made from illegal gun sales to bail you out of debt?"

No longer concerned that Lincoln would use his weapon, Archer stood. "I think you should leave now."

"You must have been in serious trouble to accept that kind of help. Or did you just feel desperate while you were going through your divorce?" Maybe Archer had used his half brother's shifty offer to try to save his marriage. "Was it her or you who wanted to leave?"

Now pure affront stormed over Archer's brow. "What does that have to do with anything?"

It must have been her. His reaction was too strong

for it to have been his. "What did you have to do for the money?"

The tightening of his mouth accompanied the emotion creasing his brow. He said nothing.

Lincoln walked toward him. "Did you know Tristan would use his generosity against you when you accepted the money?"

"You're making a lot of assumptions."

And his assumptions were probably correct. The bug he'd just planted would confirm that for him. "Are you close to him? He is your half brother."

"How do you know so much about me?"

So it was true. Lincoln didn't answer that question. "He won't be able to hold that over you after I'm finished with him."

"A producer's son is going to take down a ruthless bastard like Tristan Coulter?" He grunted a laugh. "Good luck with that."

Lincoln grinned, letting Archer know he was aware that he'd just revealed his fear of Tristan. And if he feared him, he must have personal knowledge of why Tristan was a man to be feared. No customer account manager would generate that kind of reaction in people. It would take a man of far greater ruthlessness. Criminal ruthlessness.

"If you aren't law enforcement, what are you doing here?" Archer asked.

He sensed that he'd have to give some information in order to gain trust. Because he had a feeling Archer wasn't hiding evidence willfully. Tristan was forcing him. Holding him hostage because of the money he'd given him. Had he known the money was dirty when he'd taken it? Lincoln guessed not. Tristan had essentially used him to launder it.

"I'm a bounty hunter," Lincoln said at last.

"A wannabe tough guy? Is that the closest you could come to playing a role in one of your father's movies?"

"I *will* expose Tristan." He put away his gun. "With or without your cooperation."

Archer studied him as though contemplating the actuality of his claim. But he wouldn't reveal anything. Not yet. Not until he was sure he'd live to talk about it later.

That was okay with Lincoln. He removed his wallet and took out a business card, one from his martial arts studio. Handing it to Archer, he asked, "Did you grow up with Tristan?" He put his wallet away.

Numbly, Archer nodded, looking down at the card. "We didn't get along at first, but became friends later on, especially after his dad died. I didn't see mine after my parents divorced. I don't remember him. Tristan's dad was the only father figure I had, and he wasn't much of one."

"You were close to Tristan growing up?"

Archer shrugged. "I can't say I was close to anyone when I was a kid. My mother was preoccupied with her pastry shop and domestic violence. It wasn't an ideal childhood."

"Is that why you became a cop?"

"I wanted something good in my life. Every time the cops came to our house to peel my stepdad's hands from my mother's throat, I wanted to leave with them and never come back." The edge in his tone revealed his conviction. "Anything else you want to know?"

Yeah. He wanted to know about Tristan. "Give me a call if you really want to talk." With that, Lincoln left the house.

Once in the car, he opened the laptop and plugged

in a USB device. Starting the surveillance program, he turned up the volume. Nothing.

Just as he suspected, and the purpose of the device, Archer Latoya was not going to call Tristan and tell him about the visitor he'd just had.

Chapter 9

Autumn Ivy saw the reporter in his beat-up Chevy and almost drove past Lincoln's house. Arizona was expecting her. Would she really let a reporter chase her away?

No.

Turning into the driveway faster than appropriate, the tires squealed a little as she pressed the brake. Snatching her flashy purse from the passenger seat, she alighted from her white Porsche. Her fingers caught on the door handle, and she felt a polished nail break.

"Damn!"

"Miss Ivy? Will you tell me about your relationship with Deangelo Calabrese?"

She walked faster as he took pictures, her high-heel Stuart Weitzman pumps making it impossible to move fast. Running ahead, the reporter got a face shot. She had to bite back a caustic remark. Tell him to go to hell.

At least she'd look good wearing her new fall Fendi dress.

"Why did you break up with him? Was it getting too serious? Did you meet someone else?"

As if she'd answer any of those questions. The press made her out to be a sex diva, and she was hardly that. So she dated a lot of men. Why was that news? It didn't mean she was promiscuous.

Arizona opened the door, and she rushed inside.

"Do they ever give it a rest?" Autumn asked, frustrated.

"No." Arizona locked the door.

A big yellow Lab with a smile jumped up on Autumn. She'd met Maddie when they'd all come over for dinner that night. Autumn grunted with her weight, catching her balance in the high heels and gently pushing the dog back down.

"Hey there." And then she said to Arizona. "Not much of a guard dog."

Arizona chuckled. "No." Then she eyed her outfit. "Do you ever dress down? Aren't you uncomfortable?"

"What's the matter with this?" She surveyed herself from foot to chest.

"You look like you're going to walk down a fashion runway. And then die after tripping in those shoes. You're such a girlie girl."

As the youngest sister, Arizona was about as opposite from her as could be. Autumn was the second oldest of the Ivy siblings, and the oldest sister. But their differences somehow made it natural for them to be close.

"Vandlátur." She was sure to add a tone of sarcasm.

"Where are you going this time? What is that? Greek?"

Autumn laughed and headed for the living room, a bouncing yellow Lab joining her. "Icelandic."

"What's that mean in Icelandic?"

"I just said you were nice. I haven't gotten a contract yet, but I'm expecting that soon." Sitting on Lincoln's sofa, she rested her arm on Maddie when she curled up beside her.

"So you just picked up another language so you could take this job?" Arizona sat on the other side of Maddie, arm over her rump.

"No. I've actually been studying it for a while now. I've never been to Iceland."

"Wouldn't it be easier to buy a plane ticket and take a vacation there?"

Autumn sent her an unappreciative look and refrained from saying something else in Icelandic. "I need something to do. I can't just go there and sit around."

"Most people experience the country when they go on vacation. That isn't the same as sitting around."

"I like what I do. I also like to stay busy."

Maddie moved her head so that her brown eyes looked up at Autumn and melted her heart. "Oh, look at this dog." She scratched the dog's head.

"Hard to believe her owner is a killer, huh?"

Autumn heard the sarcasm in her sister's tone. She didn't really believe Sabrina was a killer. "She might not be. We don't know the whole story."

"She said her name was Remy."

"She had a reason for that. If Lincoln thought she was a bad person, then I'd be worried. But he likes her." A lot, from what she'd seen. The way he'd looked at her could have set the walls on fire.

Arizona patted Maddie's rump. "Lincoln did say she

was being framed. And dogs *are* a good judge of people. How could she be a bad person with a dog like this?"

"I wonder if she'd bite that reporter outside. She seems fond of me." She pet Maddie's soft head and watched her red-tinted eyebrows move with the blinks and glances of her eyes. Adorable dog.

"Ignore the press."

"How? They stick their cameras in my face all the time. I get so tired of that. You wonder why I always dress up." She never knew when she was going to be the next cover photo.

"Well, then, pick a man to settle down with. They'll get bored with you and leave you alone."

"Is that what happened to you?" She sucked in a breath. "Are you and Braden getting married?"

"Not yet."

"But you are."

"Oh, yes." Arizona beamed.

Autumn had never seen her like this before. She'd never seen anyone in her family like this before. Except Mom and Dad.

"I'm not ready for that. I love men. I can't settle for one." Her youngest sister was going to beat her to the altar, and she didn't mind at all.

"That is such a weird thing to say."

"What? That I love men? I do. Especially the alpha ones. There's something about masculinity that turns me into a hot bowl of butter. Hard muscles. Stubble. Deep voices and a commanding presence. I love it all." She leaned her head back, drifting into a pleasant daydream.

"If anyone didn't know you, they'd get the wrong idea."

Anyone who didn't know her *did* get the wrong idea.

"I don't sleep with them all. I'm picky about who I get naked with. Masculinity is a turn-on, but not if they're only interested in stranger sex. I prefer them interested in what's in my head as much as my snatch."

"I think you've read that BDSM trilogy one too many times."

As Autumn laughed, the doorbell rang.

Arizona went to answer, Maddie jumping off the sofa to go after her.

She was so tired of hiding from the media. Her dad was irreplaceable, and she loved him, but he sure did make her life difficult.

"I'm Detective Jorgenson and this is my partner Smith, Denver Police, ma'am. We're here to talk to Lincoln Ivy. Is he home?"

Autumn propelled herself from the sofa and faced the door.

"No," Arizona said, startled.

"May we come in?"

Arizona glanced back at Autumn, who shrugged. Damn. The police were here to talk to Lincoln. And there was a reporter outside.

Two officers who weren't in uniform entered. But the first one was putting away a badge that he must have shown Arizona. He was tall and had a thick head of dark hair and light blue eyes. Underneath that light tweed jacket, she'd bet he was toned, too.

"Who are you?" he asked as his partner came to stand beside him in the entry.

"I'm Arizona Ivy and this is my sister Autumn."

Detective Jorgenson looked at her and then his eyes did a quick up and down. She couldn't tell if he was interested. She was.

"Lincoln is our brother," Arizona said.

Maddie nudged the man's hand with her head, and he automatically pet her.

"Where is he?"

Arizona glanced at Autumn again. "Why are you looking for him?"

"We'd like to ask him some questions about his neighbor."

"Remy?"

"That's the name she assumed when she moved here," Jorgenson's partner said. "Her name is actually Sabrina Tierney, and she's wanted for questioning in connection to a murder in Newport Beach, California."

Murder? Lincoln's neighbor murdered someone? And he was seeing her? The press was going to have a great time over this one! She walked around the man-sofa and stopped near the two detectives.

"When will your brother be home?" Detective Smith asked. He was more serious than Jorgenson. Jorgenson had a certain light to his eyes, whereas Smith's seemed to hold a haughty regard.

"He didn't say," Arizona said.

"Do you know where he is?" Jorgenson asked.

Arizona took a moment to answer. "Newport Beach."

Autumn shared her sister's reluctance. Telling the police where he was might put him at risk, but they could hardly lie to police. Would he be in trouble for helping this woman? Why was he?

Sabrina had seemed like a nice woman when Autumn had met her. Smart. A little rigid, though. Now she understood why. Autumn would be rigid, too, if she knew police were after her and she was living with a false name.

"Is he staying in a hotel?" Detective Jorgenson asked. "And do you know if he accompanied Sabrina there?"

"Yes, to both. But you should know that he's a bounty hunter, and he believes Sabrina is being framed."

"Which hotel are they staying at?" Smith asked.

Arizona told him with a snap to her tone.

Jorgenson noticed with a slight upward movement of his mouth, a very sexy mouth. Arizona didn't like Smith. Jorgenson shared the split-second humor with Autumn, and that was when she decided she had to get to know him.

"How long have you been a detective?" she asked, feeling Arizona turn an incredulous look at her.

"About ten years."

She loved this part, where the man looked at her with secret-messenger eyes and fired up a mutual chemistry.

"It must be such an exciting job," she said.

He regarded her a moment longer, not possibly missing her invitation. "Maybe I could tell you a little more about it over coffee sometime."

She smiled. Her smile was a reliable hook for most men, and had the same effect on Detective Jorgenson.

"Do you have a first name, Detective?"

"Knox."

Oh, she loved his name. She went to her purse and took out one of her business cards. Handing it to him, she said, "It's nice to meet you, Knox."

He took the card and read what it said. "You're a translator?"

"Yes. Languages have always come naturally to me."

His manly-man green eyes took in her face. "I'll call you soon as long as you promise to speak English."

Smiling wide again, she murmured, "I promise."

She loved this feeling, the newness of meeting a man for the first time. The excitement.

As his partner's disapproval entered her awareness,

she fingered some of her long, light red hair behind her ear. Arizona had her eyebrows slightly elevated in her own observation.

Jorgenson turned to Arizona. "Thanks."

"Have a nice day." There was no mistaking her sarcasm.

Jorgenson gave Autumn another sexy once-over and then followed his partner out the door.

"Really?" Arizona said. "Cops come here looking for our brother in connection to a murder and you arrange a date with one of them?"

Why was she all bent out of shape? "I didn't arrange a date."

"He's going to call you *as long as you speak English*." Arizona marched into Lincoln's kitchen.

Autumn followed. "He's hot."

"It's exhausting how many men you go through. You were just complaining about the media after you for your latest breakup. You could be a reality-show idol." She opened the refrigerator and took out a bottle of water.

"I'm not that bad. I don't hurt anyone."

"You've got a long trail of brokenhearted men behind you. You don't see it because you leave and never look back. Why can't you pick one and stick with him?"

The idea of that didn't repulse her, but it did constrict her nerves. "What's wrong with dating a lot?" She hadn't been with anyone long enough to hurt them. And the one time she had, he'd broken her heart, not the other way around.

"You're going to meet a man you should settle down with, and you'll miss out because you're so convinced that dating is all you need right now. Why are you like that?"

She made it seem as though she had some sort of health condition or something. "There's nothing wrong with me."

Arizona sighed and put down the bottle of water. "I'm sorry. It worries me that you're my oldest sister and I feel more mature than you."

Autumn smiled. "I'm a late bloomer." She stepped forward and planted a kiss on her cheek. "Don't worry about me. I'm having fun."

"Okay. Go have fun with your new toy detective then."

She was going to. "I'd better go now. I need a new outfit." She winked at Arizona as she turned.

Patting Maddie goodbye, she left the house. On her way to the car, she noticed a dark blue SUV parked across the street. There were two men inside. She reached the driver's door of her pretty Porsche and got in. Before she could back out of the driveway, the SUV did a U-turn and stopped in front of the driveway, blocking her.

Alarm triggered her pulse faster. She looked toward the front door of Lincoln's house. Should she make a run for it? Seeing the men were out of the SUV and approaching, she made sure her doors were locked and frantically dug into her purse for her phone. Why was she so afraid? Maybe they were just lost. She had a bad feeling; her instinct was warning her for a reason.

The driver of the other car arrived at her window, twirling his finger for her to roll her window down. He had dark, shaved hair and eerie pale gray eyes.

"I have to get going," she said, loud enough for them to hear through the glass.

He started to move his jacket aside to reveal the handle of a gun when Knox and his partner appeared behind him and the other man. Relief shook her. She pressed the button to move the window down a few inches.

"Are you all right?" Knox asked her.

"Yes." As long as he was there, she was.

"Are these men bothering you?"

"I don't know them. They asked me to roll my window down, and this one has a gun."

The hairless, pocked-skin man turned his face toward her, and if she could see his eyes she was sure they'd be evil.

"Do you have some documentation to carry a concealed weapon?" Knox asked.

"In the SUV."

"Why don't you show it to me, and while you're doing that, why don't you tell us why you're here?"

Smitten clear down to her toes, Autumn climbed out of her car and followed them to the SUV, standing far enough away to be safe.

"What's going on?"

Autumn jumped, not having seen her sister appear at her side. "I don't know. Those two men blocked the driveway and wanted me to roll my window down."

She watched the detectives question the men, who weren't revealing anything other than their weapons were legal. All they were saying was that the driver of the SUV wanted to meet Autumn. Knox didn't like that. He also didn't believe the man. But he had to let them go.

After they drove off, Knox and his partner walked up the driveway with them. They all stopped and faced each other, Autumn and Arizona farther up the driveway, and the detectives facing them.

"Any idea who that might have been?" Knox asked.

Beside him, his partner looked bored. Autumn imagined being constantly overshadowed by your partner would get tiresome.

"Lincoln said some men were after him." She explained the long story of Lincoln's trouble.

"Why didn't you tell us this before?" Knox was annoyed.

"I didn't think it was relevant," Arizona said. "And you might not have believed it, anyway."

A man who had to stick to the facts, Knox didn't push any further. He looked at Autumn, and she felt a surge of new attraction warm her everywhere.

"Oh, geez. I'm going inside." Arizona left them for the front door.

"I'll wait in the car." Smith vanished, too.

Knox grinned at her. "May I walk you to your car?"

"I'd love that."

They moved the two or three steps it took to reach her car. She stood in the open doorway, reluctant to sit down on the seat lest this moment end too soon.

"Thanks for that."

"Just doing my job."

He must have seen them and thought they looked suspicious. Lucky for her. What would have happened had he not done that?

"What are you doing later? I'm off duty at six o'clock."

"Looks like I'm spending some time with you."

He grinned again, sexy and lighting her up. She didn't want to wait until tonight. He didn't appear to, either.

"I don't usually do this," he said. And then he took a step closer.

"I don't, either. I mean, I date, but I—I…" She

stopped before saying, *I don't usually decide to sleep with a man on first sight.*

"It might be unprofessional," he said.

"Maybe, to some."

Slipping his hand to the small of her back, he pulled her to him. Oh. Her breath hitched and her heart flew while her body went up in flames.

With his other hand, he cupped the back of her head and then kissed her. Her lips fit his in sultry perfection. He tasted her at first, and then went in for more. She looped her arms around his muscular neck, resisting the urge to wrap her legs around him.

Slowly, he ended the kiss. Drawing back to look into her eyes, he exhaled raggedly and then stepped back.

"I'll be thinking about you all day," he said, the sound of his voice tickling her insides.

"I'll be thinking about you, too."

She watched him walk down the driveway and to the unmarked police car. Then another car caught her attention. It was the reporter. He was sitting inside snapping pictures. He'd just gotten several of her kissing the detective.

Chapter 10

When Lincoln ended the call from his sister, Sabrina could tell he was upset. From what she could glean from the conversation, some of Tristan's thugs had gone to his house and harassed Arizona and his other sister, Autumn. Two detectives had also come looking for him. Good and bad. They'd helped to scare the men away.

The threat of harming his sisters had pushed Lincoln over an edge. It was something to see, and she had to smother the way she loved that about him. His fierce protectiveness. The only problem was where it stemmed—from feelings he had for Miranda, the woman who'd died and he hadn't been able to save.

Desperate to stop Tristan, Lincoln had driven them here, where they now sat parked in front of Tristan's house in the Cadillac CTS-V rental. It was a bold move, according to Sabrina. What if Tristan or one of his men saw them?

A car passed going the other way. A woman jogged by wearing an iPod tucked into a holster clipped to her spandex shorts. Sabrina wished she was doing something like that rather than fighting to clear her name and having to go up against a man as dangerous as Tristan. At least she was comfortable. When Lincoln had said they were going on a stakeout, she'd worn something she could sit around in for a while, a black sundress. A little on the sexy side, she'd drawn a few stares from Lincoln, but that was okay.

Catching him looking again, she stole another look of her own of him. He was in tan khaki pants and a vivid blue knit shirt that really brought out his eyes. They were both dressed well for this activity. She pushed away the thought that she may have done it on purpose. Him, too. That attraction they had.

The houses on this street were good in size and nice. Nice enough for their Cadillac CTS-V rental to blend in.

Even from here she could see security cameras mounted to Tristan's house. She couldn't see any guards, but there had to be some. They were probably disguised as servants. The house itself wasn't so expensive that it would raise red flags. It wasn't anything that an upper-level manager at OneDefense wouldn't be able to afford. It was the electronics that did it. It must have cost a fortune to set it up.

"How are you going to bypass all that?" she asked.

"Don't know. For now we'll just watch." He twisted to reach into his duffel bag, coming out with binoculars.

"What if he sees us?"

"I'm not sure I care if he does."

He certainly seemed brave. Maybe his experience gave him that power. Experience and a lot of connections.

"How did you find the policeman and arrange to meet with him?" she asked. "And that background check on Tristan."

He looked through the binoculars at Tristan's house. "I just know people."

"Do you pay them?"

"Sometimes. Sometimes they prefer to swap favors."

"Huh." She nodded with a wry frown. Swap favors... What kind of favors? She looked around, not seeing anything special or significant. Or anyone.

Putting the binoculars down, he twisted again and this time retrieved what looked like a radio.

"What are you going to do now?"

"I need to have a way of listening to what he's saying in that house."

She eyed the cameras. "How are you going to do that?"

"He has a baby. With any luck, his wife has baby monitors."

Mystified, she watched him start up the radio. "Kirby told me Tristan had a baby. He's so old." Yet one more thing that disgusted her about him.

"This is a shortwave radio. It will pick up any sound in that house through the baby monitors."

"For real?"

"Yeah. Baby monitors are highly sensitive." He turned a dial on the radio.

"I don't hear anything."

"You are so impatient. I'm looking for the right frequency."

"How do you know all of this?"

"I know people who know all of this."

Popular guy. "You must have a lot of friends. All of your neighbors love you. I've noticed that much."

He stopped searching for the frequency as his eyes lifted from the task. "Most of them think I'm a pretty good guy. You're my neighbor, too." He wiggled his eyebrows, teasing her.

"I—I didn't mean *love*."

He chuckled.

Static smoothed out, and a crying baby came through the speakers. Was that coming from Tristan's house? The background report had revealed the twenty-five year gap between Tristan and his wife. Having a baby with such a young woman merely stroked his ego.

The sound of a telephone joined the crying. "Tristan," a woman's voice said. "When will you be home?" After a brief pause where only the baby could be heard, she sounded disappointed when she said, "Okay. I need to go. I can't get Everett to stop crying."

"Bingo," Lincoln said. He'd found the right frequency.

"That's amazing."

"Yeah."

"And frightening. Anyone could listen in on someone with a baby monitor."

"Some people probably do." He leaned his head back, ready to listen all night.

The baby monitor was quiet now.

"What now?" she asked.

"We wait."

"For how long?"

"For as long as it takes."

She was no good at waiting. She'd rescheduled appointments when the wait was too long. She'd bought plane tickets to escape the idle moments. Sitting here doing nothing was going to torture her.

"How long do you think that will be?" she asked.

"As long as it takes," he repeated, looking over at her.

Ignoring the fondness of that blue gaze, she leaned her head back like him.

She was really no good at doing nothing. Part of the reason she'd gotten as far as she had in her career was because she liked to be busy. She worked hard and she was efficient.

There was nothing efficient about sitting in a car waiting for a random appearance of Tristan.

Lifting her head, she rubbed her thighs, shifted on the seat, wishing she could stretch out. Resting her arm on the armrest, she tapped a tune with her forefinger to the song that kept going through her head. Feeling Lincoln still watching her, she looked over at him.

The fondness remained in his eyes. "You sure do have trouble sitting still, don't you?"

"Turn on the stereo. I have a Bob Seger song running through my head."

"That's what's making you fidgety?" He turned the key for battery power, not starting the engine, and the stereo played the latest Katy Perry song.

Sighing, she leaned her head back again, tapping her finger to the new song.

"This is better than Bob Seger?" he asked.

"Are you a classic-rock man?"

"Anything else is a bad attempt to reinvent the best."

She lifted her head off the back of the seat. "At least it's new. Don't you get tired of listening to the same thing over and over again?"

"I don't listen to music that often."

"Too busy tracking down bad guys?" To avenge Miranda?

He didn't say anything and his eyes no longer

held fondness, which told her he suspected where her thoughts were heading.

"It wasn't your fault, you know," she said. "Miranda."

"I wish my mother would keep her mouth shut."

"Not talking about it isn't healthy. It makes you do stupid things like cheat on women you date." She couldn't say he'd cheated on that poor woman, Rayna, who'd opened her heart to him in just a few dates. For some reason she just wanted to push him.

He turned his head with a derisive frown that reached his eyes. "You have a lot of anger on the subject."

About Miranda? "No, I don't."

"You're quick to accuse me of infidelity when none exists."

Oh, that was what he meant. "Trust, faithfulness and commitment are important to me." Something she doubted he'd be able to give her. "Don't change the subject."

"Why are those things so important?" he asked, anyway.

"Why isn't it important to you?" she countered.

"It is. Within reason. I'm not going to treat every woman I take an interest in as though I'm going to take her to the altar."

"I wasn't suggesting that you should. Geez, talk about anger."

He grunted a laugh. "I'm not angry. Those things become important when the relationship is serious enough to warrant it."

Which was never for him, not since Miranda. She didn't respond, her mood sinking. What a depressing thought. He'd never be serious enough about her. She tried to control the emotion but couldn't. Sometimes it was so hard to be strong when she was constantly up against love.

"I loved Miranda," he surprised her by saying.

He faced forward, elbow on the door frame, masculine fingers brushing over his mouth.

She should admire him for holding the other woman in such high regard. Instead, it kept her mood low.

At last he lowered his hand, returning to the present and looking at her. "Why are you so defensive about it?"

"About what?" Commitment?

"Cheating."

Why did he want to know? "I was cheated on, remember? Introduce me to anyone who isn't changed after experiencing that." She heard her own tone as she spoke. Defensive. Lashing out, even when Lincoln didn't deserve it. "I'm just angry with myself for allowing it to happen to me."

"Allowing it? You mean you tried to prevent it?"

She began tapping her thigh to the tune of the next song that played on the stereo. Anything to perk her mood up. "Of course. I choose the men I date very carefully. I don't date just anyone. I have certain criteria that must be met first." She had to truly know the man she was interested in before she let go.

"Trust, faithfulness and commitment?" He looked down at her tapping fingers. She bobbed her leg now, too.

"Yes. I find out the man's history as much as I can and make judgments based on that. I also ask him questions that reveal his opinion about women in general." She didn't see any harm in telling him that. They weren't dating and likely never would.

"What do you ask?"

"If he does the laundry or the dishes. Grocery shopping. Replacing the toilet paper on the holder."

He chuckled. "Really?"

"I also ask him how he feels about a woman making more money than him, and, of course, whether he's ever been unfaithful before."

"The insurance guy obviously lied."

So had Kirby. She turned away, looking out the window. It was dark now. "Yes."

"Why are you so careful? Why screen the man at all? Why not just get to know them?"

"I do."

"By interrogating them?"

"I don't interrogate." Again, her defensive tone rang in the car.

"I'd believe the insurance guy breaking your heart would make you defensive, but you were like that before the insurance guy."

Was he deliberately steering the discussion away from Miranda? It didn't matter; she answered, anyway. "I didn't want to end up like my mother." With a man who didn't respect or love her.

"You have abandonment issues," he said.

"Everyone does."

"No, yours shape how you live. You grew up without a father, and have tried so hard to avoid men like him. It's no surprise you ended up with one just like him, despite your efforts not to."

"I don't need any man to be happy and successful in this life."

"I disagree. I think your happiness depends on it. Too much. You need to let go. You won't find happiness until you do."

"I could say the same to you about Miranda."

"That's different. We were in love. She died. If she hadn't died, I'd still be with her and we'd have a family by now."

His declaration of love chafed her. She did want that from a man. Real love. True and strong enough to withstand the temptation of other women. Why hadn't she found it yet?

That was when it dawned on her that they both had some letting go to do.

A car drove by and turned into the driveway. Tristan was home from work.

"Now what?"

"We wait."

More waiting? "For what?"

He turned his head to look at her, annoyed.

Sighing, she leaned her head back again. She had to find something to do.

"Hi," Tristan's wife said over the shortwave radio. The sound of a quick kiss followed. "I kept dinner warm for you."

"I don't have time."

"What? You're going out again?"

It sounded as if Tristan had gone to the bedroom and was now changing. "I shouldn't be too late. But don't wait up for me."

"Tristan," she complained. "I was hoping we could spend some time together tonight."

"Don't pressure me. I said I wouldn't be late."

"You're always gone. It's like I live alone now. How do you think that makes me feel?"

"How do you think it makes me feel when you don't support my work?"

"I do. But you spend too much time there. You're not

even an executive. Why do you give that company so much when they give you nothing in return?"

"Stop it. It will pay off. You'll see."

"That's what you always say. I'm sick of it."

"You're sick of it?" Tristan's voice raised.

"Are you seeing someone?"

"What kind of question is that?" Tristan was really angry now, and with little provocation.

"You're always gone. I—"

The sound of Tristan hitting his wife accompanied her startled and pained gasp. Some furniture tipped over as she must have stumbled, possibly fell.

"Once again, you're out of line," Tristan growled. "I work hard so you can stay home and do nothing more than take care of this house!"

Sabrina put her hand on the door handle and was about to open it and break down Tristan's front door. Lincoln stopped her with his hand on her other arm.

"Wait," he said calmly. "He's leaving."

"What if he hits her again?"

"Wait."

"I'll be home when I want to be home." Tristan's voice came through the radio again. "What I do is none of your business."

His wife was crying and didn't respond. She was probably afraid to.

"If you would just listen to me and do what I say, I wouldn't have to do this." Now he sounded almost contrite. Sabrina felt like throwing up.

"I just want you home, Tristan."

"You don't appreciate me," Tristan spat. "If I end up with someone else, you don't have to wonder why. Stop nagging me about what I do with my time. If I want to be with another woman, I will. Is that clear?"

His wife's sobbing breath revealed her shock.

"Is that clear?" he shouted.

Sabrina imagined him raising his fist in a threat.

"Y-yes!" his wife shrieked.

The sound of Tristan's footsteps were followed by the slam of the garage door.

Tristan's car backed out of the garage and driveway. Lincoln waited for a moment before following; the sound of Tristan's wife crying filled the car.

"Turn that off," Sabrina said. "Before I kill him."

Lincoln turned the receiver off and started to follow Tristan.

Tristan led them to The Focus, a trendy nightclub in Newport Beach with a view of the ocean and a large patio off the back. Lincoln parked a good distance away.

"What's he doing here?" Meeting someone? Sabrina would not be surprised.

"Let's go and find out."

Sabrina climbed out of the rental and walked with him to the club entrance. Inside, they stayed in a dark corner near the dance floor and watched Tristan meet a woman at a table. She was about twenty years younger than him. Slender and big breasted, she had long, thick, blond hair and wore too much makeup. The V of her dress dipped inappropriately low.

"Is she a hooker?"

Lincoln smothered a laugh. "Probably not." He found them a bistro table and sat across from her.

"Can I get you something?" a petite waitress asked, wearing the short black skirt and halter top that was the uniform of the club.

"Two beers." Lincoln told her what kind.

Tristan sat close to the blonde, flirting with her in

a way that made her eyes droop sexually. A waitress dropped off two drinks.

Their beers arrived. Sabrina sipped and watched couples dance as the music slowed to a more romantic tune.

Lincoln slipped his arm around her, twirling her into the thickening crowd on the dance floor. She caught sight of Tristan. He was still involved with the blonde woman.

"He looked over here," Lincoln said.

He'd swept her into a dance to avoid being seen. She was aware of everywhere they touched. Holding her hand, his other rested on the small of her back. She reflexively moved her fingers over Lincoln's hard chest, her gaze alternating between his subtly watchful eyes and Tristan.

"What kind of man hits his wife and then goes to meet another woman in a bar?" she asked.

"Not a very nice one."

She looked up at him surveying the bar and covertly keeping track of Tristan. Lincoln wasn't the type to harm a woman. No, exactly the opposite. He hadn't intended to hurt Rayna, and he'd come to Sabrina's rescue, no matter the danger to himself.

As Lincoln danced with her in a circle, she saw Tristan kissing the woman's hand as though he were a gentleman. "That's so disgusting."

He looked over at Tristan as they danced in another circle.

"Why is he like that?" she asked, struggling to understand what made a man so despicable.

"Some men are."

"He beats his wife and cheats on her. I don't get it. Why not get a divorce?"

"Could be any number of reasons. The kids. The status symbol of keeping a wife at home. The excitement of having affairs with younger women."

And flaunting it in his wife's face after hitting her? That disgusted her even more. "He thinks that because he supports his wife, she should put up with whatever he decides to do? No matter how unprincipled and disrespectful, she's expected to bow down to him."

"There you go again with that strong opinion about infidelity," Lincoln said. "Is it Tristan or experience that makes you feel that way?"

Both, probably. She realized how angry she sounded. The man she'd trusted to love had surprised her. Blindsided her. She'd had real feelings for Chet. Trusted him. Allowed herself to believe she'd gotten it right. To find out she'd been wrong had shaken her foundation. She and Chet had ended just before she'd taken the job at OneDefense. It could be that she was still raw over that. Or it could be an indication of what she should expect for her future.

What once she'd considered solid was now broken and unreliable. Her foundation was flawed, and she didn't know how to repair it. Maybe she'd end up living alone like her mother and grandmother. Maybe she was meant to. If she couldn't choose well, she'd rather be alone. And right now she was pretty convinced that she couldn't.

How could she let go of her defenses after that?

Lincoln's gaze came into focus and she realized she'd been staring at him this whole time.

"I can understand how your boyfriend's betrayal makes you sensitive," he said, amazing her again with his insight. "But you seem to take it to the extreme."

Did she? Chet had answered all her relationship questions correctly. Did he want a future with a woman?

Was a monogamous relationship important to him? She had trusted his answers.

"I saw what a bad choice in a man did to my mother. I thought I could choose differently."

"But you didn't."

"No."

"Because you try too hard. Why not just let it happen?"

He was one to talk. "My mother did that, and look where it got her."

"If it's for real, that kind of thing doesn't happen. Your mother probably knew the kind of man your dad was, but she stayed, anyway. When he left, I bet she wasn't surprised."

"She loved him."

"Did she? Are you sure? Or was she insecure and settling for less than she deserved?"

He continued to amaze her, but her mother had been stronger than that. "If she was insecure with my dad, she wasn't after he left. She had plenty of opportunity to 'settle for less,' as you put it, after that, but no one measured up." And she'd died alone, without a man to love her.

Another love song began.

"Tristan and the woman are leaving," he said.

"Should we follow?" She craned her neck to see Tristan with his hand on the woman's rear. "Ew. Do we have to?"

Chuckling, Lincoln kept dancing with her. "No. I think we know what he'll be doing for the next few hours."

Tristan was going to cheat on his wife tonight instead of work illegal gun sales, and it probably wasn't the first time.

Lowering his gaze from a disappearing Tristan, Lincoln met her eyes, and they shared a silent speculation of where this night would lead. Slow dancing. And then what?

"There's nothing wrong with wanting to be with a man who will not only stick around but love you the rest of your life. That's all my mother ever wanted." And all Sabrina wanted. She didn't need any man who wasn't capable of giving her that.

"Most men want that, too. There may be a few bad ones out there, but if it's right, it's right."

"You talk as though you're looking for that."

"Eventually, I will."

"I don't believe you. I doubt that deep down, you even believe yourself."

He danced with her without responding. He didn't have a comeback for her. That intrigued her. She'd perplexed him, made him think more than anyone else ever had about his problem with commitment.

"You need to talk about her, Lincoln."

She felt him tense up, his fingers on her lower back flexing and his chest muscles getting harder. And those blue eyes darkened beneath his crowding brow.

"What was it about her that made you want to marry her?" she asked, despite his obvious resistance to the subject.

He looked over her head. Dancing couples surrounded them in the dim light.

"She didn't dwell on me being Jackson Ivy's son," he finally said. "That's what initially caught my attention. Well, that and she was beautiful." His brow began to smooth as he talked. "And we hit it off. We talked. We did things together."

"What did she do for a living?"

"She was between jobs." He paused. "She waited tables, but she talked about going to school to do something else."

"What did she want to do?"

"She didn't know."

Sabrina found it odd that he'd be attracted to a woman who had nothing going for herself other than a lack of interest in who his father was.

The song ended, and Sabrina was more interested in talking now than dancing close to Lincoln. She led him to the table where they'd left their beer bottles.

"Did she know who you were when you met?" she asked as she took a seat on the stool.

He sat across from her and drank the rest of his beer. "She recognized the name."

So she had known. "How long were you together before she died?"

Putting his empty beer bottle down, he sighed and looked at her, pained to have this pried out of him and yet handling it stoically. "Seven months."

That wasn't very long. Sabrina began to wonder if her death had somehow caused him to elevate what he'd actually felt for her.

"Do you really think she was the one?"

"I was going to ask her to marry me on that trip."

But they'd only known each other for seven months. It was possible that they'd fallen in love that fast. It happened. But her lack of career raised Sabrina's suspicion.

"Did she meet your dad?"

"No. My mother invited us to California for a high-profile party, but I couldn't make it."

"How did Miranda feel about that?"

"She was disappointed, but she understood."

"Did you live together?"

"We were looking for a place."

"What kind of place did she want?"

Judging by the hardening of his eyes, her time for getting answers out of him was quickly disappearing. And he'd probably caught on to what she was getting at.

"Why do you want to know?"

Should she tell him? Honesty always came first for her. It was the cornerstone of trust. "Because I think she went for you because of who your dad is."

"No, she didn't."

"What kind of house did she want with you?"

He turned away.

"A nice, big, expensive one, right?"

Then he rounded on her, defenses flaring. "She was a good person."

"Okay, but she also liked it that you were Jackson Ivy's son. She liked that you have money."

The idea that he may have missed that fought with the storm brewing in his eyes. "I thought the same about you when I met you, that who my father is wasn't important to you."

Had he? That suggested he'd been interested in her. Hadn't she sensed that? "I thought it was interesting, but not important."

"Miranda told me that, too."

"I would never want to live in a giant house. I'm not into all the things money can buy. Money is a necessary evil to me. You need it to live and plan for your future, and that's it. I spend it on frivolous things occasionally. I like a nice house. I'd spend money to decorate it. But really, I'm simple that way. I don't need to impress anyone with who I marry or what kind of house I live in. I just want to love, be loved and live a happy life." Why that was so hard for her to attain, she'd like to know.

As she spoke, his demeanor grew more restless. She was forcing him to face some truths about Miranda, and in her postmortem, worshipped status, she was too perfect to be anything less than his idolized version. He'd have to get past that if he ever wanted to have a meaningful relationship with anyone. Why did she always meet men who had something to stop her from finding love?

"Let's get out of here." He stood and threw down some cash.

She'd made him angry. She'd disrupted his idealism when it came to Miranda's death.

"I didn't mean to upset you." She trailed him out of the bar.

Lincoln was such an even-tempered man, it shocked her to see him like this.

"You must see that you have to let go of her," she continued, not understanding why.

Why was it so important to her that he let Miranda go? Why couldn't she stop trying to get him to? That suggested she might be trying to prep him to become her man. And he couldn't be her man if he was still hung up on someone else.

"Stop talking about her," he snapped.

She would. She had to. Sabrina—or any woman, for that matter—could not fix him. There was no fixing any man. Men like Lincoln had to cure themselves. He had to want to let go of Miranda, and from all she'd seen, he was nowhere near doing so. He needed more time to get over the woman he'd loved…or at least thought he'd loved.

Lincoln was not a wise choice for Sabrina. She had chosen badly once before. She damn well refused to choose badly again.

Chapter 11

Just as Pasquale had said, Cesar Castillo's wife ran a small market off Muscle Beach in Venice, California. Lincoln walked beside Sabrina down the dirty narrow sidewalk, glad for the distraction. He wished she wouldn't try to get him to talk about Miranda. It dredged up so many negative thoughts and feelings. He wasn't a believer in therapy. Talking about problems only enabled dwelling on them. He'd rather dwell on other things, like clearing Sabrina's name and exposing Tristan so he could get back to his life.

The hotel across the street looked newly renovated. Not so for Castillo's Market. A red canopy jutted out from the flat roof. The old building showed its age, with chipping brick painted white along the bottom and around the single door. Lincoln opened it for her.

Inside, it smelled like an antiques flea market. No amount of cleaning would improve the dull and scratched linoleum. Two rows of shelving were jam-packed with convenient grocery items. Some of the labels were so faded she wanted to check the expiration date to see just how long they'd been sitting there. The produce display along the front didn't offer much better promise, and flies circled the six-foot-long meat counter.

A dark-haired woman with a yellow-toothed smile appeared from the back. Short and petite, she must not eat the food here.

"Mrs. Castillo?" Lincoln asked, seeing Sabrina taking in the antiquated market.

"Yes," she answered with a slight Spanish accent.

"We're here to talk to you about your husband."

Her sales-eager smile vanished. "Do you know where my Cesar is? Have you seen him?"

"We were hoping you could tell us something about why he disappeared."

"Who are you? Are you friends of his? He usually introduces me to all his friends."

"We're trying to find out what happened to him."

"Are you a friend of his?" she repeated.

"We've never met him, but we need to find him," Sabrina said.

She eyed them strangely and then said, "The police have already been here. They are searching for him. I know nothing."

Moving down the counter, she asked a man in dirty jeans and not-so-white T-shirt, "May I help you?"

The man ordered a sandwich.

Lincoln watched beside Sabrina as the woman removed some roast beef from the meat counter. The glass was smudged. A fly flew in low over the handful she took. At least she'd put on some plastic gloves.

Removing some stiff pieces of bread from a bagged

loaf, she prepared the roast-beef sandwich, retrieving some cheese from an equally infested counter. Mayo and mustard followed. She sliced the finished product and wrapped it in paper.

The man went to get a soda from the small refrigerator in the back, and the woman rang up his purchase, which was about three dollars higher than it should have been.

Lincoln glanced around at some other products. Everything appeared to be marked up a little.

The man left beneath the ding of the door.

"Did your husband ever mention any trouble he was having at his OneDefense store?" Lincoln asked.

The woman eyed them strangely again, as though she wished they'd disappear.

"He has no trouble. He runs a good business, my Cesar."

"You seem confident that he'll be found," Sabrina said. Clever observation.

She hesitated a few seconds. "The police are looking for him. Perhaps you should go now."

She was being awfully standoffish, as though she had something to hide—or her husband did. "What about his relationship with Tristan Coulter? Did he ever talk to you about him?"

"Why do you ask about Tristan?"

She spoke his name as though it was familiar to her, more familiar than a coworker might be. Lincoln glanced at Sabrina, latching on to the fact that Cesar had known Tristan personally and wondering how much they should tell the woman. Maybe it didn't matter. If Archer Latoya learned why they'd come here, maybe it would compel him to steer the investigation toward Tristan.

"We believe he's responsible for your husband's disappearance," he answered while Sabrina swatted a fly away from her head.

The woman turned troubled brown eyes from him to Sabrina and back. "Tristan Coulter works for OneDefense. My husband runs one of their stores here in Venice."

Lincoln noticed how she spoke as though he was still here. "We're aware of that. But Tristan has been involved in some illegal gun sales, and we think perhaps your husband may have known something about them."

Mrs. Castillo shook her head. "No. My Cesar would not have been involved in anything illegal."

"We aren't suggesting he was. But he may have learned something and that's why he's missing."

"Are you saying that Tristan Coulter kidnapped him?"

Or killed him. "You know Tristan?"

"I have met him."

Why would an account manager work so closely with a OneDefense retail store? He could understand the sales link, but why Cesar? Why any store manager?

"Did Wade report to Tristan?" he asked Sabrina.

She shook her head. "They all reported to the chief operations officer. Tristan is in charge of internet sales."

"Did the COO know about the illegal sales?"

"No."

Lincoln turned back to Mrs. Castillo. "Was your husband in contact with anyone prior to his disappearance? Anyone new?"

"No. No one new. But he has many friends."

"Who are his closest?" Lincoln doubted his close friends would be involved, but maybe they'd be able to tell them something.

"The police have already gone to talk to them."

Yes, but were they asking the right questions? And who were they?

"Can you tell us about any of them?" Sabrina asked. Her gaze shifted back and forth between them.

"We want to help, Mrs. Castillo," Sabrina said. "Finding your husband may help us stop Tristan."

That was the wrong thing to say. Lincoln watched her freeze and then clam up.

"You should go now," she said.

She liked Tristan, or respected him because her husband had. Little did she know that Tristan was probably the one responsible for her husband's death.

"Tristan is not your friend, Mrs. Castillo," Lincoln said. He had to try to make her understand. "Neither was he a friend to your husband. He's a bad man."

Mrs. Castillo said nothing.

"He's selling guns illegally, and we're trying to stop him."

"Please, go." Mrs. Castillo put a pen topped with dirty, gaudy, yellow plastic daisies back into a coffee cup filled with more.

"We believe he's already killed the general manager of the Denver, Colorado, OneDefense store," Lincoln persisted.

The woman turned horrified eyes to him. "And you are suggesting that Tristan has done the same to my Cesar?"

Lincoln held himself still and quiet.

"He is a friend to my Cesar. He would not do such a thing."

"You say Cesar wouldn't do anything illegal," Lincoln said. "What if Tristan was trying to force him and your husband refused?"

A tortured gasp came from Mrs. Castillo. "It isn't true! I have met Tristan on many occasions. He has come into my home. He and Cesar were friends."

"Maybe that's what Tristan wanted him to believe," Sabrina said.

Tears sprang to the woman's eyes. "Please. You must go now. The police are looking for my Cesar. They will find him."

Lincoln shared a look with Sabrina. They wouldn't get any more out of this woman.

Sabrina faced her again. "We're very sorry for upsetting you."

After thanking her, Lincoln led Sabrina outside, taking a deep breath of fresh air. Why would anyone want to shop for food at Castillo's? He agreed it did have a certain amount of charm, being so old and close to the beach, but the risk of food poisoning was a significant deterrent.

"I think we should have gotten a can of sardines. They might have been worth some money."

He smiled. "Or a roast-beef-and-maggot sandwich."

She made a gagging sound. "How does a place like that make it here?"

Muscle Beach wasn't what it used to be. Transients walked the sidewalk along the wide expanse of sand, the ocean washing to shore in the distance.

"Must not be anything else nearby." Convenience had its price.

"Come on." She crossed the street they should have turned on to get to their rental. "Let's walk on the beach for a while."

What was she doing? Setting him up for more psychotherapy? He followed her across the street anyway and walked with her along the storefronts that faced the beach. Island music played from inside an open-front restaurant. Some tourist laughed inside, starting the day early. Hats and summer clothes hung from racks outside a shop. There weren't many people out today. A few people walked on the sidewalk—a couple holding hands, an older man with a cane and, farther up, a homeless man pushing a cart full of junk.

"Not the most romantic beach I've been to," Sabrina said.

Did she want it to be romantic? He wondered why that made him recoil. All she'd brought to the surface about Miranda not being everything he'd thought returned. Had she been with him because of who his father was? Because of money? Sweet Miranda. No. She had some good qualities. He wasn't that poor of a judge of character. But he had to agree the money and fame may have played at least some kind of a role.

When he'd first met her, she'd said she wanted all the things he did. Camping, fishing, a nice but not huge house. He'd never had a chance to take her camping or fishing, but when they'd started to look for houses, he hadn't liked her choices. Every one of them had been too big. They'd had their first argument over it. He couldn't stand it that Sabrina might be right.

"Grain of sand for your thoughts," Sabrina said.

Not again. He didn't respond. She stopped at another gift shop that had more hats for sale. Plucking one off its hook, she put it on her head. Red hair sprang out from underneath it, and her sparkling green eyes lit with playfulness.

The sight of her softened his angst.

"It's a penny," he said.

A slight gust of wind shook the hat, and she put her

hand on top of it to keep it from flying off. She laughed a little. "Sand. Piece of the moon…"

He grinned and slipped a hand to her back, pulling her against him so he could dip his head beneath the rim of the hat and kiss her. Catching himself this time, he straightened and stepped back.

"I don't know what made me do that," he said.

Her now quite wide eyes blinked into coherency. "I liked it." She put the hat back on the rack. He started walking down the sidewalk, hearing her jog to catch up.

Did she really like it that he'd kissed her? Was she beginning to change her mind about him? "I thought you had me figured for a cheater."

It took her a second to catch on to why he'd said that. He wasn't sure he understood it himself.

"I believe you would have done the right thing had Rayna not seen you and caught you exploring other, less-committing possibilities."

Less committing. "What's wrong with letting things happen naturally? Why hold back?"

And she did hold back. He'd recognized that about her.

"I had a boyfriend who naturally climbed into bed with me while he was still married."

She was talking about Chet. Her experience with him bothered her more than she admitted or was aware.

"You held back before that happened," he said. "Maybe the men you get involved with take that for disinterest."

His rationale struck her dead center, he saw, because it was accurate. She held back until it was too late. By the time a guy felt he knew her, she revealed the real her. How could that ever work?

He turned onto a narrow street. Their rental was just a block up ahead.

"Were you thinking of Miranda earlier?" she asked; for some mysterious reason she must need to know.

"Yes," he answered. "Sitting in a car doing nothing leaves little else to do but think. I think of her a lot."

He sensed her dislike of that by the nature of her fidgeting hands. "What were you thinking?"

"How much longer are you going to pry into my personal life?" If she didn't ease up, he was going to lose patience.

"You need to let her go so you can move on with your life and be happy again. That's all I'm going to say." She got in the car and faced forward, looking through the windshield. "And I don't know why I'm so curious. Sorry."

Her apology defused him. "I am happy," he said, inside feeling the untruth.

"I meant with another woman. Find someone you love and get married and have kids and live in a charming house happily ever after. That's what I mean."

Everything he thought he'd have with Miranda. Dreams like that were irreplaceable. New ones had to form, and none had for him, not yet. He glanced over at Sabrina as he moved around the hood of the rental. Until she'd come along. As soon as that thought hit him, he forced it out of his head. No dream could form with her.

Why not?

Why was he resisting it so hard with her?

Over the top of the rental he spotted a man standing on the side of the street they'd just walked up. He'd looked up pictures of the missing janitor and the woman. The man looked like Sajal Kapoor.

Abandoning the door handle, he went back around

the rental and walked toward the man. He saw him and pivoted, starting to run away.

"Mr. Kapoor?" he shouted. "Wait! We need to talk to you!" He ran after the man, veering out onto the street to avoid a pedestrian.

Sajal vanished around the corner. Lincoln cleared the corner seconds later. He spotted Sajal running around people down the sidewalk. Lincoln sprinted faster. Sajal ran onto the street where Castillo's Market was. When Lincoln followed, he felt something whiz past his head and then heard it hit the brick building. He looked back and saw a dark green Jeep Grand Cherokee on the street and a gunman aiming a weapon out the window.

Lincoln ducked as another bullet flew by. Then he saw Sabrina swing the rental car into the turn. She rammed into the Jeep, sending it swerving toward the hotel.

"Get in!" she yelled, slowing along the street.

He opened the back door and dived in. She gave the car full gas, ramming into the Jeep once more as it straightened its path on the street. Beside them, the gunman was about to fire again.

Lincoln pulled out his pistol and rolled the back window down enough to shoot. Two shots had the gunman ducking out of sight and the driver slamming on his brakes.

Sabrina sailed by and spun into a tight turn. Lincoln's head hit the back door. Sitting up, he looked for the Jeep and saw that it wasn't following.

Who was that? Tristan's men? Were they following Sajal or him and Sabrina? It had to be Sajal. Lincoln had been careful to be sure he and Sabrina weren't followed. Now Tristan would know they'd been here. And he'd know Lincoln had tried to contact Sajal.

* * *

Back at the RV, Lincoln watched Sabrina go into the kitchen and put her hands on the sink, looking through the small window there. A soft rain had begun. No one was barbecuing tonight. They would be stuck in the confined space of this RV. All her probing about Miranda had taken its toll on both of them.

There was a friction between them, born of sexual desire, a constant yearning to satisfy it. As careful as Sabrina was about the men she allowed herself to get close to, she felt threatened by Miranda and Lincoln's feelings for her. The more she questioned him, the more confused he became. Why did it bother him so much to talk about Miranda?

He moved over to Sabrina, drawn there by conflicting emotions that tugged him both to her and cautioned him to keep his distance. Why keep his distance? What about Sabrina should make him stay away? His strong desire to explore the chemistry between them? The nettling instinct that it would be good with her? Good enough for something serious? He was afraid so.

Sabrina turned to face him then, her hands on the counter edge, her eyes firing sexual invitation but her body resistant. She was fighting this, too.

Moving away from him, she went to the sofa and sat. "Is it hot in here?" She fanned her face.

He followed her, standing in front of her. "Yes, but not because of the temperature."

Did he have to be so calm when he was being blatantly honest? "Oh, well, that explains it."

"I'm going to ask you something."

A loaded question? Should she thank him for the warning?

"Do you want to have a relationship with me?" he asked.

He really wanted to know. That touched her. Was he making progress? "Maybe." Then she shook her head. "No." Forcing a smile, she grunted a laugh. "No."

He was half relieved and for a minute started to think she had a point, that he may have commitment issues. The way she laughed said she didn't mean it. A woman like Sabrina wanting a relationship with him heated his blood. He'd always thought she was beautiful. Attraction wasn't the problem. It was how far that attraction would lead that was.

He reprimanded himself for thinking that way. What was wrong with being with her romantically? It was becoming more and more difficult to resist the desire. Why not give in? At least a little?

"It's hard to say where this would go if we let nature have its way," he said.

"I've always found that nature needs some guidance."

"Or a leash." Holding out his hand, he said, "Let's put it to the test."

"What?"

"Let's give nature some guidance and see if it's any different."

When she continued to wear a blank look, he said, "Up until now, nature has had no guidance."

Breathing a laugh, she gave him her hand and stood at his coaxing. Her awkwardness warmed him. Her boldness to play along with him did far more.

Bringing her against him, he put his arms around her. She slid her hands up his chest and looped her arms around his neck. She was tall enough to fit him well.

Soft in all the right places. He felt her against his chest and tried to make his member cooperate.

"I'm going to kiss you. This is a test."

"Guiding nature. Got it."

He pressed his mouth to her still-smiling one, keeping his eyes open. She kept hers open, too. Rain tapped on the outside of the RV, picking up strength. It was cool inside, and he could smell the rain.

Moving his mouth over hers, he traced her lips with his tongue, lightly, gently. His heart beat faster, but he was still in control. Encouraged, he kissed her deeper.

Her eyes sank shut. Was it because she'd succumbed to nature or had she done that deliberately?

He closed his eyes with her and tasted her expertly. He'd kissed a lot of women and considered himself adept enough to get the job done well.

Deciding to caress her, he glided his hands over her rear.

She jerked back and opened her eyes. "I thought this was only going to be a kiss."

"Nature hasn't taken over yet."

She studied him, partially offended. "No?" Pressing her body to his, she rose up and claimed his mouth.

He felt that, all right. Her command of this kiss heated him up. With his hands still on her rear, he pressed her more firmly to him. A sound came from her that sent him further toward nature.

He kissed her hard. She answered him.

Kneading her rear, he grew near to finding a bed and instead lassoed in his control and kissed her neck, holding her head in his hand.

Hearing her ragged breathing made him put his mouth on hers again. He kissed her softly. The urgency began to build. Where before the urgency had begun before a kiss, now it gathered slowly.

She pulled back, gazing up at him with half-closed eyes. She stepped back.

"Nature lost that time," she said.

And he didn't know whether to believe her or not. Had she maintained control the entire time or had she been close to forgetting her reasons for rejecting him? Even more disconcerting, why did he consider this a rejection?

Chapter 12

Isadora's heart finally stopped racing when she rode her bike down the street that would lead her to the field where Candra had said the party would be. If her parents found out what she was doing she'd be in so much trouble. Well, if her mom found out. She didn't know where her dad was. That conversation she'd heard bothered her. Was her dad okay? Her mom was really worried, too. Isadora had asked her about it, and her mother had said she couldn't tell her anything specific, that her dad would be okay, he was doing what he had to do. It was essentially what she'd heard him say that night he and her mother had talked.

It was a little cool tonight. Isadora wore a hooded sweatshirt and hiking boots. She pedaled onto a dirt road and spotted the bonfire. She heard voices. Teenagers laughing and talking loudly. The sound of a car approaching made her twist to look back. A car slowed on the road.

For a moment she thought she should ride away from here. If the party was broken up by police, she'd be in even more trouble than if she were just caught sneaking out to come here. But the car picked up speed and drove past the dirt road.

She breathed deep a few times in relief. Nearing the bonfire, she stopped the bike and climbed off, walking with it a few feet before setting it down next to some others. About twenty teenagers huddled around the warmth of the fire. Flames lapped at the night air, reaching three or four feet high and flickering light on the faces of gatherers.

Isadora spotted Candra among the throng. Rubio stood behind her, his arms around her. There was a boy beside them. Blond hair, trim body, sort of tall. He had his fingers in the front pocket of his jeans, thumbs hanging out. His head lifted, and he saw her.

Candra noticed and turned. She smiled wide.

"You made it!" she exclaimed when Isadora came to stand beside them.

"Yeah. It was easier than I thought. My mom must sleep like a rock."

Rubio lifted a bottle of beer and swigged, one of his arms still around Candra.

"This is Darius," Candra said.

Very adultlike, Darius removed one of his hands from his pocket and offered it to her. She took it for a shake.

"Hi," she said.

"Hey." His deep voice was nice enough, but she detected a slur and his eyes were a little bloodshot.

Rubio moved with Candra so that Isadora stood next to him. She began to feel it was a mistake coming here. The fire was awesome, though. She watched the other teenagers drinking beer and having a good time. Most of them appeared older than Candra and her.

"I've seen you around school," Darius said.

Had he? She hadn't seen him. There were a lot of kids in her school. Plus, she didn't pay much attention to the older boys.

"You're a pretty nice-looking girl."

Her Indian complexion was smooth and the color of creamy mocha coffee. Her mom always told her she had pretty brown eyes.

"I like the way you dress, too," he said.

He sure wasn't afraid to say it outright. "Thank you." She didn't think she dressed any different than the other girls. Sometimes she wore hats or scarves. And she wasn't popular, not by any stretch. Her dark skin tone set her apart from a lot of the other kids. Some just didn't accept her as easily as others, and Isadora wasn't exactly outgoing in school. She did well in her studies and had a few friends, but she didn't put much importance on being recognized by everyone. She was more interested in the subjects she learned. Well, most subjects. She didn't like physical education or art.

Removing his other hand from his pocket, he bent for a bottle of beer he'd set down on the ground. Alcohol intrigued her in a dark sort of way. What did it taste like? Why did kids like to drink it?

Seeing her watch him, he asked, "Do you want one?"

She glanced at Candra, who'd heard and gave her a nod. Then she showed her the beer she now held. Candra was trying beer, too.

She turned back to Darius. "Okay."

He grinned, real cute-like. Putting his bottle of beer down, he went to a cooler to grab her one. Nervous about trying something new that her parents had always warned her about, she rubbed her hands on her jeans. At least the beer would take care of her dry mouth.

Darius returned, twisting the cap off and handing her the bottle. The bitter smell wafted upward, assaulting her nose. She barely stopped a grimace. Darius drank some of his beer as though he'd drunk many before this. A practiced beer drinker. Isadora wasn't impressed. Was she supposed to be?

She looked over at Candra, who daintily sipped her beer and flirted with Rubio. She seemed to try too hard for approval. If that was why she'd tried the beer, Isadora didn't think that was a good enough reason. She didn't want to drink the beer she held, but it was too late to turn back now. Lifting the bottle, she met Darius's entertained eyes and took a sip.

She could not stop a grimace this time. "Ew!" She handed him the bottle. "That's horrible."

His esteem drained away as he took the bottle. "You're going to be one of those fruity drinkers, huh?" His eyes went down her body and back up as though the idea appealed to him in a purely male way. He finished his beer and tossed it to a trash can sitting near the fire. He made it in with a loud clatter. There must have already been a ton of bottles in there.

"You might like ganja better," he said.

Ganja? What was he talking about? She breathed a half laugh to cover her ignorance.

"You want to try some?"

Insecurity reared up. She couldn't agree to anything unless she knew what ganja was. What should she say now?

After finishing the beer she'd handed him, he set that aside and then reached into his sweatshirt pocket, procuring a strange-looking pipe. He sure was drinking fast.

Isadora searched for Candra and found her talking close with Rubio. Looking around, she realized she didn't know anyone other than Candra here.

Batting down fear, more interested in the exploration, she took the pipe.

Fumbling some, she glanced at Darius. He was nice. She sensed it. Alcohol scared her, but this wasn't alcohol.

When he handed her a lighter, she hid her befuddlement. Of course the pipe had to be lit. She looked at the partially charred contents of the bowl. Some of them were green. Dried, but leafy.

She lit the lighter and put it to her lips. Inhaling just a bit, she handed him the pipe back.

"That wasn't a hit," he said.

It wasn't?

He grinned in that way, that nice way. "You haven't smoked before, have you?"

Isadora had been raised to always tell the truth. "No."

Darius took the lighter. "Are you sure you want to do this?"

She thought about it, appreciating that he cared enough to ask. "It's different than alcohol, right?"

"Yeah. It relaxes you like that but it's not as—I don't know—out of control."

That made her feel better. He made her feel better. She put the pipe to her mouth and leaned toward him. He lit the lighter, and his eyes captivated her as he put fire to the ganja.

She inhaled deep.

"Hold it," he said, his voice dark and warm.

She held her breath.

When she felt her mind go a little feathery, she exhaled. At first it was okay. Nice, even. Then the smoke sort of engulfed her. She could see everything so clearly but felt so...what was it?

Slow. Zombie slow.

She didn't like it.

"Yeah," Darius applauded in a drawn-out way.

He liked it that she was turned into a zombie. Great.

"I think I should go now," she said.

"What? You just got here."

"Yeah, but..." If she said this wasn't her thing—something she'd just discovered—would it get all over school that she was a bore?

"Does the weed scare you?" He seemed genuinely concerned.

"No." She wasn't scared. This was just...off somehow. Not right.

Her parents often talked about drugs and alcohol. They were afraid she'd get addicted or something. Isadora hadn't understood why they'd hammered it in so hard, but she was beginning to now. Not that she'd ever get addicted. She didn't like ganja.

"After you do it a few times it gets nice. Real nice."

A few times? She was pretty sure once was enough for her. Dulling her brain didn't appeal to her. That it did for Darius made her wonder if he was stupid. Then she remembered his low-grades reputation and wanted to go home more than ever.

She had to figure out a way to get out of here without seeming uncool.

"Let's go sit over there." Darius pointed to a pickup truck someone had backed up to the fire pit. No one was sitting there, as most were close to the warmth of the fire.

"Okay." She trailed him to the truck, where he lifted her by her waist to seat her on the back of it.

If she was thinking clearer, what would she do? She wished she had the answer to that.

"Hey, your dad is a janitor over at that gun company, isn't he?"

Why was he asking that?

"I read about the CEO," he said. "He was murdered, huh?"

"Yeah." She didn't pay much attention to her dad's job, but now she thought of the way her parents had talked that day she'd come home from school. Did her dad know something about that?

"Has your dad said anything? Janitors can go anywhere in a building."

"He hasn't said anything."

"Well, the news said he was murdered at his girlfriend's house. Some girlfriend, huh?" He smirked a laugh.

"I don't watch the news." And she didn't find that story funny. Looking toward the fire, she saw Candra walk away with Rubio. Their forms became little more than shadows as they approached some parked cars on the other side of the bonfire.

At the older model Honda Civic, Rubio moved to stand in front of Candra, putting his hands on her waist and then kissing her. Candra didn't seem to mind. In fact, she looked as if she was having a good time. She lifted her arms around his neck.

Isadora had never kissed a boy before. Seeing her best friend do it gave her mixed feelings. Then she realized she and Darius were apart from the crowd around the bonfire, too. And Darius had likely done that on purpose, drawn her away so they could be alone.

"Hey, Darius."

She looked with him to a boy who threw a bottle of something at Darius. Darius caught it.

"If she doesn't like beer, maybe she'll dig that."

"Thanks, Aaron." He caught another bottle Aaron threw with his free hand, a beer.

Darius rolled the first bottle in his hand until the label was clear. It was a wine cooler. The boy must have been standing close to them when Isadora had tried the beer. Would it be all over school what a baby she was?

Darius opened the bottle and handed it to her. It smelled good.

She sipped. It was tangy and fizzy like a soda.

"Mmm." She liked it much better than the beer.

Darius twisted the cap off his beer, foam bubbling up from being jostled.

"How much have you had to drink?" she asked.

He shrugged. "Four or five."

That sounded like a lot. "Are you drunk?"

"A little. Not much. It takes a lot for me to get drunk." He looked down at his body. "I'm not exactly small."

Boys were bigger than girls. She supposed it would take more, but five?

"Is that your sixth, then?"

After studying her face and apparently figuring she was judging him, he said, "What are you, the sobriety police?"

"I was just wondering." She sipped the wine cooler.

He sat quietly beside her. She had no way of knowing what he was thinking, and it made her uncomfortable. Had she offended him by asking how much he'd had to drink?

Lights from the road caught her eye. She watched a car drive by real slow. Was the driver looking at them?

She didn't see how they wouldn't be caught here. Except, that road was pretty isolated. There was a big ranch at the end of it. Was the owner driving by? Or was it someone else?

"Are you one of those smart people in school?" Darius asked, diverting her attention.

"I get good grades."

"I wish I could get good grades."

"Why don't you?"

"I try. It's just... I don't know. School is so boring."

Boring? She didn't think it was boring. Math and science were fascinating. That things about the universe could be explained with math was amazing. And history. She *loved* history. It was anything but boring.

"Is there nothing you like?" she asked. "What's your best subject?"

"Gym."

Figured. She looked toward her bike and saw car lights go out in the distance. Had the car that had passed disappeared over a road or had it stopped and parked?

"Did you see that car?" she asked Darius.

He looked with her. "There've been a few cars driving by. Nobody's stopped so far. They probably think it's the rancher having this party and wish they could join us."

That made her feel marginally better.

"Don't get out much, huh?" he teased.

This was her first time sneaking out.

He leaned closer to her. "I like that."

"What do you like about it?"

"Is this your first time out without your parents knowing?"

"Yes."

"Then I'm the lucky guy who gets to be with you tonight."

Flattered, she breathed a laugh. "I wouldn't go that far."

"I would."

He was so close. The wine cooler and weed had her head so fuzzy. Was he going to—

He kissed her.

The shock of it paralyzed her for a second. When his hand touched her arm, she pulled back. This was not how she'd imagined her first kiss would go.

"Don't do that."

"What? It was just a kiss."

Isadora jumped off the back of the truck. Putting the wine cooler down, she pivoted and ran to her bike.

"Hey!" Darius came after her. Grabbing her arm, he stopped her a little roughly. "What's the matter?"

"I don't even know you."

"It was just a kiss," he repeated.

Isadora tried to pull her arm free. "Let go of me."

"Come on. Let's go back to the truck. We can talk more."

So he could persuade her to kiss him? No way. "I'm going home now."

His brow gathered in an ugly frown. A mad frown.

"All I did was kiss you."

Yeah, and she wasn't about to tell him that was her first. He was a jerk. She yanked her arm and freed it. Seeing some of the other kids around the fire had noticed them, she turned away in embarrassment. This was sure to get all over school. Why had she even come here tonight?"

"Izzie?" Candra called.

Isadora saw her rushing toward her and paused after lifting up her bike.

"What's wrong?" Candra looked from Darius to Isadora.

Darius shrugged in irritation.

"Nothing," Isadora said. "I just need to go home. I don't want to get caught. My mom hasn't been sleeping very well at night. She's going to find out I'm not there."

Candra didn't seem to buy that, but she slowly nodded. "You want someone to take you home?"

She shook her head. She just wanted to get out of here. "No. I'll call you tomorrow."

"Okay."

Climbing on her bike, she'd never felt more relieved in her life. Getting away from this place was all that mattered. She pedaled hard, riding fast down the dirt road. At the paved road, she headed for home.

That was when she spotted the car she'd seen earlier. It was still parked there. Her brief sense of relief scattered. She pedaled as fast as she could and veered wide around the car, seeing there were three people inside.

As she rode down the street, she heard the car roll into motion. Was it coming after her? Feeling paranoid, she tried to calm herself.

But when the car appeared next to her and both the passenger in the front and back looked at her, all-out fear consumed her. She rode as hard and fast as she could. She wasn't far from home. Just three or four blocks.

The car drove ahead of her. Were they going to leave her alone? No such luck.

It pulled over, blocking her path. The man in the backseat got out.

Isadora rode to the other side of the street, but the

car moved with her and blocked her path there, too. She rode into the field. Her front tire hit something, and she lost control.

Oh, no.

She flew off her bike and landed hard on her arm and side. Pain shot up her arm.

The man who'd gotten out of the car lifted her before she could get her bearings. She screamed loudly.

"Shut up, kid!" the man growled.

She kept screaming. "Help me! Somebody help me!"

The man threw her into the backseat of the car and got in after her. The car moved before he had the door shut. Isadora kicked him with both feet.

He hooked her ankles one-armed and then blocked her flying punches. Then the man in the front turned a gun on her and said, "Stop moving or it ends right now."

Isadora stared at the gun, in a surreal place. This couldn't be happening. But it was. These men had abducted her. What were their plans? Her mouth was dry and her heart beat so fast she felt light-headed and sick to her stomach.

"Where's your daddy?" the man with the gun asked.

"I don't know."

"Wrong answer. Where is he?"

She shook her head frantically. "I swear I don't know. He left and wouldn't tell us where he was going. He said he was in trouble." He hadn't, but he may as well have.

The man scrutinized her. "Well, then, you're going to be staying with us for a while." He gave a nod to the man in the backseat with her. He lifted a black bag and stuffed it over her head. They didn't want her to know where they were taking her.

About forty-five minutes later, Isadora was forced

out of the car. She smelled wet ground and heard no sounds of the city.

A door was unlocked with a key on a chain with a few more, jingling as the lock snapped open. The man holding her shoved her, and the other pulled off the bag. She stumbled into the dark room.

As the door closed and the lock clicked into place, a light came on, and she found herself looking at a woman. She was older than Isadora by about twenty years.

"Who are you?" the blonde snapped. She wasn't afraid. Inconvenienced, maybe.

"I'm Isadora Kapoor. Who are you?"

"Tory Von Every."

Sajal Kapoor started to berate his wife for calling him when her frantic voice stopped him. Tristan could trace these calls.

"Isadora is gone."

Isadora was…

"What?"

"She's gone. She's not in her room."

It was after three in the morning. Where could she have gone? Several possibilities ran through his mind. Had she sneaked out? She was an honor student. Well behaved. That didn't seem viable. Had someone taken her from her room?

"I didn't hear anything," his wife wailed.

Just then his phone beeped, indicating a call waiting. He checked the number and didn't recognize it. Who would be calling him at this hour? With his daughter missing, it had to be related.

"Darling, I have another call."

"Someone is calling you?"

When she began to cry, he knew she'd drawn the same conclusion.

"I'll call you right back."

"Come home, Sajal. I need you."

Could he risk it?

"Come home. Now. Please."

He could not refuse her. "I am on my way."

He disconnected her call and connected the new one. "Sajal Kapoor," he answered.

"Ah. Sajal. Ever the polite man."

Tristan. Anger began to build in Sajal. He could not allow this to continue. But what could he, a simple man with no experience in these matters, do? He'd do anything to spare his family, including dying for them.

"I have something that belongs to you."

"If you hurt her, I'll…" Sajal struggled for control of his fear.

"You'll do what?"

As long as Tristan had his daughter, he was helpless. "I'll do anything. Just tell me what you want me to do."

"I thought that's how you'd respond. I'm glad, Sajal. I actually like you."

"Don't hurt my daughter."

"She'll be fine as long as you do as I say."

"Anything."

"I need you to come and meet me."

"Will my daughter be there?"

"Yes. She will."

Tristan gave him directions to the same building where he'd been taken the last time he'd had to face off with him. While Sajal wrote them down, he was certain of two things. One, his daughter would be fine until he reached the meeting place, and two, neither of them would be spared. Tristan would kill them both.

Sajal knew it in his core. The man was crazy. A mass murderer. Killing for him was simple and easy. He had no empathy. He had no heart. He had only greed. Greed fueled his purpose, and anyone unfortunate enough to cross his path, however briefly, would find themselves in life-threatening peril. As Sajal had.

But, oh, as a father and a husband, Sajal vowed he'd go to his grave fighting for what he held dear.

He needed a miracle. He needed help. But who could he turn to? All the way to the building where Tristan had directed him, Sajal despaired. He was powerless against a man like Tristan.

Passing along the front of the building, he saw two men waiting outside. He couldn't see any weapons but was sure they were concealed somewhere. They wore jeans and zip-up sweatshirts, hoodlums in a Los Angeles alley. Sajal parked his truck along the street and got out.

The old building looked cleaner than last time. Trash was picked up, windows were washed and the bum was gone. A sign over the door gave good enough disguise. Easy Pawn, it read.

The two men approached.

"Hands up," the short Mexican man said.

Sajal lifted his hands while the other man patted him down. Finding no weapons, the two led him inside. The storefront had been renovated. The drywall was repaired, flooring replaced with faux wood and shelves and countertops held a variety of pawned goods, no doubt put there for show. No one stood behind the checkout counter.

Another hoodlum stood in front of the door that led to the back room. Seeing them, he opened it and stood aside, nodding to the two escorting Sajal. Through the doorway, Sajal searched the room for his daughter. This room had been renovated also, and furnished into a sort of studio, with a seating area and double bed. The only thing missing was a kitchen.

Isadora sat on a sofa next to another woman. One more man stood before them, and he wasn't Tristan. Sajal took heart that he at least had some time. They'd have to wait for Tristan. Or would they? Did Tristan mean to kill him and his daughter? Never in all the years he'd worked for OneDefense would he have dreamed he'd be introduced to this side of the man.

"Daddy!" Isadora sprang up from the sofa and ran to him. Sobbing, she threw her arms around him.

Sajal's heart roared with love and anger as he took her into his arms. His precious girl. How dare anyone frighten her this way.

"I'm here, Izzie. Everything's going to be all right now," he said.

"They're going to kill us," she wailed.

"You don't know that."

"Tory said so. She said they're only using us for now."

And now that he was here, would they kill him and his daughter or wait? He had to figure out a way out of here. Looking around the room, he didn't see how. There were three guards.

He looked over his daughter's head to the woman on the sofa. Why hadn't Tristan killed her? Why was he holding her captive as he was Sajal and Isadora? Perhaps they had more time than Sajal thought. Perhaps Tristan had other plans for them. If only Sajal knew what.

Chapter 13

Sabrina was so tired of sitting in this car. She and Lincoln had been parked outside Tristan's house for hours. Nothing stirred and it was late. They had taken turns drifting off to sleep. It was close to dawn. Tristan's wife wasn't home, and Tristan himself hadn't spoken to anyone, at least not while he was here. And maybe the baby monitors were turned off. Lincoln's radio receiver was awfully quiet.

"Do you think he knows we're listening?" Sabrina asked. Tristan was probably sleeping now, but earlier he had been quiet, too.

"I don't see how."

Really. Radio waves were invisible, and unless he actually saw them out here, Tristan wouldn't know they were using his wife's baby monitor to listen in on him.

Sabrina was getting impatient. "Maybe we should call it a night. The sun is starting to come up."

"Yeah." But Lincoln didn't move to start the car or drive away. She wasn't anxious to go back to a place where there'd be beds, either. Bad enough that she had to sit next to him in this car, ever aware of him over there, his muscular thighs, his washboard stomach, his powerful arms. Those blue eyes. His hair. His voice when he spoke. What he liked to do when he wasn't working or sitting here chasing a gun trafficker. Practically everything about him turned her on.

He was perfection to her heart. At least her head wasn't steering her wrong. This could only be perfection if he felt the same, and clearly he didn't. For him it was the opposite—his mind might tell him they'd be great together, but his heart was steering him wrong.

That was a new one. She'd never been involved with anyone who stopped his attraction to her. She'd dated plenty of men she'd liked but hadn't liked her, but their heart and head worked in tandem, not against each other.

What was Lincoln so afraid of? Falling in love again only to lose it? Failing the one he loved? She looked over at him, fiddling with the receiver.

"Have you ever been to the South Platte River?" he asked.

All this time she'd been lamenting over her feelings for him and he was thinking about a river?

"No."

"My parents took us on a camping trip to a place along its bank. I was fourteen. That's when I discovered the glory of fishing."

"What made you think of that?" Fishing, of all things, at a time like this. Okay, so not everything he liked to do turned her on.

"There are so many other things I'd rather be doing right now."

Than watching for Tristan? Or being with her?

"You'd rather be fishing?" Maybe for Christmas she'd get him one of those goofy bumper stickers.

"Fishing. Camping. At home with your dog watching a hockey game. Anything but waiting for a lawbreaker to lead us somewhere."

"I haven't been camping in a long time." She and her mother had gone every so often.

"You like to camp?" He sounded surprised.

"Love it. Maddie especially does."

She saw him grin. "Do you fish?"

"No. I can't understand why people call fishing a sport. All you do is stand there with a line in water."

"It requires some physical activity. Hiking. Maybe rowing. Reeling in the big ones."

She'd concede to that. "I'm not ridiculing the activity. Fishing goes hand in hand with camping. But I don't like catching the fish."

"Too slimy for a girl?"

"Yes. I'd rather read."

"But you haven't been camping in a while."

"No." Now that she thought of it, she missed doing things like that. Camping with her mother and their dogs had made her feel part of a family more than any other. She'd loved that about it.

"What was camping like with your parents?" she asked after a bit.

"In a fifty-foot motor home. Luxurious. Too much food. Not enough nature."

"You prefer a tent?"

"I have a nice one."

She smiled. He was so down-to-earth. "What a shame that it's only gathering dust."

The only thing left to say was "we should go sometime," but neither spoke.

Camping with Lincoln would be romantic. So much alone time. Just the two of them in nature, comfy on a camping bed, cozy under the covers. Naked...

As soon as her mind wandered there, she stopped the imaginings.

Damn it. She'd concentrate on exposing Tristan, not her uncontrollable feelings for Lincoln.

As though on cue, Tristan's garage door opened and his car rolled out. The sun was well on its way to rising.

"Get down," Lincoln said.

Sabrina sank down on the seat and listened as the car drove by. When it was safe, Lincoln sat up and made a U-turn in the street. Tristan's taillights disappeared over a hill. When they breached that, Sabrina saw Tristan turn.

Lincoln kept a safe distance behind as they merged onto a freeway.

"You're good at this," Sabrina commented. "Tailing people."

"Lots of practice."

"Do you always get your man?"

"Always."

The way he said it confirmed what she'd guessed all along. Every time he captured a bail jumper, he avenged Miranda. How many did he have to capture before it was enough?

"Doesn't your martial arts studio keep you busy enough?"

He glanced over at her, knowing why she'd asked.

She didn't need him to answer. His studio would

keep him plenty busy. He didn't need the bounty hunting to supplement it.

Traffic jammed up, and they slowed to twenty miles per hour. Amazing how she could be more interested in him than in the danger of following Tristan.

They both couldn't cook. They had both stumbled into their professions, his bounty hunting excluded. And they both preferred simple things. Lincoln was rich because of his parents and always would be, but he didn't need money, and he didn't allow money to dictate his destiny, although it almost had without his consent with Miranda.

Something inside of her supported her attraction, as though he'd be a good choice in a partner, or worth a chance. But that went against all she believed. She never took a chance on men like him, especially when the threat of them looking for other women reared its ugly head. Lincoln hadn't actively looked for that woman Rayna had seen him with. Deep down, Sabrina had to acknowledge that it was her, not Lincoln's actions, that created a barrier. It was her own lack of trust, her own unwillingness to take chances that created the barrier. Her cardinal rule was never to become too attached to men whose interest could wander. But what if Lincoln's would not wander?

All the men she'd dated hadn't liked camping. Chet hadn't. He preferred fancy hotels and restaurants. He wore suits. She'd never seen him in shorts and a T-shirt. Looking back, she couldn't see what had attracted her. Other than his passing of her worthiness-test questions. His answers about fidelity.

Was she so obsessed with not ending up with a man like her father that she based her decisions solely on that? If a man looked good enough to her, all he had to do was pass the Trust, Faithfulness, Commitment test?

Chet had been a practiced liar. Sabrina hadn't been the first woman he'd duped. He enjoyed a steady woman with excitement on the side. He'd actually told her that after she'd caught him. He didn't want a monogamous relationship.

Thinking of him now, she couldn't come up with a single thing about his personality that she liked. In fact, she didn't like anything. He had been selfish and cold. Never held her hand. Their conversations had been all about him. When she'd talked about herself, he'd frequently cut her off and changed the topic back to himself. He'd been nice in some ways, though. His attention had come in the form of flowers and dinners and weekend trips. He'd complimented her on her looks and had been a gentle lover.

Lincoln listened to her. She looked over at his strong hands on the wheel and then ahead at the packed freeway. Tristan's car was barely visible, but he was stuck in traffic, too.

"What do you look for in a woman?" She had to know.

Lincoln glanced over at her. "Compatibility, mostly."

"And looks." She grinned over at him.

"Yeah. But finding someone who wants me for me and who I want the same way is more important. Why do you ask?"

"Just curious." She looked out the window at the other cars moving at a snail's pace.

"Saying your thoughts out loud?"

He'd read between the lines and guessed where her thoughts had been to make her ask that question. What kind of woman would cure him of his commitment problem? Make him forget Miranda and learn how to love again. When the idea of her being the woman who had what it took to win him surfaced, she grew depressed. She didn't welcome anything that made her feel insecure, and that did. Chances were she would not have what it took. No woman would. Not until he, and he alone, came to grips with Miranda's death.

She didn't answer, hoping he'd let it drop.

"What do you look for in a man?"

Drat. "The same thing, plus morals."

"Ah. That again."

"No." She decided not to hold back. What did she have to lose? Nothing she'd ever have, anyway. "I did focus too much on that. Truth is, I don't know what to look for in a man. I mean, how do you know if you're compatible?" As she spoke she realized more and more that she was still hurt over Chet. Not because she'd loved him; because he'd lied and she hadn't seen that about him. Had her mother been as poor a judge of character? Was that why she'd lived alone most her life? And was Sabrina fated for the same destiny because she'd never learned not only what she needed in a man, but how to find him?

She'd put Lincoln to task over needing to get over Miranda when she was in just as dire need to do the same with Chet. And perhaps even more, her father. Maybe she did have abandonment issues.

Traffic began to open up, and she noticed Lincoln hadn't answered her. A glance at him presented a thoughtful profile, brow marginally low, mouth firm. He couldn't answer her. He didn't know.

They both didn't know what to look for in a partner. They'd thought they had. Until now.

Tristan took the next exit and Lincoln followed. This

wasn't the best area of L.A. Sabrina watched all the old, run-down stores pass by her window.

When Tristan drove into an alley next to a pawn shop, Lincoln drove by and turned a corner to park.

"What's he doing down here?"

"Good question. Why don't you wait here while I find out?"

"I'll go with you." Waiting here would be just as dangerous as going with him. What if someone recognized her, or one of Tristan's men noticed her? Besides, sticking together was better than separating.

Lincoln didn't argue, but as they walked toward the Easy Pawn he took out his gun and kept it at his side, looking around. There were a few people walking the street, and cars drove by, but no one took notice of them. A bum leaned against the front of a vacant store three doors down. When he saw them, he headed down the street as though he knew trouble was on the way.

In front of the shop, Lincoln peered into the window. A closed sign was visible on the door. He removed a tool from its compact case.

"What if there's an alarm?" Sabrina whispered.

"Then the cops will come," he said.

"Isn't that a bad thing?"

"Maybe not. Depends on what is going on in here."

And whatever that was, they'd be walking in blind.

Compact and light, the blade worked quietly as he sliced a circle in the glass of the door. A suction cup helped remove the hand-size piece from it. Taking out the piece of glass, Lincoln put the tool away and reached his hand in the door to unlock the dead bolt.

Sabrina went inside after him. Pawned items filled shelves and display cases. There was a door leading to the back that was closed, but she could hear voices. Urgent tones, sometimes rising. A girl was crying softly.

Lincoln stopped and faced her. "Please, wait here."

She nodded.

He leaned down and kissed her mouth, brief and hard. Then he looked into her eyes, passing a sultry message before getting back to action.

She moved to the side of the door, near the checkout counter. With one more look, he opened the door a crack. A man stood with a teenage girl. Sajal. Who was the girl? Sabrina moved just a bit and saw a blonde woman. The door blocked sight of Tristan and whoever else was in there with him. There were at least two other men. Sabrina could hear them moving, and one of them coughed.

"Go outside and keep watch," Tristan said to someone.

The sound of a door opening and closing followed. At least one man had left the room.

"You're a fool if you think you can get away with this," a woman's voice said, the blonde woman.

"Shut up," Tristan growled.

"How many people do you think you can kill before you get caught?" the woman persisted.

"I haven't killed anyone."

"No, but you pay people to do it for you. Wade found out too much about your new friends, so you killed him. What did Cesar Castillo do?"

"He disagreed with me," Tristan said.

In other words, he'd refused to go along with whatever Tristan had planned for him and his store.

Sabrina exchanged a look with Lincoln.

"What have these two innocent people done?"

The blonde was trying to save Sajal and his daughter. Who was she?

"Kill them. Leave her here."

"Daddy," the young girl pleaded, scared.

"It's okay, Izzie," Sajal said, wrapping his arm around her.

They were going to kill a young girl and her father? As Tristan moved into sight, Sabrina jumped back, startled and afraid he'd see her or Lincoln. She tripped, her hand going down onto the checkout counter for balance and bumping a pen holder. It clattered to the floor.

Horrified, she met Lincoln's equally incredulous eyes. He had moved to the side of the door when Tristan came into view, pistol aimed down toward the floor.

"Go see what that was." Tristan's angry voice sent Sabrina's pulse into rapid beats. "Why is that door open? Wasn't it shut when you came here? I told you to keep it locked."

"Sorry, sir," a man said.

Footsteps approached.

Fear paralyzed Sabrina. Lincoln readied himself.

A man opened the door wider and peered into the shop, spotting her.

Before the man could move, Lincoln swung his arm and expertly planted a strike on the man's face. Then he drove his knee to the man's sternum and pounded the back of his head with his gun. The man dropped.

Lincoln stepped over him and entered the back room. He shot another man in the leg, and Tristan ran for the side door. At that moment, Sajal pushed the young girl toward the shop doorway. Sabrina grabbed the girl's wrist and pulled her safely out of the way, tucking her behind her. She was close enough to the door to see the blonde crouching at the end of a sofa. Sajal joined

Sabrina and the young girl behind the protection of the wall.

"Get me out of here!" Tristan shouted to what must have been the guard outside the side door.

The guard fired at Lincoln, who fired back three times. The side door slammed shut, and Tristan and the other man got away.

Lincoln ran to the front of the store. Tristan's car swung out into the street.

In the back room, the woman who'd crouched by the sofa now had the shot man's gun and aimed it at him as he groaned in agony and held his bleeding knee. The man Lincoln had knocked unconscious remained unmoving.

Sabrina joined Lincoln at the front window as he put his gun away. Sajal and the young girl followed.

Sajal put his hand on Lincoln's shoulder. "I don't know who you are, but I owe you my life for saving my daughter."

Lincoln faced him. "You don't owe me anything. Tristan Coulter has caused enough trouble for all of us. I'm just sorry he got away."

"You saved my daughter," he said. "I cannot repay you enough for that."

The sincerity pouring from the man touched Sabrina. He was so genuine. She sensed it about him. This was a good and honest man.

"Tristan has to be stopped," Lincoln said, Sajal's gratitude rolling off him. He'd done it out of necessity, out of duty to do what was right.

Sajal put his arm around the young girl. "This is Isadora, my beautiful, precious daughter." He kissed her forehead. "I would be so lost without you."

Isadora began to sob. "Daddy."

He wrapped both arms around her. "I love you. You are safe now. You are safe."

"Hello?" the blonde called from the back of the pawn shop. "I'm not exactly partying back here."

"Who is that?" Sabrina asked.

"Tory Von Every," Lincoln answered.

He'd recognized her? He was that good at hunting people. Sabrina once again fought her appreciation for him that went far beyond casual.

Lincoln headed for the back of the pawn shop, where the blonde held the injured man at gunpoint. Sajal remained in the front of the shop, where he preferred to wait for police with his daughter.

Lincoln took the gun from Tory, holding it at his side after making sure it was ready to fire.

The injured man turned his grimacing face up to him and spat a vulgar curse.

Lincoln knelt before him, his forearm draped over his knee, gun hanging from his hand. "What is Tristan planning to do with the guns?"

The man responded with more vulgarities in Spanish.

"When is his next big sale?" Lincoln tried again.

The man only stared at him, glazed with pain and anger.

"Where will he go now that the police will be looking for him?" Lincoln didn't expect an answer and received none. The man refused to cooperate. Maybe the police would have better luck.

Lincoln straightened and faced Tory, checking Sabrina to see how she'd react in the company of the woman who'd had an affair with Kirby while seeing her. A woman who was in love would react differently than one who wasn't. Instinct told him she hadn't been in love with Kirby, that their relationship was more complicated than that, complicated enough to keep secret.

"Why did Tristan kidnap you?" he asked Tory.

Tory glanced at Sabrina almost apologetically. "I was having an affair with him."

Sabrina looked confused. "What about Kirby?"

After a pained hesitation, Tory said, "I was having an affair with him, too."

She was married and having an affair with two men? Lincoln caught a hint of disgust from Sabrina, and, though he agreed, he stayed his course. "Did Tristan find out about you and Kirby?"

Tory turned to him. "Yes. And he was furious."

"When was that?"

"Just before Kirby was killed."

Lincoln looked at Sabrina. Tristan had more motive to kill Kirby than what she'd overheard and Kirby's attempt to protect her. And then he'd kidnapped Tory... to force her to remain with him?

"I tried to break it off with Tristan," Tory said, confirming Lincoln's assumption. "When I told him I didn't want to see him anymore, he lost it. I made the mistake of going to see him at a house he rented in Venice. He wouldn't let me leave. That's where he kept me until tonight. I think he was going to kill me after he was finished with me, and I think he would have been finished with me after tonight."

"Why after tonight?" Sabrina asked.

"He's been planning a big sale. He never discussed details in front of me, but I could tell by how anxious he was that he's close to completing it."

It wasn't enough information. Of course, Tristan would be careful.

Lincoln checked on the injured man. He still lay holding his knee, but appeared to be fading from loss of blood. He was Mexican. Come to think of it, a lot of Tristan's men were Mexican. Was that a coincidence?

"I blew it with Kirby," Tory continued. "I could tell he was starting to lose interest, so I began to sleep with Tristan. I shouldn't have done that. I should have fought for him. My marriage was over. Kirby once told me he wanted me to get a divorce. I put it off. I loved my husband, but, well... He knew about my affairs." And there was no repairing a marriage that faced that kind of betrayal, when the affairs were compulsive, addictive almost. Tory had a problem in that regard. "But Kirby would have been worth fighting for. If only I hadn't lost him before I started seeing Tristan." She turned to Sabrina. "That was because of you, wasn't it?"

"Kirby and I were just friends," Sabrina said.

"Oh, I don't think so. If you were the one who drew him away from me, he must have had strong feelings for you. Kirby hated it that I was married and hadn't left my husband." She sighed in exasperation, short on empathy. "I was torn over that. I have an unusual connection to my husband. There are things about him that I love, especially the way he loves me, but there were others... I wasn't getting all that I needed."

As in sexually.

"Now I have no one," Tory said. "I don't think my husband will ever forgive me."

The man on the floor groaned. Lincoln hadn't called for help yet. He'd wanted to talk to Tory first.

"It doesn't sound like you deserve him," Sabrina said to Tory. "He gave you trust and love and you gave him multiple affairs with other men and all the lies that go along with that betrayal."

Lincoln supposed her red gloves would always come out when confronted with infidelity.

"You don't understand," Tory said.

"I understand you consider sex more important than your husband's feelings. You have no concern for anyone other than yourself."

Lincoln touched her arm, stopping her brutal honesty. They needed Tory to tell them all she knew about Tristan.

She blinked with her cooling ire. "Sorry."

He grinned at her. "It's okay. Just put the gloves away now."

Her brow twitched at first in confusion, then she realized what he meant and that he was teasing her. She smiled back, and a spark of heat flashed before he tightened his control.

Turning back to Tory, who'd taken note of the exchange, Lincoln asked, "Is there anything else you can tell us about Tristan? Aside from his gun operation. Is there anything that might help the police find him?"

Tory shrugged, her gaze going around the back of the pawn shop. "He's an abusive man. He didn't treat me that way until I rejected him. That man has serious issues. He's dangerous."

She didn't look abused now. If she had been beaten, there were no marks.

"He hates his mother. What kind of man hates his own mother? You should have heard him talk about her. Pure hate."

"She was his stepmother," Lincoln said.

"She was the only mother he had," Tory argued. "She was his mother."

Lincoln glanced at Sabrina and sensed her thinking

what he was thinking; maybe it was time to go talk to Tristan's stepmother.

"What's her name?" Sabrina asked Tory. "Do you know where we can find her?"

Tory told them her name. "I don't know where she lives. Tristan never said, and he never went to see her."

"Please," the man on the floor said, in pain and bleeding.

It was time to leave. Taking out his phone, Lincoln pressed in a number.

"Cash. Lincoln Ivy. Tristan Coulter has abducted three people and held them captive in a place called the Easy Pawn. Sabrina Tierney and I rescued them and Tristan got away. Two of his guards will need medical attention." He told him the address and answered several questions from the detective.

Archer Latoya would not be able to protect Tristan after this. There were three victims who could testify against him, reveal his crimes. They weren't illegal gun trafficking crimes, but they'd be enough to turn suspicion off Sabrina and on him.

He disconnected and then turned to Sajal. "When the police get here, tell them exactly what happened."

Sajal nodded. At last things were turning in their favor. This time he and Sabrina had witnesses.

Lincoln searched their surroundings, putting a hand on Sabrina's back as they made their way along the sidewalk to Archer Latoya's white, two-story home.

"Do you think he'll talk?" she asked.

"One way to find out."

Sunlight warmed the air under a clear blue sky. It was about midmorning now. All the houses were built close together here, and the front yards were small, many fenced in. Most had only single-car garages. Mature trees shaded the street and yards. The curtains were closed in the two dormer windows on the second level, and in the bay window on the lower level. The roll-down blinds on each of the narrow windows beside the double front door were also closed.

Here lived a man afraid to go outside.

They reached the front door.

Archer opened it before they knocked. In his early fifties, slight wrinkles creased his brow and mouth. An average-height man with a fairly trim body and no signs of gray in his brown hair, Archer stepped aside. "Come in."

No resistance? Why did he seem so...welcoming? Or was it welcoming? Had he already heard about the kidnappings? He could have a police scanner, or someone could have called him. Cash? Perhaps to gloat? To push him into a corner? He didn't appear to feel pushed.

Leading them past a laundry room that led to the garage door and into the living room off the front entry, Archer went to the front window Lincoln had seen from outside and stood there. The curtains were sheer, but made it difficult for anyone to see inside during the day.

He glanced around the average-size home. Behind him, all was as it had been the last time he was here, except this time it was daylight. A portion of one wall had been opened up to the kitchen. A small, round table sat before a glass sliding door. A stairway along the side of the dining area led upstairs. In the living room, the flat-screen TV that hung on the wall was dark this time. It was quiet in the house. Archer didn't have much, a sofa and a chair with an ottoman, and he didn't clean very well.

"We just came from Easy Pawn," Lincoln said.

"I heard what happened. Cash Whitney responded to the call." Archer remained standing at the window, resigned, and not happily so.

"Who told you?" Lincoln asked.

With a pass of his gaze to Sabrina, Archer put his hand on the window frame and sighed.

Sabrina moved beside Lincoln at the end of the sofa and coffee table, slipping her arm so that it hooked comfortably with his. Why she did that, he couldn't guess, but he suspected she'd sensed the same as he had about Archer.

"I'm off duty today, but another officer called," Archer finally said, still with his back to them.

"You must know I couldn't have killed Kirby," Sabrina said.

With that, he dropped his hand and turned. "Yes. I know." More of that resignation.

Sabrina's fingers flexed on Lincoln's arm and did more than make him feel protective. Heat flickered for her. He doused it before it could grow into an all-out blaze.

"I've known it all along."

"Then why—"

"Tristan Coulter is my half brother," he cut Sabrina off.

"We know that," she snapped.

"We were never close," he replied, unaffected by her tone. "Ours was not a family of close ties. Tristan and I grew up together and that's the extent of it. He never liked me. I never liked him or his sister. Both of them were conniving backstabbers. My mother left my father when I was young and took up with Tristan's father shortly thereafter. She didn't know he was abusive until after they were married. Tristan and I were angry with her for different reasons, but it was no pact."

"Then why protect him?"

"After we left the house, we got to know each other. Grew closer, especially after his father died." He spoke with bitterness now clipping his tone. "I didn't realize until it was too late that he'd planned it that way. He never wanted to be close to me. He only wanted someone to control, someone in law enforcement. And at the time, I was vulnerable. My marriage was failing. I had no one to turn to."

And Tristan had used that to his advantage, become the only one Archer could turn to.

"So you let him pay off all your debt?"

The depressed resignation hung over Archer's brow. "He offered to loan it to me. Said I could pay him back over ten or twenty years, no interest. I was desperate. My wife had a credit card problem. She spent more money than we made. Not that I was any better. I've never been good at managing money. I spent it, too, on different things. We were in big trouble, going under fast with no rope to pull ourselves out. We were three months late on the mortgage payments, and even further behind on the credit cards and car payments. Creditors were calling multiple times a day. And then my wife came to me one night and said she was leaving me. She had her bags packed and had spent the day going through our things. Anything she wanted was already gone."

Falling silent as he lamented over the memory, Archer continued after a moment. "My lawyer said I'd be stuck with half of everything. Most couples split profits from property and bank accounts. We were talking nothing but debt. The debt was staggering. Over a hundred thousand after you added in our upside-down mortgage. Half was crippling."

He looked from Sabrina to Lincoln as though checking to see if they understood. Then once again, he continued. "About a month after the divorce was final, I found out she had been seeing another man and planned to marry him. He was a doctor and made a lot of money. That's how she paid her half of the debt. I wondered why she was so calm about it, not worried over how she was going to pay her half. She didn't care that I was left with the other with no way of paying for it."

Archer rubbed his hands together, a jaded man.

"And Tristan came to your side," Sabrina said.

Without looking up from his morose contemplation, Archer nodded.

"How did he threaten you to hide evidence?" Lincoln asked.

Now Archer looked up with the feral eyes of a caged wild animal. "A few weeks before he gave me the money, he invited me over to what he called his friend's house. We spent an hour there talking. Tristan and the man disappeared for a short while into an office. I didn't think anything of it then. But after he gave me the money to pay off my debt, he brought a picture of me shaking hands with the man he'd introduced me to."

The money he'd given him had come from a gun sale, an illegal one.

"If the chief learns about that, I'll lose my job," Archer said. "And you can bet that if I betray Tristan, he'll do his best to make that happen, or worse. For all I know, he's fabricated enough evidence to show I was the one who made the gun deal." He looked at Sabrina. Tristan had done the same to her.

"So you'd send an innocent person to jail?" Sabrina

didn't fall for the sympathy ploy, if that was what Archer had intended. "You'd throw someone else in jail to save yourself?"

Archer's demeanor softened, and the same resignation that had shrouded him when they'd first arrived came over him again. "No. I wouldn't have allowed that to happen. An apology may seem shortcoming, but you have it. I've been trying to find a way out from under Tristan's control ever since he double-crossed me. But you must understand why I have to be careful. Tristan has no empathy. He kills without remorse, whenever it suits his needs or he feels threatened. He'll do it himself or have one of his men do it for him. And he's destroyed my life far more than it would have been with my wife leaving me and being left with debt I had no way of paying. I'd like nothing more than to expose him, but I'd also like to survive doing so."

Sabrina folded her arms and didn't respond, her indecision over whether to believe him evident.

Lincoln put a stop to his adoration and mentally ticked off all the points Archer had raised that he'd like to question. "Has he asked you to do anything for him before this?"

"No. But if I don't stop him, it will never end. I can't live like this," he said to Sabrina. "I can't live under Tristan's control."

"How is it that he has so many men working for him?" Lincoln asked.

Archer turned to him. "Gun trafficking is lucrative to those who know how to work it. I managed to find out about one man. Cesar Castillo. He's a gang member."

Sabrina inhaled a shocked breath.

"The *Avenidas,* they call themselves," Archer went

on. "It's Spanish for the Avenues. Castillo was their leader."

Spanish. There was the link.

"Was?" Lincoln queried.

"I haven't found his body yet, but you can bet Tristan had him killed."

"Tristan and Cesar were friends?" Sabrina said it as she absorbed the information.

Archer scoffed. "Tristan doesn't know how to be a friend. He saw an advantage to befriending Castillo. Selling guns. But Castillo refused him."

"Who is their leader now?"

"I don't know."

"Why would Tristan befriend a street gang leader?" Lincoln asked.

"The *Avenidas* aren't like other gangs. Their main focus is to support Mexicans. They could almost pass as businessmen. They're educated and have honest jobs. They aren't centrally located, don't wear colors or have a strict hierarchy. That makes them hard to catch. They look like you and me."

"What makes them dangerous?" Lincoln asked.

"Don't let their appearance fool you," Archer said. "The *Avenidas* are an extremely violent gang. Warring against other gangs, protecting their criminal activity. They've murdered innocent bystanders, people who were at the wrong place at the wrong time. They like money. Something they share in common with Tristan, and Tristan has a business mind. He can make them a lot of money."

"What kind of criminal activity?" Sabrina asked.

It had to be guns, at least in part.

"Some of their members have been arrested for gun trafficking. Mostly straw purchases. Drugs, too. But it's their ties to Mexico that drew Tristan in. The *Avenidas* are closely connected to the Tres Equis Cartel."

Triple X Cartel. Sometimes referred to as the 3X Cartel, or just 3X. Lincoln had heard of them. Tristan had wormed his way into a very large, very successful and very dangerous organization. No wonder he felt so untouchable, killing those store managers and planning to kill Sajal and his daughter, and probably his estranged lover.

Even more disturbing, had Sabrina uncovered that detail on her own, she'd have had no chance against a Mexican drug cartel. She'd have no chance with only Lincoln, either. Just the two of them couldn't stop Tristan with that kind of backing. But the police were swaying to their side. Tristan's true nature was coming to light. And now that a street gang and a Mexican drug cartel were involved, the feds would be brought in. Tristan would have to take refuge in Mexico to escape that kind of manhunt.

Archer moved away from the window and came to stand before them. "I've been trying to find out when Tristan is planning to sell them a big shipment."

"Alone?" Lincoln questioned.

"What choice do I have?"

"You have one now."

"Wade must have learned of the cartel," Sabrina said, mirroring what he'd already thought. "That's why he was killed."

"Wade wanted to partner with Tristan," Archer explained. "Tristan isn't interested in partners, but he can't kill every *Avenida* to take over the operation. He needs them."

"Why a gang?" Lincoln put the question out there.

"Cesar worked for OneDefense. Tristan discovered

the cartel through him. He wanted to be in charge of the sale, and Cesar wasn't going to let him. Cesar wanted to control the sale."

But Tristan wanted to be in control. And an idea had formed, one he'd nurtured into fruition to what it was today, a money maker. Money was the main motivator for Tristan. He had no family, not one he revered in any fashion. He'd blackmailed his half brother and was estranged from his stepmother. His wife was a trophy, and Lincoln doubted he cared about his infant child. He didn't know how to love anything other than material things. And himself. How any man could love himself for being the kind of human being Tristan was today was beyond Lincoln's grasp. Without love, what did a man have when his last day came?

If Sabrina were listening to his thoughts, she'd say he didn't have love. How could he when he couldn't commit?

He could commit. He'd marry a woman who fit him that way.

Wouldn't he?

What if he loved Sabrina? Would he marry her?

He didn't know her enough to say. Or was that an excuse?

Frustration made him sigh hard. He was letting her get to him too much. He'd take a day at a time as he always did. He didn't love Sabrina, not yet. But he could. He was falling for her.

"Can I get you anything? I was making some coffee when I received the call. Should be finished by now." He walked into the kitchen.

Lincoln picked up on his nervousness. He had a lot to lose. His life, if Tristan found out before the police caught him, and his job.

"We could both use a cup. Make it a latte for Sabrina."

When she glanced back at him in surprise, he winked at her. He'd been paying attention to what she liked.

Sabrina didn't touch the dining table, dusty and full of dried drops of liquid and crumbs of food, but went to the back door. Archer had a view of a single tree in his small backyard and the neighbor's two-story house that was similar to his, only yellow.

Lincoln's wink had her a little flustered. With just that playful gesture after asking for her favorite flavor of coffee, he'd set her on fire.

But now wasn't the time to entertain that temptation. Were it not for Archer tampering with evidence and painting her a murder suspect, she'd have never gone to Denver and gotten into this mess. Tristan would have been arrested.

But then she'd have never met Lincoln, and Kirby would still be dead.

She wasn't sure how to feel about any of it, but the anger and resentment she'd first felt when she'd arrived was gone. Archer was just as much of a victim of Tristan's evil ways as she and Lincoln were.

Someone offered her a steaming cup. It wasn't Lincoln. Taking it, she looked into Archer's eyes that sought forgiveness.

"Why talk now?" she asked.

"There are witnesses now. Tristan is on the run. He isn't in control anymore." Archer looked pleased, cynically so, and sipped his coffee.

"Are you going to tell the truth to police?"

His gaze broke from hers as he lowered his cup to the filthy table. She felt like getting some cleaner and paper towels and wiping it for him. His entire house, for that matter.

"I suppose I don't have a choice in that, either."

"Do you expect us to lie to Cash?"

He looked back at Lincoln, who'd taken a perch against the kitchen counter, his head turned toward them. "No." Then Archer said to Sabrina, "You found the right man to help you with your situation."

Lincoln.

"He's my neighbor," she said. "Like you, he doesn't have a choice other than to help me. Tristan's gang members are after him, too."

Archer nodded grimly. "It will be a day of celebration when he's brought down. I should have known better than to trust him, especially after those two boys were killed."

Sabrina straightened, and Lincoln put his cup down and approached, coming to stand at Archer's right.

"The two that died in a car accident?" Lincoln asked.

Sabrina was still recovering from shock. Of course Archer would know about that. He'd grown up with Tristan.

Looking from one intent face to the other, Archer said, "Yes. Tristan was bullied all through school. He was awkward and homely back then. He had to grow into his looks. Doesn't look so bad now that he's filled out, but when he was a scrawny fifteen-year-old, he wasn't a pretty sight. Couple that with being bookish and a loner, and you have the perfect recipe for bullying."

"Did you see how it affected him?" Sabrina asked.

"After a bad day, he'd come home mad. He'd throw his backpack and books and bang around in his room.

One day he threw a glass of milk at our mother when she asked what was wrong."

"Did he act on his temper often?" she asked.

"He threw things. He never mistreated animals or hurt anyone."

"He threw a glass of milk at his stepmother." Was he desensitized over that sort of thing? Sabrina watched him.

With the lowering of his eyes and hesitation, Archer must have realized how she had come to that interpretation. "Yes, and he was wrong for that. You have to remember the environment we grew up in. I was angry with my mother and Tristan hated her. That doesn't excuse the way we treated her, Tristan worse than me. I mainly avoided her."

Sabrina had grown up without a father, but she hadn't had dysfunction. She'd had love from her mother. Still, she could understand his lost sense when he spoke of his adolescence.

"Don't you think I don't have regrets over how I behaved back then? I wish I'd have known then what I know now."

"What is that?"

"That my mother did the best she could and never meant to be with men who didn't treat her children right. She had her share of getting the short end of the stick. She struggled to provide a good life for us. She failed. That's all. I don't blame her, or resent her in any way."

"It's good that you made amends with her."

"There were no amends made. My mother refuses to see or speak to me. She refuses to see or speak to Tristan, too."

"Still? When was the last time you tried?"

"I try every year at Christmas. She never answers

or returns my calls. She's changed her number a few times."

But as a cop, he could find it. He wanted to have a relationship with his mother, one he'd never had before.

"I've written letters. I've gone to see her. Going to see her upsets her terribly. She screams for me to leave. I don't go to her in person anymore. I hope someday she changes her mind and gives me another chance. My aunt keeps me apprised of her health. She's doing well for now, but she's getting older."

Thinking of her own mother, Sabrina reached out and touched his forearm. She couldn't imagine her mother dying without any contact with her. Before coming here, she'd thought poorly of Archer. She'd placed him in the same category as Tristan. Bottom dweller. Not worth any decent person's time or consideration. Trash to be taken out. Period. Talking to him today had changed her mind. Underneath his forced actions to incriminate her resided a good man.

He put his hand over hers. "I'll tell my chief everything I know this afternoon."

Sabrina could only nod, grateful and worried for him at the same time and not fully understanding why. He was Tristan's half brother. Nothing like him, but still related. And yet, there was something about him that instilled trust. Tristan was good at fooling those around him. Was Archer the same?

She looked over at Lincoln. They'd go talk to Archer's mother and see what she had to say. Maybe she should have thought to do that a long time ago.

"We should go." Lincoln extended his hand to Sabrina.

They said goodbye to Archer and left.

Outside, Sabrina asked Lincoln, "Do you think he'll suffer much because of Tristan?"

"He'll have to deal with the consequences of tampering with evidence, and even though he was blackmailed, he never went to the police when he discovered where the money came from that Tristan gave him. But maybe the chief will be lenient, given he was coerced." And then he said, "It's hard to say."

Sabrina walked with him toward the rental. "What if Tristan is never caught?"

"Then you and Maddie will have to move in with me," he answered.

Hearing the joking in his tone, she studied him to see if that was a mask for what he truly felt. "Have you ever lived with a woman?"

"In my twenties. We grew apart."

"How does a man get to be forty-two without ever marrying?"

They reached the rental, and he stopped with her in front of the passenger door.

"I suppose I've been looking for what my parents have." He grinned. "Minus the paparazzi."

He'd been searching for love, real love. "That's nice." And it was. Except Miranda's death had destroyed his belief that he could find it. Not only had he had a solid example of what love should be, he'd found a good match with Miranda, who'd been killed. His love had been ripped apart, taken away. Would he ever feel like searching for love again? Was his belief that it existed still intact? Was it buried in him somewhere? Would any woman be able to exhume it?

As her thoughts ran free, she became aware of him watching her. His blue eyes captivated her as always, and a familiar heat expanded. With him it was so natural, her reaction to him, a man her body and mind found so stimulating. Why him? Why did it have to be him who did that to her?

She hadn't felt that way with Chet. It hadn't been natural. Methodical was a better word to describe what they'd had. Logically they should have fit, but their hearts hadn't connected. Not like this. Not the way her heart connected with Lincoln.

What if she just let go and let happen whatever would happen? What was the worst outcome if she did? She could fall in love with him, and he could turn away and leave her brokenhearted. On the other hand, he could fall in love with her, too. He couldn't possibly be unaffected by her. The heat generating between them right now could not be from just her. She could see it in his eyes.

Was he worth the risk?

Chapter 14

Archer's mother wasn't home, so Lincoln took Sabrina across the street to a small hamburger place, aptly called Buns. Archer's mother lived above a pastry shop. She lived alone, according to the young girl working the counter at the shop.

Standing in line, he tried to take an interest in all that surrounded him except Sabrina, but that proved impossible. Something kept nagging him, something that she'd said.

He handed Sabrina her hot dog and they went to stand by some tall tables where there were no stools. All the seating was outside, except for four small tables that ran along the window inside the cramped space of Buns.

Everything was finally coming together with Tristan. As soon as Archer confessed and revealed Tristan's blackmail, the law wouldn't be after them anymore. They could both go home and resume their lives. Well, he could resume his in Denver. Her life had been here until she'd been forced to flee. What would she do after this was over?

Living without her next door didn't appeal to him much. Somewhere along the way he'd grown attached to her. Her curly red hair, her green eyes, her sexy body. Her brave independence and the need for companionship hindered by a self-imposed barrier. Her dog. Her inability to sit still.

She took a bite, ketchup smearing her mouth and onions falling to the napkin she'd put on the table. He reached up and used his thumb to wipe the ketchup, sucking it off when he finished. She laughed softly and reached up and did the same for him. The way she leaned, her breasts touched his forearm, one more than the other.... She licked her lips, still smiling.

All of it fueled his earlier realization that he was well and truly falling for her.

"You should do that more often," he said.

"What?" she cajoled.

"Let your guard down." He was perfectly serious.

Her smile faded into understanding. She was careful who she picked to date and who she picked to have a relationship with. Too careful, in his opinion. "You're beautiful when you're like that."

She blinked a few times, his compliment soaking in. He enjoyed that he was the one who did that to her. Maybe too much. All of it was too much. Everything about her.

Bending, he put his lips on hers to taste where her tongue had been. He heard her stalled breath, felt an instant of stiffening and then the melting of her. He kissed her fully, not caring who saw. Both of them held what remained of their hot dogs. With his free hand, he molded his palm to her lower back. With hers, she touched the side of his face, and then slid it into the ends of his hair at the back of his neck.

He could stand here and kiss her for an eternity…or until he had to find a place to take it to the next level. Lifting his head, he savored the way her eyes reflected light and radiated heat, the energy of her desire, the essence of her. This was something few men ever saw— Sabrina with her guard down. That he could do that to her made him reel with answering passion.

But then the barrier was back up.

Moving back, she eyed him peculiarly. "Why did you do that?"

She didn't know? Blind passion. Adoration. Love…

He put his hot dog down, no longer hungry.

Love?

Where had that come from? He couldn't possibly love her. She'd only just moved in next to his house a couple months ago. It had to be the constant presence. They'd been together nonstop since this whole situation began. He hadn't had sex in a while, either. That was it. It was superficial.

The lump in his throat loosened. He was in no danger of falling for her.

Why was he worried he would?

Miranda's bloody body flashed in his mind, followed by the echo of her laughter and loving eyes, the life of her. He didn't remember feeling like this with her, the way he felt with Sabrina, kissing her, just being with her.

A big woman wearing a flowing dark pink dress came out of the pastry shop across the street and picked up a chalkboard that had all the early-morning specials written on it. Carrying that inside, the door swung shut.

Dark-skinned, Archer's mother was around five foot ten and on the heavy side. Lincoln could see her jewelry from here. Big, like her.

"Let's go." He didn't wait for her, all too glad for the interruption.

She walked with him over to the shop. He held the door for her. Inside, he saw Archer's mother with the girl they'd spoken with earlier.

"That's them," the girl said. "They're the ones who were asking for you."

Archer's mother eyed them curiously, if not suspiciously. "Can I help you?"

Her hair was bleach blond and thick and curly. She had tanning-bed skin—wrinkled and unnaturally brown. Big, silver hoop earrings sagged her earlobes, and the huge, bright yellow chain necklace might've complemented the dark pink of her dress if it wasn't so bulky. She looked like a secondary character in one of his father's worse street-gang films.

Lincoln introduced himself and Sabrina. "We're here to talk to you about Tristan."

Coldness ran all over her, eyes chilled, body jolted ever so slightly. And then she snapped, "I have nothing to say about him. Not to anyone." Then to the girl, "Sarah, you can go on and go now."

"Thanks, Tia." The young girl all but skipped through a back door, anxious to be free for the rest of the day.

"Tia Coulter?" Lincoln asked.

"I ain't got nothin' to say about that boy." Her high-pitched voice sounded gangster in a Rhea Perlman kind of way. "You two may as well turn around and get out of here."

He hadn't expected a warm welcome, but this was hostile. "We aren't friends of Tristan's."

"Then why are you here?" she snapped. "To tell me about what kind of trouble he's in? Because if that's it, I don't want to hear it."

Sabrina stepped forward. "Mrs. Coulter—"

"Don't be callin' me no Mrs. Coulter. That man is dead. Ain't nobody missin' him, neither."

If she felt that strongly about it, why hadn't she changed her name? "Tia. We—"

"We've just spoken with Archer," Sabrina cut him off. "Before you kick us out, please, listen."

Tia closed her mouth and cocked her head. "You have five minutes."

Lincoln doubted she gave either one of her sons that much time.

Sabrina began a methodical explanation of everything that had occurred, from Kirby Clark's murder to Archer revealing Tristan's blackmail.

"Archer has been trying to be free of Tristan ever since his divorce," Sabrina said. "And now I have to find a way to clear my name. It wasn't Archer you should have shut out of your life, Tia. It was Tristan."

Tia stood calmly behind the counter, staring at Sabrina, taking it all in. When she'd finally absorbed what she needed, she boomed, "Come upstairs with me."

Tia ambled her heavy frame over to the front door and flipped the closed sign so that it faced the window. Locking the entrance, she led them to the back. Lincoln trailed the women, diving through ugly beads and entering a work area that also served as a docking station. He climbed a narrow stairway, his face excruciatingly close and near eye level to Sabrina's rear.

Tia unlocked a worn-out white door at the top of the

steps. There was barely enough room for two people to stand on the landing, so Lincoln waited on the top stair.

Opening the door, Tia led them into a surprisingly quaint apartment. An antique-finished yellow-and-pastel-green table had a vase of white lilies in the center and tasteful yellow-cushioned chairs. Straight ahead, the narrow kitchen had been renovated. Glass doors in faint-green-painted cabinets revealed neatly stored white dishes and an assortment of glasses.

There was a giant white rug with thin brown-and-muted-green stripes spread in the small living room, a white sofa with colorful pillows, and a glass coffee table full of travel books. Light poured in from the living room window, white blinds up. A white bookshelf and glass TV stand completed the room.

The entire eye-catching decor clashed remarkably with the woman who lived here.

Tia removed a pitcher of iced tea from the refrigerator and poured it into three drinking glasses with ice. She didn't ask if they wanted any, just handed them over. She seemed nervous.

"Tristan was always a handful, you know. Smart, though." Tia smacked her lips with a sip of tea. "That boy was quick as a whip."

She sat at the dining room table, so he and Sabrina did the same.

"I tried my best to help him. He was already in trouble when I married his daddy. Kids teased him mercilessly. He'd be rich by now if it hadn't been for that. Smart as he was. Mmm-hmm." She drank more tea.

"About the bullying." Sabrina had her forefinger lifted. "Can you tell us what happened to those boys?"

"Jared and Dakota. Yes. Sad, that story is. They were out with some friends that night. Doing what kids do when their parents aren't lookin'. Drinkin'. Smokin'. Toxicology reports confirmed it. Went over to a friend's house and had themselves a good time. On the way home they lost control of their car and drove right into a ravine. Head-on with a big boulder at the bottom. Musta died instantly."

"That's terrible," Sabrina said, more of a way to keep her talking, it sounded to Lincoln.

"Yes, I imagine, for the families. Can't say I could pretend remorse at the time, I'm afraid. Tristan was a handful, but I had such high hopes for him."

"Where was Tristan that night?" Lincoln asked.

"He told the police he went to the party those two boys were at before they wrecked their car."

"The police questioned him?" Sabrina asked.

"Not whole lot. Tristan saw them at the party, and that's it. He said they dumped a bowl of punch on him. Tristan never gave up trying to fit in. Ended up subjecting his-self to a lot of misery that way."

"Did the police suspect foul play in the accident?" Sabrina asked.

Lincoln sat back and let her do the questioning. She was doing a fine job of it.

"Something mechanical went wrong with the car. Severed brake line or somethin'. I suppose that's why they talked to everyone at the party."

"Did anyone tell them that Jared and Dakota bullied Tristan?"

"The punch bowl came up. Police asked Tristan about it. He said it was all in fun. The car was damaged pretty bad in the accident, so in the end it was ruled an accident."

The bullying hadn't come up. Not the full extent of it.

"Did you ever wonder if Tristan may have…" Sabrina didn't finish.

Tia didn't need her to. Her gaze met Sabrina's, wary, hesitating. "The thought did cross my mind a time or two. Especially after…"

"After what?"

Tia stood. "Let me show you somethin'." Lincoln got up with Sabrina and trailed Tia to a spare bedroom. Tia went to a closet and retrieved a box from the back corner.

Lincoln took it from her when her grunts of exertion accompanied heavy breathing. He set it on the lime-green-and-brown-covered double bed. Some of Tia's personality had made it into the bedrooms. There was a painting of a bright pink flower above the bed. Gaudy, but nice in a weird way.

Lincoln opened the box, and Tia began removing items. A baseball glove. A photo of Tristan with a dog. Some books. And then a wood jewelry box. Setting that on the bed, Tia opened it.

"Here are some pictures of Dakota and Jared. And a notebook," Tia said.

Sabrina took the photos while Lincoln flipped open the notebook.

The first page had a date on it.

"He started that after those boys were killed," Tia said.

Tristan had made a journal about all of his bullying experiences. Most were done by Dakota and Jared. The last entry was an exposé on the accident that killed the boys. It began with, "If I were the one who killed Dakota and Jared, this is how I'd do it…."

He showed the notebook to Sabrina, who lifted her eyes to his when she finished.

Spotting something shiny in the box, Lincoln leaned forward and saw that it was a pocketknife. Severed brake line...

"Do you mind if we take this with us?" he asked Tia.

"Why?" She looked worriedly from Sabrina to Lincoln.

"I'm going to give this to the police," he said. "Just in case."

"You think Tristan..." Tia didn't finish. "I suppose it's nothin' less than I ought to have suspected."

She should have given this to police as soon as she'd found it. Why hadn't she? She'd estranged herself from Tristan and Archer. There must have been at least part of her that harbored hope they'd come around.

"When I first married Tristan's father, his kids were my kids. I wanted us all to be a family. It's what I always wanted." She sighed and dropped the baseball glove she'd held on to. "I guess that jus' wasn't in the cards for me."

Sabrina reached out and touched Tia's arm. "Archer regrets treating you badly, Tia. He wants to make amends. Now that Tristan won't pose a threat, maybe it's time you gave him another chance. He is your only son. You're only *real* son. You can still have a family."

Tia stared at her, her big, blond hair as unmoving as she was right now. And then she broke down and cried.

"I've made mistakes in my life. Lord knows I have. I ain't never dreamed I'd see the day when my boy had a change of heart."

Sabrina wrapped her arms around the big woman. "Give him a chance. You'll see he has."

"Thank you, girl." Tia leaned back, mascara beginning to run down her overly made-up face.

Sabrina wasn't a touchy-feely kind of person, at least

not when her guard was up. More and more she was beginning to let it down. What would happen if she let it down with Lincoln?

Sabrina went with Lincoln to meet Cash Whitney, and they gave him the notebook and pocketknife. He told them he'd make sure the accident was reopened as a homicide investigation. Police would be looking for Tristan in connection to that as well as the kidnappings.

It was a great feeling. After all this time, it was finally over. She was free of Tristan forever. He'd be arrested, and she'd never have to see or hear from him again.

Falling back on the hotel bed, Sabrina stretched with a long sigh, happy that she'd be able to reclaim her life. Her lease was month-to-month in Denver. She could go back to Denver or she could stay here. One thing was for sure: she was quitting her job in Denver. Maybe OneDefense would hire her back.

Did she want that job? Should she look for a job in Denver or in California? She didn't know what she was going to do. Lincoln appeared in the room. Their suite was good in size and very nice, the luxury of being once again innocent. No law chasing after them.

Looking down, she saw Lincoln lean against the wall near the doorway, legs crossed at the ankles, watching her. She could feel his tension. His eyes smoldered, but his thoughts were too heavy. She wished there was a way to woo him, to make him feel the way she felt for him.

And how was that?

As panic welled, she reasoned with herself. Her life was at a crossroads. Would it include Lincoln? Did she want it to? As she continued to look at him and he at her, that heat rising again, she decided she was going to find out. He was a good man. He was worth the risk.

Bounding off the bed, she said, "Let's go out tonight."

"Isn't it a little early to celebrate?"

Tristan hadn't been caught yet. Was he worried if it was safe? Tristan would be busy running from police. How stupid would it be to chase them? Sabrina wondered if the real reason Lincoln hesitated was that he'd be with her. Celebrating.

Was he afraid he'd brush too close to commitment, spending time with her without the purpose of tracking down Tristan? Tonight, the only purpose would be to enjoy the night...together.

That made her mad, and she rebelled. "We're going out." She scooted off the bed and went to the bathroom to shower. When they'd gone shopping she'd bought a couple dresses in case they had to go somewhere that warranted it. She'd say tonight warranted it. She was going to push Lincoln as much as she could. Torture him with sexiness. And see what happened.

They were going somewhere nice for dinner. And then they'd come back here and...then what?

Sabrina paused in the act of turning on the shower. Maybe she should think about this. She straightened, naked and ready to get sexy for Lincoln. Tall, muscular Lincoln. Blond-haired, blue-eyed, nice, patient, masculine Lincoln.

Would he be patient in bed? Was it worth the risk to find out?

When an answer didn't come, she leaned into the shower and turned on the water.

Lincoln had changed into dress slacks and a matching white linen jacket with a blue shirt. No tie. And now they'd parked in front of the Kibalti Museum, a mansion of a Jewish family who'd moved here from Nazi Germany. He couldn't pay attention while the tour guide led them through one spectacular room to the next, detailing the family's escape from Germany, subsequent rise to wealth in the United States and the tragic end of the parents' lives in a plane crash. Their three children had donated the mansion to a nonprofit organization. All quite interesting, but not as interesting as Sabrina in her little black dress. It showed off her thighs and breasts, an onyx pendant flirting with the top of her cleavage.

She'd had him when she'd stretched out on the bed. He didn't need this added stimulus of her beautiful body in tight black spandex. He found himself struggling to keep from getting hard in the most inappropriate places. Here, for example. The tour was ending, thank God.

Seeing Sabrina's happy smile as they left, he faced a new challenge. Her stunning face and the knowledge that his idea of bringing her here had lit it up.

He drove as fast as he could to the restaurant, which she had chosen. There was no stopping what would transpire once they returned to the hotel. He'd resigned himself to that, and hoped he wouldn't feel the way he had before every time he'd touched her. Trapped. His insides twisted with equal amounts of apprehension and anticipation, whenever he thought of being inside her.

The drive to the restaurant was quiet. Sabrina thanked him for taking her to the museum and he said, "You're welcome." The rest of the way, they took turns sneaking peeks at each other.

At the restaurant, he parked and they sat there, neither getting out, even after seat belts were removed. Lincoln could tell she was as hot and bothered as he was. When she reached over and put her hand on his thigh, he spun over a precipice.

Twisting toward her, she met him between the seats, and they kissed. Holding the back of her head, he devoured her the way he'd been craving to for nearly the past three hours. He slipped his hand inside her dress and felt her breast. He had to have her.

"I want to take you back to the hotel room right now," he said.

"Yes," she answered.

"Are you sure?" He looked into her eyes, holding her head between his hands.

She nodded. "I don't want to leave California without doing that."

Whatever happened after that didn't matter. She was letting her guard down all the way. For him. She wasn't holding back.

It seared him with uncontrollable desire. He kissed her hard. She reached over and cupped his crotch, panting when she discovered him achingly ready for her. He couldn't take it any longer. Breaking the kiss, he shoved the rental in Reverse and peeled out of the parking space. Racing for the highway, he caught sight of Sabrina, hand on the door handle, lips parted and breathing with passion. She wanted this, too.

He sped down the interstate, weaving in and out of traffic. Someone honked as he veered in front of them, leaving ample room, but probably startling them.

Sabrina laughed lightly.

Ten minutes later he turned the car over to valet parking. Taking Sabrina's hand, he hurried with her inside. In the elevator, she backed him to the wall and kissed him. He put his hands on her backside and pressed her to his hardness.

"See what you've done to me?" he rasped.

"You already know what you do to me." She kept kissing him as he grew hotter, remembering her wetness from last time.

The elevator doors slid open. Lincoln moved his hands up Sabrina's back as an older couple stood outside the doors. They didn't move to enter. The doors slid shut.

Chuckling with her soft laughter, he kissed her again. The elevator stopped at their floor.

Sabrina wrapped her legs around him as he walked with her down the hall, her dress hiking up her legs, indecently exposing her, but he loved it. She wasn't wearing any underwear.

At their door, she used the keycard to unlock it, and he carried her inside. They'd been able to stay in luxury again. Their hotel suite had a bedroom, a kitchen area and a spacious seating area with a wall of windows that offered a spectacular view of the ocean.

She kissed Lincoln as he carried her to the bedroom. He put her down onto the bed. She shimmied up the mattress, green eyes hot and sultry, knowing that he loved watching her. He took off his jacket and shirt while she stretched again, waiting and watching.

He took off his shoes and pants and underwear. Naked, with his erection jutting out, he savored the way she looked him over before getting on his hands and knees over her. Taking the hem of the dress, he pulled it up her body, slowly revealing skin as he did. Tossing the dress aside, he unclasped the front hook of her bra, easing her out of it while he looked at her breasts, nipples pointing out toward him, perched on the round globes that begged for his mouth.

He took one in and caressed her with his tongue.

While she moaned, he treated the other to the same loving. She opened her legs, and he went between them, lifting off her breast to look at her face while he entered her. She was so wet. A couple firm pushes and he sank into her.

He had to shut his eyes to the mind-numbing, incredibly intense sensation. He may have even groaned, he couldn't be sure. It wasn't going to take him long. He slid in and out.

"Wait," she rasped, pushing his chest.

He rolled onto his back, fighting the onset of a powerful orgasm.

Straddling him, she took his thickness into her again.

"You think that will prolong it?" he asked her.

Smiling, looking down at him, she slid herself up and down, her hands on his chest. He gritted his teeth and held still.

Then she began to grind herself on him.

He swore, unable to keep still anymore. Pumping his hips, he rammed into her, eliciting cries from her. At the last second, he rolled her onto her back.

"Don't stop. Don't stop," she urged.

"I'm not going to." He shoved into her again and resumed his hard penetration. Back and forth in rapid repetition.

She cried out as she came, and he thanked the heavens it hadn't taken long. He came with the next thrust, collapsing onto her, still moving in and out as the pulsing eased.

With his head next to her, he kissed her neck.

"I guess we shouldn't have waited so long," she said.

He chuckled and moved to lie next to her, spooning. He'd think about what all this meant after they went back to Colorado. And he sensed Sabrina would do the same. For now, he planned on spending some time right here in this bed. Maybe in the shower. Maybe on one of those chairs in front of the window.

Chapter 15

"You mean, you don't live here?"

Autumn Ivy looked across the table at Knox Jorgenson, the sexy, blue-eyed detective she'd met at Lincoln's house. She'd love to run her fingers through his thick, dark hair.

"Not exactly," she answered. "My parents have a house in Evergreen. I stay there sometimes. I also stay at a loft downtown. I rented it because I come here so often. This is where we meet as a family all the time."

"Where do you live?"

Autumn braced herself for this part. This was when a guy either made it to the second date or he shot himself in the foot. "I'm Jackson Ivy's daughter."

His blank look gave her hope. The instant heat he'd felt when she'd first met him returned.

"The movie producer? *The Last Planet? Rebound?*"

His blank look continued, or had it shifted to shock? "You're kidding."

She shook her head and lifted the glass of red wine for a sip, loving his face, and encouraged that there just might be something to this.

"You have a big family?" he asked.

She smiled, setting down her glass, also loving the first coherent question that followed his knowledge of how rich her family was. "There's eight of us, not including Mom and Dad."

"Mom and Dad," he murmured, still absorbing. "Where do you live?"

"New York City. I have an apartment there."

She watched him register how expensive that apartment must be.

"That's pretty far away," he said.

She couldn't tell if his ego was struggling to keep up with her. As a detective, he couldn't compete with her financially. She clearly made more than he did. Well, technically she didn't make the money. Her parents gave it to her in a big trust fund. But he'd focused on how far away she lived rather than the cost of her home.

"I can find a place here if I need to," she told him.

"Yeah, I'll bet you could."

Had his interest in her changed? Money and fame had a way of doing that to people. She'd had conversations with Lincoln about it. He hated dealing with that, too. Most of her siblings did. Except Jonas. He fed off the attention he got. But maybe not so much anymore. When she'd seen him at Lincoln's, he'd seemed different. More down to earth.

"Does that bother you?" she asked.

He shook his head. "No, but you might have to buy your own wedding ring."

Why was he talking wedding rings? They barely knew each other.

Then he chuckled. "Just making a point."

She relaxed. "Oh." She might be accustomed to expensive things. She was accustomed to shopping for clothes and accessories, but she didn't need a man for that. She didn't need a man to buy her anything.

"Let's see where this goes," he said, defusing her even more.

She liked that. He made her feel comfortable. Taking it easy was her motto. She needed time to get to know a man.

"Okay."

"Where did you grow up?" he asked.

"California." She didn't have to say it was in a mansion.

"I grew up in a little fishing village in Delaware. My parents still live there. My sister stayed nearby, but my brother left for college in Michigan. He's in Chicago now. He's a doctor there."

"Wow." She was impressed. "You must have had such an idyllic childhood."

She could see the love shining in his eyes as he thought of his parents. "Yeah. My parents are great. Hardworking, good morals. My dad was a fireman before he retired. He's the reason I wanted to become a cop."

"You wanted to be a hero?"

"What little boy doesn't?"

"Is it all you dreamed about?"

He grunted derisively. "I think you know the answer to that."

It wasn't. Fighting crime was a difficult job. He must have seen some terrible things.

"How did you end up here?" she asked.

"The Rockies. And not the baseball team."

She laughed. "What a relief." He seemed so normal. She'd thought that before about men, though, and found herself wrong.

He paid for dinner and they walked down the 16th Street Mall, other people walking past them and on the other side of the tram, some dressed up, some looking rougher. A horse and buggy clip-clopped by. It was a nice night for this time in fall.

He took her hand, which she thought was a sweet gesture. Recalling that he'd kissed her the first time they'd met, she wasn't sure she should let him keep it. But his physical presence wooed her. He was tall and lean, with muscles in all the right places. She began to warm again, that electric magnetism firing up.

"Have you seen any sign of those men anymore?"

He was asking about the men who'd come to Lincoln's house. "No. Arizona told me that Lincoln said police and FBI are looking for them now. Or, at least, the one they worked for." She told him all about the ordeal her brother and Sabrina had been going through in California, leaving out her speculation that there was serious romance blooming between her brother and Sabrina.

"Good. I was beginning to wonder if I'd have to continue my police protection."

What? She angled her head to eye him. "Police protection? Have you been spying on me?"

He grinned, the manly crease along his mouth distracting her. "Spying isn't the word I'd use."

She hadn't even noticed. How scary was that? It was nice to know he was watching her, but it almost felt… creepy. If he wasn't a cop she would have ended the date right now."

"Why didn't you tell me?" she asked.

"I figured you'd feel more comfortable not knowing."

"Yeah, but…you were spying on me."

"Not spying. What do you think I'd do? Assume those men wouldn't try to come back?"

"It's Lincoln they're after." He'd known she was staying at the loft. If he was spying on her, had he already known about her family?

"You already knew who I was, didn't you?" she asked.

He let go of her hand and stopped. "No." He sounded emphatic. "I didn't look into your background. I just followed you home. I wanted to make sure you were all right."

He'd followed her. Was that weird?

Putting his hands on her shoulders, he said, "I wouldn't do anything to ruin this. Meeting you was…"

Yeah. Indescribable. She tipped her head back when he leaned in for a kiss.

The rapid shutter snaps of cameras went off. Autumn broke away from Knox to find herself caught by a reporter.

"Is this your next boyfriend, Autumn?" he asked.

Autumn stepped back, taking Knox's hand as she tugged him toward his car. "Let's get out of here."

"Detective Jorgenson," the reporter called, coming after them. "Did you know Autumn just broke up with Deangelo Calabrese? Aren't you worried she's on the rebound?"

"Kind of hard to be rebound when we only dated a few times." Autumn tugged harder on Knox, who held back and seemed interested in what the reporter had to say.

"That's all it takes with you," the reporter teased, snapping more pictures.

"Leave us alone!"

"You dated Deangelo Calabrese?" Knox asked.

"She didn't tell you?" the reporter smiled. "He's not the only one. There's a long list of men she's tossed aside. I'd be careful if I were you."

At last they reached Knox's Chevy Malibu. Inside, he started the engine but didn't move to drive away. The reporter snapped a few more pictures, probably hoping to catch an argument.

"Get us out of here," Autumn pleaded.

Knox backed the Malibu up and began to drive away.

"What was he talking about back there?" he asked.

"Nothing." Autumn bit her knuckle, her elbow on the door.

"You have a reputation for dating lots of men? I mean, I wouldn't be surprised. You're beautiful, but..."

"It's the media. They lie about everything."

Chapter 16

Tristan still hadn't been caught. Sabrina stood at the wall of windows with a view of the beach and ocean. It didn't work to distract her. Two days had passed since she and Lincoln had devoted themselves to sex and she'd made the stupid decision to try to seduce him into wanting a commitment with her.

Last night, she'd sensed his withdrawal, and it was intense.

He'd been quiet and absorbed in thought, thinking about *her,* no doubt, that woman he'd loved and planned to marry. Sabrina had given him space, hoping he'd come to terms with the tragedy once and for all, but this morning he was even quieter and wouldn't look at her.

She turned. He still sat at the table. The more they were together, the more serious this felt. She couldn't be alone in this. The sex was too strong.

The morning after that first time, Lincoln had woken

her with soft kisses. After climbing onto her and entering her while she was still half-asleep, he'd told her to roll over. His deep voice had lulled her into obedience. She'd rolled over, and he'd lifted her onto her knees.

"Stay on your elbows," he'd instructed.

And he'd separated her knees. She had long legs, and the spread had been adequate. She could still feel his hands on her hips, the glide of one around to her abdomen, his fingers on her clit. And then he'd pushed into her from behind. Rubbing her clitoris, he'd made love to her gently. It had gone on for several minutes like that. He'd bring her to near eruption and then slow down, removing his fingers to just go in and out. And then he'd heat her up again. Finally, she'd been a tight channel of sensitivity, tingling like mad. With circular motion, his fingers had worked their magic as he'd penetrated her harder. Faster. Deeper. He'd kept himself deep inside her while she'd yelled her release. Only after the long, deep spasms had eased had she realized he'd come at the same time.

They'd watched TV for an hour and taken a shower, where he'd sat down and made her straddle him.

They'd spent the entire day in the room. Making love. Eating. Sleeping.

Yesterday, they'd packed a picnic and spent the afternoon on the beach. They'd found a secluded spot and spread a blanket out. He'd made love to her there, too. On the soft sand, the day warm for fall, he'd kissed her endlessly and then pulled her bikini bottoms down. He'd untied her top, but not removed it, just pushed it to the side to expose her for his pleasure. She'd stretched her arms over her head and waited for him to look his fill. He had, his smoldering blue eyes on fire. Then he'd looked around to be sure no one could see, and kneed her legs open. She'd pulled his trunks down, caring only about him, pleasuring him as much as he was pleasuring her. He'd slid inside her, keeping watch around them until the passion grew to be too much and neither of them were aware of anything except his erection mind-blasting them both into oblivion.

If anyone had walked by along the beach, they would have seen them. No one had, and the day had turned into a fantastic memory. And then night had come, and he'd begun to withdraw. She didn't think it was his feelings for Miranda that put a wedge between them; it was the tragedy. Losing Miranda to murder. Losing love. He didn't want to lose love again.

All Sabrina had ever wanted was to find love. She wasn't afraid of losing it once she had it, only never finding it.

The realization came in that instant. She'd never thought of it that way before, that she was searching for love so that she didn't have to live alone like her mother and grandmother. That was why she was always so careful about the men she chose. But she was going about it all wrong. This was the closest she'd ever felt to love. That was why letting go with Lincoln had been so easy. And as soon as she had, their love had begun to sprout. It would be powerful with him, if he'd allow it to keep growing.

There was nothing she could do to make him, though. She couldn't just stand by and watch him throw it away.

Well, she didn't have to stay here and do that. She could watch him throw it away from her front porch. At least there she could go inside and spare herself some agony.

Making up her mind, she went to pack her clothes. There was nothing they could do here, anyway. The police would catch Tristan if they could, and who knew how long that would be? She wasn't waiting here. At home she'd have Maddie and the task of finding a new job.

Realizing she'd subconsciously decided to stay in Denver, her mood plummeted. Did she harbor hope that Lincoln would come around? She had to resolve herself to the possibility that he might not.

"What are you doing?"

Realizing he'd stood and come to her, she stopped packing. "I'm going home."

He stared at her. She watched him rationalize their relationship, the gripping sex, the magnetism that brought them close and the fact that Tristan wasn't going to be easy to catch. His face went cold. And then he nodded.

Disappointment crushed her. She resumed packing, refusing to give her feelings power; not now. Maybe when she arrived home and he wasn't around, she'd allow some time for sorrow. But right now she just wanted to focus on getting home.

Sabrina sat curled on her couch with Maddie, the television on, a laptop on the ottoman in front of her. She'd spent the past hour looking for jobs both here and in California. The flight home had been pure torture.

Lincoln had noticed a change in her. She doubted he'd ever been with a woman who could switch it off as masterfully as she could. While she'd taken great care in getting good at that, she wasn't proud. She'd just been raised by women who had to do that to survive. It was in her blood.

"Are you okay?" he'd asked on the plane.

"Fine. Why? Are you?" she'd countered.

He'd missed her underlying meaning. She'd be fine. It was him who wouldn't if he didn't learn how to deal with his commitment issue.

"You just seem…quiet."

"You're quiet, too, Lincoln."

That had shut him up. He'd fallen into another long bout of thinking. By the end of the trip, she'd practically had to bite her tongue off to keep from saying something.

"If I hear anything, I'll let you know," he'd said when they'd arrived home.

"That won't be necessary. I'll find my own way of keeping track of Tristan's capture."

"Are you sure you're going to be all right?"

She hadn't been able to stop her sneer. "I was fine before you came along. I'm sure I'll be fine now."

"Yeah, real fine, huh, Mad?" Sabrina scratched the dog's ear, seeing her looking up with knowing eyes. She could sense her master's mood. Sitting up on the sofa, Maddie gave her a soft, drooless kiss on her cheek, which instantly lightened Sabrina's spirit.

"I know, snap out of it, right?" she said.

Maddie licked her again, and Sabrina went back to looking for a job, stopping yet again as she wondered if staying in Denver was such a good idea. Right next door to Lincoln, the man she'd had repeated sex with for a few days, and that was all that had come of it. She'd taken the risk. She'd let go.

And lost.

"Win some, lose some," she said to the room. "Might as well get used to living alone."

Was there such a thing as fate? Was she fated to live the same as her mother and grandmother?

A news program began coverage of a murder in California. She heard the name Castillo and sat straighter. The body of Cesar Castillo had been found in a farmer's field. Castillo's wife had identified him and wasn't available for comment. It came as no surprise to Sabrina that the man had been murdered. She'd expected to hear that at some point. There were no suspects, and the authorities were investigating it as a gang hit. It may have been that, but it was related to Tristan's gun dealings. The police were surely aware of that by now. It just hadn't made the news.

While she began to wonder why Mrs. Castillo wasn't available for comment, Maddie growled and hopped down from the sofa. Sabrina went on full alert as she watched her dog move slowly toward the kitchen, the hair along her back raised.

Lincoln stood staring through his kitchen window at Sabrina's house. She'd shut all her blinds on this side of her house. He'd seen her once yesterday when she'd come home from the grocery store. He'd seen her carry a few bags into her garage. She hadn't seen him or looked at his house.

She'd seemed so accepting of his brooding. He couldn't tell her the thoughts that had plagued him, that still plagued him. He was afraid of continuing their relationship. As she probably knew, it would develop into something serious. He wasn't prepared for that.

His thoughts were so jumbled. He thought of Miranda, her death and losing her. Guilt consumed him, and he didn't understand why. Was it over his love for her or the way she died? She was gone, and he had to move on. He clung to her memory too tightly. Those realizations were what had him in a conundrum. He felt guilty, and then he felt justified in letting her go. Which was it? And where did Sabrina fit in it all?

Somewhere new.

She was brand-new territory. What he felt with her was completely different than what he'd felt with Miranda. That was where the guilt came in. How could he feel more for Sabrina than he had with Miranda when he'd known Miranda longer?

Not that much longer.

Why was he having such clarity, and clarity that was so much different than it had been before he'd met Sabrina?

It was time to let Miranda go. He hadn't loved her as much as he'd thought. Making love with Sabrina had proved that. He hadn't been able to admit it until now.

So what was he going to do?

Pursue Sabrina? Was it too late for that? His heart palpitated. Apprehension. Excitement. Passion. It scared him to think of falling in love again.

Sitting at his kitchen table, Lincoln put his head in his hands. Not much scared him, but that did. He felt weak and silly for feeling that way, but glad he was able to face it. He would feel the fear and do it, anyway. Go after Sabrina. Love her. Have her. Make a family with her. More palpitations assaulted him with each idea. Passion and happiness assured him of his path.

Barking made him lift his head. Maddie was at the back window, rising up on her hind legs and pawing the glass. She looked frantic. Panting.

Lincoln shot up and opened the door. Maddie barked and ran inside, bounding around him, jumping up on him.

Sabrina...

He should not have left her alone.

"Okay, girl." Lincoln ran to the front of the house in time to see a man stuffing Sabrina into the back of a white Lexus.

Grabbing his gun, he ran for his BMW SUV, Maddie on his heels.

"No, Maddie!" It was too late to put her back in the house. He let her jump in and started the engine as he backed out of the garage. He drove normally so as not to alert the other driver he was going to follow. He could see Maddie's head in the rearview mirror. Luckily, he wouldn't have to drive like a madman. He'd follow at a good distance so as not to draw attention. The driver of the Lexus didn't speed. He hadn't noticed the tail.

Lincoln managed to remain unseen all the way to the Denver OneDefense store. The Lexus rolled to the back, where a truck was backed to a loading dock. Lincoln stopped in the alley and watched two people get out, one dragging a struggling Sabrina with her. Lincoln recognized Castillo's wife. He'd heard on the news that her husband's body had been found.

How well she'd covered her lies. She was in on the sales with the gun cartel. With Tristan. Her husband had not agreed with the sale. He hadn't thought setting his *Avenidas* members up to act as mules to transport guns across the border a wise activity. Maybe he'd meant to keep the gang away from any allegiance with a Mexican cartel. Some cartels were known to use U.S. citizens to bring weapons to them from the United States. What better source than a street gang whose members were already corrupt?

After calling 911 to report Sabrina's kidnapping and giving the location, Lincoln twisted to see Maddie.

"You stay." Her ears perked, and she didn't move.

Leaving the windows down, he got out of his BMW and walked toward the back entrance to the store. He couldn't leave Sabrina in there alone. Every second counted right now. No matter what kind of trap he was walking into, he had to do something. He could not wait for the police to arrive. Looking around him to make sure he hadn't been seen, he noticed the truck backed to the loading dock had its rear door open. Had it been unloaded or did Tristan have a shipment of arms planned?

At the door to the store, he tested the knob. It easily turned. Nothing like a welcome sign.

Lincoln removed his pistol and entered the building. There were shelves around the perimeter, and crates filled the center. Mrs. Castillo stood behind one of them, Tristan beside her and facing Lincoln. Tristan grinned. Stepping farther into the room, Lincoln saw Sabrina around a stack of shipping crates. She was tied to a chair and gagged. Her eyes were large, and she shook her head. Then she looked toward the stack of crates as though to warn him.

Tristan had planned to lure him here. This was about revenge. He'd suspected as much.

"Hand over the weapon," a voice said behind him at the same time he felt a metal barrel against his head.

Lincoln did as requested, having anticipated this.

A chair was procured and put next to Sabrina. Lincoln went there and sat. Sabrina was trembling. She was afraid. He removed the gag from her mouth and threw it aside.

"Lincoln. He's going to kill us both. What are you doing here?"

"Don't worry."

"Don't worry?" she rasped.

Tristan approached. "You've both caused me a lot of trouble. You nearly cost me this sale to the Tres Equis Cartel. Lucky for you, they are giving me this opportunity to get rid of you." He stopped before them, Mrs. Castillo staying back by the crate, a rifle draped over one arm. "Apparently they believe you won't stop until I am arrested, and they fear my arrest will lead to them."

"The police won't stop looking for you," Lincoln said. "And since we're talking about a Mexican cartel, you should probably include the FBI with that."

"You have a smart mouth for someone who is about to die."

What was he waiting for? And where the hell were those cops?

Tristan's gaze went to Sabrina. "I have only one question I need answered first."

Lincoln glanced at Sabrina. Tristan had a question for her? He had a feeling all her secrets were about to be revealed.

"Why?" Tristan asked.

Lincoln checked on the man with the gun on him. He was the only one other than Mrs. Castillo.

"Why did you stick your nose in my business?" Tristan asked.

"You framed me for murder."

Tristan leaned over, putting his hands on his knees and studying her closely.

What the...

"No. You stuck it in my business before that."

"I don't know what you're talking about."

Lincoln heard the lie right along with Tristan.

"Oh, yes, you do. Kirby told me where he met you." When she didn't respond, he said, "The gun show?"

"So?"

"You met him deliberately." Tristan straightened but didn't move back.

"No, I didn't."

"There was something he wouldn't tell me about you. He knew something. But he was falling for you, so he decided to protect you. Try, anyway. Why? What did he know, Sabrina? Did you tell him why you singled me out?"

Lincoln watched Sabrina keep a cool face. Her stoic resolve was impressive. And she was no longer afraid. Whatever had driven her to OneDefense burned deep inside her. Determination. Certainty.

Tristan pulled a gun out from behind the smooth lapel of his jacket and raised it to Lincoln's head. "Tell me or he dies."

Sabrina's breathing increased, scared again. For him. She believed Tristan would do it. So did Lincoln, so that was a plus. If he made a move now, he could take the gun from Tristan and shoot the other man, but would he be able to take out Mrs. Castillo in time? She watched with a sort of bored interest, having no intention of using her rifle.

"Stop," Sabrina said.

Lincoln moved his gaze to her. She met it briefly and then said to Tristan, "You're my father."

That detonation worked to stagger Lincoln as much as it did Tristan.

"You're lying."

Sabrina shook her head. "No. My mother was divorced when she met you and in the process of reinstating her maiden name. You didn't know her maiden name. It's Tierney. I was born after she changed it."

Tristan took a step back, staring incredulously at her.

"After my mother died, I searched for you," Sabrina

continued. "I found you, but I wasn't sure if I would tell you who I was. You didn't seem to care that I existed. That's when I met Kirby. He approached me at the gun show, which made it easy. He was a kind man, and I used his attraction to me to get close to you." She turned to Lincoln. "Not something I'm proud of."

That explained her mood every time the subject of Kirby came up. She hadn't had feelings for him, but she had felt bad about using him.

She turned back to Tristan. "When I discovered the kind of man you were, I wanted nothing to do with you. I decided that you didn't deserve to know who I was."

"Was that before or after you heard me talking to Kirby?" he asked.

"Before. I know now that he wanted to stop you, but he was afraid of you."

"And you weren't?"

"I despise you. After you killed Kirby, I vowed to expose you. Somehow. Some way. That's why I came here and went to Wade. Kirby said he was someone I could trust."

Tristan grunted a laugh. "Kirby didn't know as much as he thought, then."

Meaning he hadn't known Wade wasn't someone Sabrina could trust. Lincoln saw her absorb that, her eyes softening. Kirby had been good, as she'd originally thought.

"Did he know I was your father?"

Sabrina hesitated. "Yes." She looked at Lincoln. That had been her secret. Then she turned back to Tristan. "I'd have kept it to myself my entire life."

She would have denied Tristan was her father. He may as well be dead to her.

Tristan's mouth hardened in reaction to the insult.

Part of him cared that Sabrina was his daughter. He may never admit it, but he did care. Lincoln chose that moment to move. He used his foot to strike him in the sternum and slam his hand against Tristan's wrist and his nose with the other. Ripping the gun from his grasp, he hooked an arm around his throat and pointed the gun to his head, backing up to put himself in front of Sabrina, protecting her.

Both the man and Castillo's wife aimed their weapons.

"Drop the gun and untie her," he ordered.

The man looked at Tristan, who said, "Do it."

The man dropped his gun and went to Sabrina, keeping his eyes on Lincoln as he untied her.

Sabrina stood and put her hands on Lincoln's back just as a swarm of police entered, one of them yelling, "Denver Police, drop your weapons!"

Lincoln stepped back with Sabrina, slowly lowering the gun to the ground. Then he stepped back some more, lifting his arms so the police could see them, Sabrina doing the same beside him.

Tristan turned lethal eyes to Lincoln and then Sabrina as Castillo's wife and the other man lowered their weapons and raised their hands into the air. Police cuffed the three as Lincoln explained who he and Sabrina were.

"We were briefed on the way here," one of them said. "We know who you are. If you could wait outside, we'd like to ask you a few questions."

"Sure." Lincoln took Sabrina outside, seeing her look back once at her biological father. She'd regret not having a father she could respect, but she would never regret bringing him to justice.

Now probably wasn't the time to tell her what he'd been thinking before Maddie had come to his door. But as soon as they got home, he'd find a way to make her listen.

Chapter 17

Sabrina went to where Maddie wagged her tail and barked in a soft, playful way, looking up and back at her and then down at the patio through the glass.

"What's out there?" Sabrina asked as Maddie peered through the glass. Maddie was being playful, but there still could be something out there. Or someone. It would be a while before Sabrina felt totally safe. The FBI had captured most of the people involved in Tristan's operation. A few of the gang members had talked to get a deal.

Seeing nothing terrible through the darkness, she opened the door.

Maddie bound outside and stopped where a biscuit lay on the patio. She chewed and then sniffed the air.

Why was there a biscuit on the patio? Maddie trotted with her nose down toward the edge of the patio. She found another biscuit and chewed happily, tail wagging faster now.

Looking down at her bare feet and nightie that went to her knees, she contemplated making her dog go back inside with her. The trail of biscuits had her too curious. She followed Maddie to the still-broken gate, where another biscuit lay.

Sabrina started to smile. Somebody had put them there, and that someone could be only one person. Lincoln.

Two more biscuits led into Lincoln's backyard, and one more was on the back step. The back door was open.

Maddie went inside.

"Crap." She folded her arms. The nightie wasn't see-through, but it was soft and comfortable and she wasn't wearing a bra.

Rationalizing that he'd seen a lot more of her, she stepped inside. The lights were turned low, and Sinatra-like music played quietly. She walked through the kitchen. No one was in the living room, but when she looked to her right, she spotted Lincoln standing there, dressed sharply in a black suit and tie, his gaze taking her in as she appeared. Candles flickered on the dining room table, which was set in white, rose-petal-shaped china. A bucket held a bottle of something.

"You're going to make Maddie fat."

"I see you dressed for the occasion," he said.

Wary of him, she approached. "And what occasion is that?"

"Join me for dinner, and I'll tell you. You can change…if you want."

She could tell he preferred that she didn't go change. He wouldn't have gone to all this trouble if he hadn't had a major epiphany. Going to him, she stopped.

"Okay, I've joined you," she said, standing close.

His gaze once again swept her form. But this time

she was standing so close that all his eyes could feast on were her breasts.

"I've done some thinking."

"Yeah?"

"You're right. It is time for me to move on."

"Really," she coaxed.

"Yes. And I have to tell you…I've never felt this way for anyone before."

That tripped her up a bit, but she managed to keep it light. "What way is that?"

He slipped an arm around her, bringing her closer and pretty much guaranteeing they wouldn't make it to dinner. "Lost without you."

Lost. Her heart did a happy flip. She looped her arms over his shoulders. "It's Maddie, isn't it?"

"And her owner. My suggestion is we all live here."

"Yeah?"

"I own this house. You're renting over there, and—"

She kissed him hard. He wrapped his arms around her and held her closer while he kissed her in return.

"I'm not finished yet."

"I am. And I'm not hungry." She stepped back, taking his hand, meaning to lead him upstairs to find his bedroom.

"Wait." He didn't move, serious now.

She was, too. Just knowing he wanted to live together was enough for her. He was ready to get past his commitment issues.

He pulled out a ring box from his coat pocket.

"Lincoln…" she breathed. Wasn't this a little fast?

"We don't have to get married right away," he said. "This is just a symbol of how much I mean what I say when I've never felt this way before."

He opened the box. It was a diamond flanked by

smaller ones. Not Hollywood huge, but just enough to dazzle.

While delight and excitement raced along with her many thoughts, he slipped it on her finger.

"Oh, Lincoln. It's beautiful." She held out her hand to admire it.

"Now we can go do what you want. Dinner will be waiting for us."

"You didn't cook, did you?" She laughed softly.

"No. I had it brought in."

She took his hand and led him up the stairs.

A month later, Lincoln's mother called to invite them to a brunch in Evergreen. He agreed to be there as he always did, having given up asking her to give him notice for her events. She never listened. She preferred the spontaneity.

Leaving the circular driveway and the sound of water falling over stone in the center fountain, he led an awed Sabrina up several sweeping stairs toward the mansion entrance. Sabrina was slow to follow, busy taking in copper gutters and ground-to-roof stone turrets, not to mention the flower garden between the driveway and the front door.

The door opened before they reached it.

"Hi, Berto," he greeted the doorman, a tall, thin, balding white man in his late fifties.

The man smiled. "Welcome, Mr. Lincoln." He always used everyone's first names as a surname. Otherwise they'd all be Mr., Mrs. or Ms. Ivy. Maybe that was because he preferred to keep his job impersonal.

"Miss." Berto gave Sabrina a bow.

"Hello." Sabrina glanced almost sheepishly at Lincoln.

He chuckled and put his hand on her lower back, ushering her inside. She smiled up at him as they entered.

"Oh, my...." Sabrina's eyes grew round as she took in the huge front entry.

Lincoln thought it was cold, with hardly any furniture, just a shiny spread of marble and high ceiling trimmed impeccably in white. There was a quaint and colorful parlor to the right and a library to the left, both for the public to use. There was another library for private use.

"Your parents are in the entertainment room downstairs," Berto announced. "Mr. Macon and Mr. Jonas are here, as well."

Macon was here?

"Thanks, Berto." Lincoln led a gawking Sabrina through an open panel of six doors that folded like an accordion.

Taking Sabrina's hand, he walked beside her through the mansion, passing a dining area and reaching a curving staircase. Down that, they passed through another giant room filled with art collections, and then a Churchill style room.

Catching Sabrina's gaze as she glanced from the grandeur of the estate to him, he noticed her glowing behind all her fascination. Everyone was going to notice that. And her ring, of course.

Smelling food, he realized how hungry he was. An archway led into the rec room where his family gathered for things like this. The room had everything: a beautiful bar with leather stools, pool table and plenty of seating.

"Hey, Lincoln." Jonas got up from a sofa before a giant television playing a football game.

Macon sat on a theater chair adjacent to that, not

moving to get up. He had a tall drink in one of the chair cup holders, glancing over at Lincoln with a nod before returning his attention to the TV.

Lincoln hugged Jonas with a hard pat on his back. Then he introduced Sabrina.

Jonas took her hand and kissed the back of it like the son of a duke, his green eyes dancing with vitality. Then he noticed the ring.

"What's this?" Straightening, he looked at Lincoln for an answer.

Sabrina slid her hand free from Jonas's.

"Exactly what it looks like."

"When did that happen? Does Mother know?"

"She will tonight."

"I have a new sister." Jonas beamed one of his famous smiles that had adorned the cover of many magazines at Sabrina. "A pleasure to meet you."

"Thank you. You, too."

Then Jonas said to Lincoln, "First Arizona, now you."

"Maybe you'll be next." He grinned.

When Jonas raised his eyebrows, Lincoln added, "For real this time."

"No, thanks. Too much trouble. I'm going to keep busy with my singing for now. I don't have time for women." He turned apologetically to Sabrina. "No offense."

Sabrina smiled. "None taken."

In jean overalls with a white T-shirt underneath and stylish boots, his mother appeared from outside, bobbed blond hair swinging. "Savanna said it was too far for her to drive." She leaned in for a hug with Lincoln. "What's this I hear about Arizona?"

"Lincoln's getting married," Jonas said.

From the chair, Macon turned a sharp look at them. Of all the Ivy clan, he had the least going for him. Drugs and alcohol robbed him of life. His mother had sent him to rehab more than once. Nothing worked. Right now his family tolerated him, and felt sympathy and help-lessness over the whole mess.

The press had a great time with him, though. He was the quintessential bad boy of Hollywood. He'd done some interviews, and his photos sold millions to ad-miring women. But the truth was far less glamorous.

His mother recovered from shock. "Are you?" She looked from Lincoln to Sabrina.

"We haven't set a date yet, but yes." She glowed even more radiantly than before.

His mother inspected the ring and then looked at her son. "You must have picked this out."

He lifted a palm. "Guilty."

His mother turned to Sabrina. "He's such a conser-vative."

"That's good, because so am I." She smiled and Lin-coln's heart did a flip.

His mother kissed his cheek. "I'm so happy for you." She patted his cheek. "You had me worried for a while."

"Mother…"

"Maybe you and Arizona should have a double wed-ding?"

He wasn't sure how he felt about that. Checking on Sabrina's reaction, he couldn't tell if she liked the idea or didn't mind it.

"Or not. I'd love to plan two weddings if you need any help. Arizona turned hers over to me."

Lincoln had to laugh. "She knows how much you like doing that sort of thing."

"That sort of thing is the beginning of the rest of your

life." She patted his cheek again. "Your dad's manning the grill. I'd better go help him."

As she left them, Lincoln asked Jonas in a low voice, "Why is Macon here?"

Jonas shrugged. "Mom called him like she usually does, and he showed up. She thinks he came because she told him about me, how I've changed my *direction*." He snorted. "You know how she can be."

"Lincoln, Jonas and Macon!"

Before Lincoln could go over and talk to Macon, he heard Autumn make her entrance. What a live wire.

She hugged him and then Jonas, and then went over to Macon and forced a hug onto him, leaning over so he didn't have to get up.

"You smell like booze," she told him.

"Nice to see you, too, Autumn. I read about you and that dude Deangelo."

"You know none of it's true."

"None of it's true about me, either. I also read about some new guy. What's his name?"

"Knox." She didn't look happy.

"Uh-oh…" Jonas said. "Is that ending, too?"

Ignoring him, she turned back to the others. "Has Mom told you?"

"Told us what?" Jonas asked.

"I'm going to Iceland! I got a translating job." She bounced happily up and down in her high, red shoes.

"That's fantastic," Lincoln said. "Who will you be working for?"

"A commercial developer needs someone to translate to some of their workers."

"Why didn't they hire someone local?" Someone who lived there.

"They're a U.S. company."

"How did you find that job?" Sabrina asked.

Lincoln answered for her. "She's been wanting to go to Iceland for a long time."

Sabrina looked perplexed. "Then…why not just go there?"

Jonas and Lincoln shared a knowing look, and together they said, "That's Autumn."

Autumn was going on an adventure. Lincoln met Sabrina's eyes. His adventure was being right here with her.

* * * * *

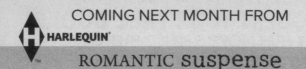

REQUEST YOUR FREE BOOKS!
2 FREE NOVELS PLUS 2 FREE GIFTS!

ROMANTIC suspense

Sparked by danger, fueled by passion

"What if someone is still using that poison?" she said as soon as she saw him.

He leaned back against the counter, folding his arms. For the first time she noticed he was armed with both knife and pistol. "My God," she whispered.

He looked down, then looked at her. "I wasn't going out there without protection. Want me to ditch this stuff?"

"Ditch it where?"

"I can put it by the front door with my jacket, or take it home."

She met his inky gaze almost reluctantly. He really did come from a different world. Well, not totally. Plenty of people hereabouts had guns, and some wore them. But somehow this felt different. Maybe because she hardly knew this man and he was in her house?

Still, why this reaction?

Because there was only one reason he would have carried those weapons today. And it explained why he'd eaten lunch with his parka still on.

"I'll go home," he said.

"No." The word was out almost before she knew it was coming. "I'm just surprised." That was certainly true. "I don't have any guns. Well, except for the shotgun in the attic. It was my dad's."

"A moral objection?"

"No. This is gun country. I'd have to object to most of my neighbors if I felt that way. I'm just not used to seeing weapons inside my house."

"Then I'll get rid of them."

"It's okay. Really. This is you, right?"

Something in his eyes narrowed. "Yeah," he said, his voice rough. "This is me. This is me on high alert. I don't need to be on alert in your kitchen."

"I hope not."

Without another word, he unbuckled his belt and removed both holsters from it. The sound of leather slipping against denim, the sight of him tugging at his belt, caused a sensual shiver in her despite the situation. She repressed it swiftly.

**Don't miss
DEADLY HUNTER by *New York Times*
bestselling author Rachel Lee,
available March 2014 from
Harlequin® Romantic Suspense.**

HARLEQUIN®

ROMANTIC suspense

DEGREE OF RISK
by *New York Times* bestselling author
Lindsay McKenna

Love leaves no one behind

Black Hawk pilot Sarah Benson was born brave.
A survivor from the start, Sarah is known for her
risky flights to save lives, and SEAL Ethan Quinn
is just one more mission. But when she needs
rescuing, it's Ethan who infiltrates enemy
territory, and her heart.

Look for the next title from *New York Times*
bestselling author Lindsay McKenna's
Shadow Warrior series, DEGREE OF RISK.

Available March 4, 2014,
wherever books and ebooks are sold.

Heart-racing romance, high-stakes suspense!

HRS27861